Tucholsky Wagner Zola Scott Sydow Freud Schlegel

Turgenev Fonatne

Wallace

Twain Walther von der Vogelweide Fouqué Friedrich II. von Preußen

Weber Freiligrath Frey

Fechner Fichte Weiße Rose von Fallersleben Kant Ernst Richthofen Frommel

Hölderlin

Engels Fielding Eichendorff Tacitus Dumas

Fehrs Faber Flaubert Eliasberg Ebner Eschenbach

Feuerbach Maximilian I. von Habsburg Fock Eliot Zweig

Ewald Vergil

Goethe Elisabeth von Österreich London

Mendelssohn Balzac Shakespeare Dostojewski Ganghofer

Trackl Lichtenberg Rathenau Doyle Gjellerup

Mommsen Stevenson Tolstoi Hambruch Droste-Hülshoff

Thoma Lenz Hanrieder

Dach Verne von Arnim Hägele Hauff Humboldt

Karrillon Reuter Rousseau Hagen Hauptmann Gautier

Garschin Defoe Baudelaire

Damaschke Descartes Hebbel

Wolfram von Eschenbach Schopenhauer Hegel Kussmaul Herder

Bronner Darwin Dickens Rilke George

Melville Grimm Jerome Bebel Proust

Campe Horváth Aristoteles

Bismarck Vigny Barlach Voltaire Federer Herodot

Gengenbach Heine

Storm Casanova Tersteegen Grillparzer Georgy

Chamberlain Lessing Langbein Gilm

Brentano Lafontaine Gryphius

Strachwitz Claudius Schiller Kralik Iffland Sokrates

Bellamy Schilling

Katharina II. von Rußland Gerstäcker Raabe Gibbon Tschechow

Löns Hesse Hoffmann Gogol Wilde Gleim Vulpius

Luther Heym Hofmannsthal Klee Hölty Morgenstern

Roth Heyse Klopstock Kleist Goedicke

Luxemburg Puschkin Homer Mörike

La Roche Horaz Musil

Machiavelli Kierkegaard Kraft Kraus

Navarra Aurel Musset Moltke

Nestroy Marie de France Lamprecht Kind Kirchhoff Hugo

Laotse Ipsen Liebknecht

Nietzsche Nansen Ringelnatz

Marx Lassalle Gorki Klett Leibniz

von Ossietzky May vom Stein Lawrence Irving

Petalozzi Platon Knigge

Sachs Poe Pückler Michelangelo Kock Kafka

Liebermann

de Sade Praetorius Mistral Zetkin Korolenko

The publishing house tredition has created the series **TREDITION CLASSICS**. It contains classical literature works from over two thousand years. Most of these titles have been out of print and off the bookstore shelves for decades.

The book series is intended to preserve the cultural legacy and to promote the timeless works of classical literature. As a reader of a **TREDITION CLASSICS** book, the reader supports the mission to save many of the amazing works of world literature from oblivion.

The symbol of **TREDITION CLASSICS** is Johannes Gutenberg (1400 – 1468), the inventor of movable type printing.

With the series, tredition intends to make thousands of international literature classics available in printed format again – worldwide.

All books are available at book retailers worldwide in paperback and in hardcover. For more information please visit: www.tredition.com

tredition was established in 2006 by Sandra Latusseck and Soenke Schulz. Based in Hamburg, Germany, tredition offers publishing solutions to authors and publishing houses, combined with worldwide distribution of printed and digital book content. tredition is uniquely positioned to enable authors and publishing houses to create books on their own terms and without conventional manufacturing risks.

For more information please visit: www.tredition.com

Three Thousand Years of Mental Healing

George Barton Cutten

Imprint

This book is part of the TREDITION CLASSICS series.

Author: George Barton Cutten
Cover design: toepferschumann, Berlin (Germany)

Publisher: tredition GmbH, Hamburg (Germany)
ISBN: 978-3-8495-2160-8

www.tredition.com
www.tredition.de

CONTENTS

PREFACE

The present decade has experienced an intense interest in mental healing. This has come as a culmination of the development along these lines during the past half century. It has shown itself in the beginning of new religious sects with this as a, or the, fundamental tenet, in more wide-spread general movements, and in the scientific study and application of the principles underlying this form of therapeutics.

Many have been led astray because, being ignorant of the mental healing movements and vagaries of the past, the late applications, veiled in metaphysical or religious verbiage, have seemed to them to be new in origin and principle. No one could consider an historical survey of the subject and reasonably hold this opinion. It is on account of the ignorance of similar movements, millenniums old, that so much, if any, originality can be credited to the founders.

The object of this volume is to present a general view of mental healing, dealing more especially with the historical side of the subject. While this is divided topically, the topics are presented in a comparatively chronological order, and thereby trace the development of the subject to the present century.

The term "mental healing" is given the broadest possible use, and comprehends any cures which may be brought about by the effect of the mind over the body, regardless of whether the power back of the cure is supposed to be deity, demons, other human beings, or the individual mind of the patient.

It is hoped that this may contribute to the knowledge of a subject which is of such wide-spread popular interest.

George Barton Cutten.

Wolfville, Nova Scotia,
December 1, 1910.

ILLUSTRATIONS

THREE THOUSAND YEARS OF

MENTAL HEALING

CHAPTER I

INTRODUCTION — MENTAL HEALING

"'Tis painful thinking that corrodes our clay." — Armstrong.

"Oh, if I could once make a resolution, and determine to be well!" — Walderstein.

"The body and the mind are like a jerkin and a jerkin's lining, rumple the one and you rumple the other." — Sterne.

"I find, by experience, that the mind and the body are more than married, for they are most intimately united; and when the one suffers, the other sympathizes." — Chesterfield.

"Sublime is the dominion of the mind over the body, that for a time can make flesh and nerve impregnable, and string the sinews like steel, so that the weak become so mighty." — Stowe.

> "The surest road to health, say what they will, Is never to suppose we shall be ill; Most of those evils we poor mortals know From doctors and imagination flow." — Churchill.

The fact that there is a reciprocal relation between mental states and bodily conditions, acting both for good and ill, is nothing new in human experience. Even among the most crude and unobserving, traditions and incidents have given witness to this knowledge. For centuries stories of the hair turning white during the night on account of fright or sorrow, the cause and cure of diseases through emotional disturbances, and death, usually directly by apoplexy, caused by anger, grief, or joy, have been current and generally accepted. On the other hand, irritability and moroseness caused by 4 disordered organs of digestion, change of acumen or morals due to injury of the brain or nervous system, and insanity produced by bodily diseases, are also accepted proofs of the effect of the body on the mind.

Recent scientific investigation has been directed along the line of the influence of the mind over the body, and to that phase of this influence which deals with the cure rather than the cause of disease. In addition to what the scientists have done along this line, various religious cults have added the application of these principles to their other tenets and activities, or else have made this the chief corner-stone of a new structure. There are some reasons why this connection with religion should continue to exist, and why it has been a great help both to the building up of these particular sects and the healing of the bodies of those who combine religion with mental healing.

We must not forget that in early days the priest, the magician, and the physician were combined in one person, and that primitive religious notions are difficult to slough off. Shortly before the beginning of the Christian era there were some indications that healing was to be freed from the bondage of religion, but the influence of Jesus' healing upon Christians, and the overwhelming influence of Christianity upon the whole world, delayed this movement, so that it did not again become prominent until the sixteenth 5 century. About this time, when therapeutics as a science began to shake off the shackles of religion and superstition, another startling innovation was noticeable, viz., the division of mental healing into religious and non-religious healing. This change came gradually, and as is usual in all reform, certain prophets saw and proclaimed the real truth which the people were not able to follow or receive for centuries.

Paracelsus, who lived during the first half of the sixteenth century, wrote these shrewd words: "Whether the object of your faith is real or false, you will nevertheless obtain the same effects. Thus, if I believe in St. Peter's statue as I would have believed in St. Peter himself, I will obtain the same effects that I would have obtained from St. Peter; but that is superstition. Faith, however, produces miracles, and whether it be true or false faith, it will always produce the same wonders." We have also this penetrating observation from Pierre Ponponazzi, of Milan, an author of the same century: "We can easily conceive the marvellous effects which confidence and imagination can produce, particularly when both qualities are reciprocal between the subject and the person who influences them. The cures attributed to the influence of certain relics are the effect of this imagination and confidence. Quacks and philosophers know that if the bones of any skeleton were put in the place of the 6 saint's bones, the sick would none the less experience beneficial effects, if they believed they were near veritable relics."

What seemed to be a movement whereby mental healing should be divided so that only a portion of it should be connected with religion proved to be too far in advance of its time, and not until the advent of Mesmer was this accomplished. Healing other than mental, however, did obtain its freedom at this time. While Mesmer and his followers emphasized non-religious mental healing, it should not be thought that mental therapeutics was ever entirely separated from the church. There have always been found some sects which laid particular emphasis on it, and both Roman Catholic and Protestant orthodox Christianity have always admitted it. It has been considered, even if not admitted, that the power of the Infinite was more clearly shown by the healing of the body than by the restoration of the moral life. It is natural, then, that the sects which showed this special proof of God's presence and power would grow faster than their spiritual competitors, but that they would decline more rapidly and surely than those which espoused more spiritual doctrines.

On the other hand, it is not difficult to see why mental healing would be helped by its connection with religion. Religion grips the whole mind more firmly than any other subject has ever done, and when one accepts the orthodox conception of God, 7 he naturally expects to come in contact with One whose sympathies are in favor of the cure of his diseases, and whose power is sufficient to bring about this cure. With this basis there is set up in the mind of the patient an expectancy which has always proven to be a most valuable precursor of a cure. The devout religious attitude of mind is one most favorable for the working of suggestion, and persons of the temperament adapted to the religious expression most valued in the past are those who could be most readily affected by mental means. For these reasons, it can be easily understood why mental healing has continued to be associated with religion, and why when thus associated it has been so successful.

To those not very familiar with mental healing, it has seemed strange that any law could be formulated which would comprehend every variety. In the following pages many different forms will be described, and in examining the subject it will be found that many and varied are the explanations given for the results produced. We find also a general distrust of all the others, or else a claim that this particular sect is the only real and true exponent of mental healing, and that it produces the only genuine cures. Those which claim to be Christian sects, however divergent the direct explanation of their results, give the final credit to God, and base their *modus operandi* upon the Bible 8 — in fact, they claim to be the direct successors of Jesus and his disciples in this respect.

We find, however, that the healer connected with the Christian sect has no advantage over his Mohammedan or Buddhist brother, and that neither is able to succeed better than the non-religious healer in all cases. We recognize that when one class of healers fails in a case another may succeed, but the successful one is just as liable to fail in a second case when the first one cures. What particular form of suggestion is most effective in any given case depends upon the temperament of the individual and his education, religious training, and environment. When we consider the whole matter we are forced to the conclusion that mental cures are independent of any particular sect, religion, or philosophy; some are cured by one form and some by another. Not the creed, but some force which resides in the mind of every one accomplishes the cure, and the most that any religion or philosophy can do is to bring this force into action.

As a general rule, one sharp distinction is noticed between the religious and the non-religious healers, viz., the religious healer sees no limit to his healing power, and affirms that cancer and Bright's disease are as easily cured, in theory at least, as neuralgia or insomnia; the non-religious healer, sometimes designated as the "scientific healer," on the contrary, recognizes that there are some diseases which 9 are more easily cured than others, and that of those others some are practically incurable by psycho-therapeutic methods.

14

The line has been drawn in the past between functional and organic diseases, the former including diseases where there is simply a derangement of function, like indigestion, and the latter comprehending the diseases where the organ is affected, like ulcer of the stomach. The more we know about diseases the less sure we seem to be about their classification; some of which we were formerly sure have recently caused us considerable doubt. For example, we have formerly classed cancer as an organic disease and consequently incurable by mental means. The question is now asked, "Is cancer an organic disease, or is it some functional derangement of the epithelium tissue which causes it to grow indefinitely until it invades some vital organ?"

A further question arises due to further study. Some of the latest investigators claim that most if not all persons have cancer at some time in life, but that anti-toxin or some other remedy is supplied by the body itself, and the growth is stopped and the tissue absorbed. The question then seems to be pertinent, "If the body can produce the cure within itself, and this would be functional, why cannot mental means stimulate the body to produce it?" or "Does not mental influence stimulate the body to produce it?" What the cancer experts tell us of 10 the wide-spread extension of the disease and its spontaneous cure, the tuberculosis experts affirm of tuberculosis, and certainly of the latter disease spontaneous cures are not uncommon. We also know that mental influence may, in fact does, have an indirect but no less beneficial influence in the cure of tuberculosis. From these examples one seems to be forced to either one of two conclusions, either of which is contrary to generally accepted ideas, viz., first, that these are not organic diseases; or, second, organic diseases are aided or cured by means of mental healing. In general, however, the distinction holds good; the so-called functional cases are amenable to cure by mental means, and the organic are much less so.

Coming back, then, to the common law which underlies all cases or forms of mental healing, we find two general principles upon which it is built—the power of the mind over the body, and the importance of suggestion as a factor in the cure of the disease. The law may be tersely stated in the first person as follows: My body tends to adjust itself so as to be in harmony with my ideas concerning it. This law is equally applicable to the cause or cure of disease by mental means. To apply this law in a universal way as far as mental healing is concerned, we should notice that however the thought of cure may come into the mind, whether by external or auto-suggestion, if it is firmly rooted so as to im 11 press the sub-consciousness, that part of the mind which rules the bodily organs, a tendency toward cure is at once set up and continues as long as that thought has the ascendancy.

Hack Tuke quotes Johannes Mller, a physiologist who lived during the first half of the last century, as follows: "It may be stated as a general fact that any state of body which is conceived to be approaching, and which is expected with certain confidence and certainty of occurrence, will be very prone to ensue, as the mere result of the idea, if it do not lie beyond the bounds of possibility." This is a fair statement of the law from the stand-point of consciousness, but does not include all of the vast influence of subconscious ideas which are so potent in the cure of diseases by mental means. Mller's observation was in advance of his times, but could not be expected to include the results of the latest researches of modern science.

For a great many years physicians have recognized that not only are all diseases made worse by an incorrect mental attitude, but that some diseases are the direct result of worry and other mental disturbances. The mental force which causes colored water to act as an emetic, or postage-stamps to produce a blister, can also produce organic diseases of a serious nature. The large mental factor in the cause of diseases is generally admitted, and it seems reasonable to infer that what is caused by mental 12 influence may be cured by the same means. There is no restriction in the power of the mind in causing disease, and should we restrict the mind as a factor in the cure? The trouble seems to be in the explanation. People ask, "How can the mind have such an effect upon the body?" and to the answer of this question we must now turn our attention.

We all recognize that involuntarily certain bodily effects take place. We blush when we do not wish to; we betray our fears by our blanched faces. Some other factors of mind than the conscious mental processes have charge, and rule certain functions. The heart, the respiratory apparatus, the glands, and digestive organs all carry on their regular functions during sleep and also better without our direction when we are awake. What is the explanation of this? We have recently been saying that the subconsciousness rules these physical organs, and through this that the effects already referred to take place. So much has been written recently regarding the subconsciousness that anything more at this time would be superfluous; suffice it to say that the general conclusions on that subject are accepted as the basis of faith cure. We may, however, go further in our endeavor to explain.

In such mental troubles as psychasthesia much has lately been heard about psycho-analysis and re-education. What does that mean in the language of the psychology of a few years ago? In cases of 13 unreasonable fears or phobias, for example, there is a firmly rooted system of ideas which refuses to depart at the command of consciousness. We analyze the mental store to find out the cause of the unreasonable persistence, and sometimes, quite frequently in fact, have to resort to hypnosis or hypnodization to find the initial trouble. It is then corrected, and re-education consists in living over again from the first experience, the events connected with that fear and correcting them up to date. In this process minutes only are used where the original experiences took weeks. Putting it in other words, we have certain systems of ideas; as a psychological fact of long standing we know that other elements may be injected into that system so as to change it, or that one system may be destroyed and another system built up to take its place. This is the secret of cures of this nature — of mental troubles — the irritating factor, the thorn in the mind, is extracted.

We have heard in modern psychology of the hot and cold places in consciousness, or, to use other terms for the same idea, the central and peripheral ideas, meaning the ideas which dominate consciousness, and those which are in the background. The mind can readily attend to only one thing at a time; if that be pain, for example, that takes up all of our attention. On the other hand, if for some reason some other ideas suddenly become central, then the 14 pain is driven away to the periphery and we say we have no pain, or we have less pain. The sufferer from neuralgia experiences no pain as he responds to the fire alarm, and the toothache stops entirely as we undergo the excitement and fear of entering the dentist's office.

Serious lesions yield to profound emotion born of persuasion, confidence, or excitement; either the gouty or rheumatic man, after hobbling about for years, finds his legs if pursued by a wild bull, or the weak and enfeebled invalid will jump from the bed and carry out heavy articles from a burning house. The central idea is sufficient to command all the reserve energy, and that idea which has suddenly and unexpectedly become central may remain so. What Chalmers called "the expulsive power of a new affection" in the cure of souls, is the precise method of operation in the cure of some bodily ills.

I have here made two suggestions which may help to show how mental healing may be brought about. Not simply the alleviation of bodily ills, but the complete cure may result from the influence on the subconsciousness. A large number of cures are brought about by faith in certain religious practices, this faith amounting to a certainty in the minds of the patients before the cure is started or while it is in progress. Trustful expectation in any one direction acts powerfully through the subconsciousness because it absorbs the whole mind, and 15 thus competition with other ideas, either consciously or subconsciously, is largely excluded. It is this which acts in mental healing under the caption of faith, although some abnormal conditions may also arise to assist the suggestion.

That this confident expectation of a cure is the most potent means of bringing it about, doing that which no medical treatment can accomplish, may be affirmed as the generalized result of experiences of the most varied kind, extending through a long series of ages. It is this factor which is common to methods of the most diverse character. It is noticeable that any system of treatment, however absurd, that can be puffed into public notoriety for efficacy, any individual who by accident or design obtains a reputation for a special gift of healing, is certain to attract a multitude of sufferers, among whom will be many who are capable of being really benefited by a strong assurance of relief. Thus, the practitioner with a great reputation has an advantage over his neighboring physicians, not only on account of the superior skill which he may have acquired, but because his reputation causes this confident expectation, so beneficial in itself.

There have been fashions in cures as in other things. At one time a certain relic, or healer, would attract and cure, and shortly afterward it would be deserted and inefficacious, not because it had lost its power, but because it had lost its reputation, 16 and the people had consequently lost their faith in it. Some other relics would then acquire a reputation, spring into popular favor, and the crowds would flock to them. We have many modern instances of this kind. If sufficient confidence in the power of a concoction, a shrine, a relic, or a person can be aroused, genuine cures can be wrought regardless of the healing properties of the dose.

The whole system of mental therapeutics may be divided into two parts; what we may designate as metaphysical cure denies that either matter or evil exists, and heals by inspiring the belief that the disease cannot assail the patient because he is pure spirit; the other class, faith cure, recognizes the disease, but cures by faith in the power of divinity, persons, objects, or suggestion.

Without doubt the best example of the former theory and the most successful application of it are found in Christian Science. Perhaps it is not so difficult to understand the frame of mind which brought about this theory on the part of Mrs. Eddy. Here was an hysterical, neurotic woman who knew nothing all her life but illness and misfortune. She had suffered much from many physicians and was none the better but rather worse. One physician had called her disease one thing, another had designated it another, until confusion and uncertainty were increased with every physician consulted. She began to despair of ever either knowing about her 17 disease or of having it cured. As a last resort she went to Quimby, and he told her there was no disease and no need of suffering. He denied the suffering, and she accepted his teaching; she followed him in denying disease and then matter, and kept on with her theory of negation and denial until she evolved her present theory. It was a natural reaction from all conceivable pains characteristic of hysteria, to no pain; from all conceivable diseases which different physicians had opined, to no disease; from the infirmity of body with its inhibitory discomfitures, to no body. The history of the founder of Christian Science is its best *raison d' être*, especially from a psychological stand-point, and the rather strange thing is that a reaction from an abnormality, going as it naturally does to another abnormality, should find a response in the religious cravings of so many; the philosophy undoubtedly would not attract as it does were there not connected with it, in the practical working of the system, the lure of mental healing.

Faith cure, the other form of mental healing, has such a variety of forms that it is practically impossible to describe a typical one. Faith in some power, or, what amounts to the same thing, the uncritical reception of suggestions concerning the cure, is the common factor in all forms.

The question naturally arises, Which is the best form of mental healing? There is no best form for 18 all diseases and all persons. For example, it matters not how new associational systems are formed so long as they are substituted for the pernicious ones. It may be in the common experiences of every-day life, through the pleading of a friend, during sleep or trance, in some abnormal state of a hypnotic character, or during religious ecstasy, and we cannot well say in any given case that one form will be more efficacious than another. Mental healing creates nothing new, but simply makes use of the normal mechanism of the mind and body. The question then is, What method of mental healing is most likely to stimulate the mental mechanism so that physiological processes will be set up leading to a cure? The great power of faith and expectancy may decide the question, and the answer may be in favor of the form in which the patient has the most faith, either on account of its reputation, or on account of some prejudice on the part of the patient.

19

CHAPTER II

EARLY CIVILIZATIONS

"The office of the physician extends equally to the purification of mind and body; to neglect the one is to expose the other to evident peril. It is not only the body that by its sound constitution strengthens the soul, but the well-regulated soul by its authoritative power maintains the body in perfect health." — Plato.

"Aristotle mapped out philosophy and morals in lines the world yet accepts in the main, but he did not know the difference between the nerves and the tendons. Rome had a sound system of jurisprudence before it had a physician, using only priest-craft for healing. Cicero was the greatest lawyer the world has seen, but there was not a man in Rome who could have cured him of a colic. The Greek was an expert dialectician when he was using incantations for his diseases. As late as when the Puritans were enunciating their lofty principles, it was generally held that the king's touch would cure scrofula. Governor Winthrop, of colonial days, treated 'small-pox and all fevers' by a powder made from 'live toads baked in an earthen pot in the open air.'" — Munger.

"There is nothing so absurd or ridiculous that has not at some time been said by some philosopher. Fontenelle says he would undertake to persuade the whole republic of readers to believe that the sun was neither the cause of light or heat, if he could only get six philosophers on his side." — Goldsmith.

A glance at the history of medicine will show three fairly well defined periods. The beginning of the first is hidden in the uncertain days of prehistoric ages and the period continues down to early Christian times — perhaps the end of the second century when Galen died. The second period extends from this time to the fifteenth or sixteenth centuries, and the third period embraces the last 20 three or four centuries. The second period was almost wholly stationary, and this, we are ashamed to say, was largely due to the prohibitive attitude of the church. The science of medicine, then, is almost wholly the result of the investigations and study of the last period. This means that medicine is one of the youngest of the sciences, while from the very nature of the case it is one of the oldest of arts.

From the beginning of the art of therapeutics, mental healing has been a large factor in the cure. This was not recognized, of course, for only in the last century has the psychic element been admitted to any extent as a therapeutic agent. We can read back now, however, and see what a large element this really was. The cruder the art, the more powerful was the mental influence. The ways of primitive therapeutics are completely hidden from us except what we can gather from the races which retained their primitive practices in historic times. We can well understand, though, that the concoctions of medicine-men and witch-doctors could have little effect except in a suggestive way. Snakes' heads, toads' toes, lizards' tails, and beetles' wings have a small place in the pharmacopœia of to-day, except as placebos, and it is extremely doubtful if they were ever valuable for any other purpose.

The object of the primitive practitioner seems to have been to make an impression upon the patient 21 either by the explanation of his disease or by the effort made to effect a cure. The explanation most frequently given was that demons were responsible for the trouble, and the cure of the disease was an attempted exorcism of the demon. The more fantastic the ceremony, the more likely the cure, on account of the mental influence upon the patient. The primitive man's religion and therapeutics were inextricably interwoven and, unless we make an exception of the past few years, this has always been an unprofitable union for one or both. All the early civilizations with the exception of the Greeks, as well as the Christian nations up to the sixteenth century, were handicapped by this partnership, and it was only by divorcing the two that therapeutics was able to make the great advance during the last period. The nature of the primitive religions was responsible to a great extent for the nature of the method of healing, therefore, appeasing the offended deity and exorcising the demon were therapeutic as well as religious ceremonies.

The Chinese of to-day, except in some of the seaboard cities, must be classed among the earliest civilizations, for their mode of living has not changed much in the last two or three milleniums. Their system of medical practice partakes of the character of that found among the early people, with some slight modifications which show some relationship to the European practice during the Dark Ages. 22

All sorts of disgusting doses are administered, and incantations and exorcisms are among the most effective methods of healing. For example, Hardy reports that a missionary told him of his being called in to see a man suffering from convulsions; he found him smelling white mice in a cage, with a dead fowl fastened on his chest, and a bundle of grass attached to his feet. This had been the prescription of a native physician.

Medicines are made from asses' sinews, fowls' blood, bears' gall, shaving of a rhinoceros' horn, moss grown on a coffin, and the dung of dogs, pigs, fowl, rabbits, pigeons, and bats. Cockroach tea, bear-paw soup, essence of monkey paw, toads' eye-brows, and earth-worms rolled in honey are common doses. The excrement of a mosquito is considered as efficacious as it is scarce, and here, as in Europe in the Middle Ages, the hair of the dog that bit you is used to heal the bite and to prevent hydrophobia. An infusion from the bones of a tiger is believed to confer courage, strength, and agility, and the flesh of a snake is boiled and eaten to make one cunning and wise. Chips from coffins which have been let down into the grave are boiled and are said to possess great virtue for catarrh. Flies, fleas, and bed-bugs prepared in different ways are given for various diseases. Medicines are given in all forms, and not infrequently pills are as large as a pigeon's egg. If any of these medicines ever had any beneficent 23 effect it must have been through mental rather than through physical means.

Nevius has left us in no doubt concerning the belief in demons among the Chinese, and of the effect this belief has on their theory of disease. Certain forms are daily observed to drive away the evil spirits. For this purpose Taoist priests are hired to recite formul欠ring bells, and manipulate bowls of water, candles, joss-sticks, and curious charms. Sometimes the family insists that one of the priests shall ascend a ladder, the rounds of which are formed of swords or knives with the sharp edge uppermost, and go through his exorcisms at the top. Instead of the priest, the mother may make a fire of paper and wave a small garment of her sick child over it.

A relative or friend of a sick person will visit a temple and beat the drum, which notifies the god that there is urgent need of his help. To be sure that the god hears, his ears are tickled, and the part of the image which corresponds to the afflicted part of the sick person's body is rubbed. Some ashes from the censor standing before the image may be taken to the sick-room and there reverenced. Holy water is brought from the temple, boiled with tea, and drunk as a certain cure for disease. Spells are written on paper and burned;

the ashes are then put into water and drunk as medicine. Charms and magical tricks of all kinds are tried in order to drive away the demon. 24

There were schools of medicine in Egypt in the fifteenth century before the Christian era, and the Egyptians made great progress in the study and practice of medicine. Notwithstanding this, we find many examples of mental healing, or at least attempts at healing by mental means, among the recipes and prescriptions which have come down to us. Poor and superstitious persons, especially, had recourse to dreams, to wizards, to donations, to sacred animals, and to exvotos to the gods. Charms were also written for the credulous, some of which have been found on small pieces of papyrus, which were rolled up and worn, as by the modern Egyptians.

The Ebers papyrus, an important and very ancient manual of Egyptian medicine, has thrown much light on early Egyptian practices. It shows that an important part of the treatment prior to 1552 B. C., consisted in the laying on of hands, combined with an extensive formulary and ceremonial rites. The physicians were the priests, and among the interesting contents of this manuscript are several formul栴o be used as prayers while compounding medicaments. Some of the prescriptions given here are accompanied by exorcisms which were to be used at the same time. Many of the prescriptions could have had little but mental influence because the remedies recommended consisted of horrible mixtures of unsavory ingredients, the theory, if we can judge by the medicines, being that the more dis 25 gusting the dose the more efficacious the remedy; this is true from a mental stand-point.

Demonism was not unknown; in fact, it underlay much of the treatment. People did not die, but they were assassinated. The murderer might belong to this or to the spirit world. He might be a god, a spirit, or the soul of a dead man that had cunningly entered a living person. The physician must first discover the nature of the possessing spirit, and then attack it. Powerful magic was the weapon used, and the healer must be an expert in reciting incantations and skilful in making amulets. On account of this, the Egyptians became the most skilled in magic of any people, and have their equals only in the Hindus of to-day. The experiences of Joseph and

Moses, as recorded in the Bible, give us some idea of their skill at that time. After the exorcism the physician used medicine to relieve the disorders which the presence of the strange being had produced in the body.

Masp麒 gives us the following information: "The cure-workers are divided into several categories. Some incline towards sorcery, and have faith in formulas and talismans only; they think they have done enough if they have driven out the spirit. Others extol the use of drugs; they study the qualities of plants and minerals, describe the diseases to which each of the substances provided by nature is suitable, and settle the exact time 26 when they must be procured and applied; certain herbs have no power unless they are gathered during the night at the full moon, others are efficacious in summer only, another acts equally well in winter or summer. The best doctors carefully avoid binding themselves exclusively to either method." 1

Among the early Egyptians the human body was divided into thirty-six parts, each of which was thought to be under the particular government of one of the aerial demons, who presided over the triple divisions of the twelve signs. The priests practised a separate invocation for each genius, which they used in order to obtain for them the cure of the particular member confided to their care. We have the authority of Origen for saying that in his time when any part of the body was diseased, a cure was effected by invoking the demon to whose province it belonged. Perhaps this is why the different parts of the body were assigned to the different planets, and later to different saints. It undoubtedly accounts for the fact that an Egyptian physician treated only one part of the body and refused to infringe on the domain of his brother physician.

Incubation was commonly practised at the temples of Isis and Serapis as it was afterward among the Greeks. This "temple sleep" was closely akin 27 in its effects to hypnotism and was undoubtedly efficacious in the case of some diseases.

The Babylonian system of therapeutics was not unlike the Egyptian as far as incantations were concerned. Many of these have been discovered. The formulas usually consist of a description of the disease and its symptoms, a desire for deliverance from it, and an order for it to depart. Some draughts were given which may have had some medicinal effect, but they were supposed to be enchanted drinks. Knots were supposed to have some magical effect on diseases, and conjurations were also wrought by the power of numbers. The Book of Daniel shows the official recognition given to magicians, astrologers, and sorcerers.

The Jews seem to have got their early medical knowledge from the Egyptians, and changed it only in so far as their religion made it necessary, for with them as with others the healing art was a part of the religion, and the Levites were the sole practitioners. Much valuable medical knowledge was mixed with much that could only have had a mental influence. Disease was considered a punishment for sin, and hence the cure was religious rather than medical. The disease might be inflicted by God direct, and the cure would be a proof of his forgiveness; it might also be inflicted by Satan or the spirits of the air with the permission of Jehovah, and the cure would then be brought about by exorcism.

28 There seems to have been a rather elaborate system of demonology among the Jews, who were at one time the chief exponents of the doctrine, and consequently the principal exorcists. Among the Jews a prominent "demoness of sickness is Bath-Chorin. She touches the hands and lower limbs by night. Many diseases are caused by demons." According to Josephus, "to demons may be ascribed leprosy, rabies, asthma, cardiac diseases, nervous diseases, which last are the specialty of evil demons, such as epilepsy." Incantations were in use among the later Jews, and amulets of neck-chains like serpents and ear-rings were employed to protect the wearers against the evil eye and similar troubles.

In India, medicine became a separate science very early, according to the sacred books, the Vedas. Notwithstanding this, demonology played a large part in the production of disease according to their theories, and religious observances were helpful in the cures.

Among the oldest documents which we possess relative to the practice of medicine, are the various treatises contained in the collection which bears the name of Hippocrates (460-375 B. C.). He was the first physician to relieve medicine from the trammels of superstition and the delusions of philosophy.

The Greeks undoubtedly believed in demons, but, different from the nations around them, considered 29 the demons to be well-intentioned. Homer (c. 1000 B. C.) speaks frequently of demons, and in one instance in the Odyssey tells of a sick man pining away, "one upon whom a hateful demon had gazed." Empedocles (c. 490-430 B. C.) taught that demons "were of a mixed and inconstant nature, and are subjected to a purgatorial process which may finally end in their ascension to higher abodes." Yet he attributed to them nearly all the calamities, vexations, and plagues incident to mankind. Plato (427-347 B. C.) writes of demons good and bad, and Aristotle (384-322 B. C.), the son of a physician, speaks directly of "demons influencing and inspiring the possessed." Socrates (470-399 B. C.) claimed to have continually with him a demon—a guardian spirit.

In Greece, in early days, physicians were looked upon as gods. Even after the siege of Troy, the sons of the gods and the heroes were alone supposed to understand the secrets of medicine and surgery. At a late period Yculapius, the son of Apollo, was worshipped as a deity. When we speak of the art of healing in Greece, one naturally thinks of the apparent monopoly of the Yclepiades, who ministered unto the Grecian sick for centuries.

The original seat of the worship of Yculapius was at Epidaurus, where there was a splendid temple, adorned with a gold and ivory statue of the god, who was represented sitting, one hand holding a 30 staff, the other resting on the head of a serpent, the emblem of sagacity and longevity; a dog crouched at his feet. The temple was frequented by harmless serpents, in the form of which the god was supposed to manifest himself. According to Homer, his sons, Machaon and Podalirius, who were great warriors, treated wounds and external diseases only; and it is probable that their father practised in the same manner, as he is said to have invented the probe and the bandaging of wounds. His priests, the Yclepiades, however, practised incantations, and cured diseases by leading their patients to believe that the god himself delivered his prescriptions in dreams and visions; for this imposture they were roughly satirized by Aristophanes in his play of "Plutus." It is probable that the preparations, consisting of abstinence, tranquillity, and bathing, requisite for obtaining the divine intercourse, and, above all, the confidence reposed in the Yclepiades, were often productive of benefit.

The excavations of Cavvadias at Epidaurus have furnished us with much interesting material concerning the cures performed at this ancient shrine, five hundred years before the beginning of the Christian era. If the modern physician still recognizes Yculapius as his patron saint, he must have great respect for mental healing. It appears certain from inscriptions found upon "stel栢that were dug up at Epidaurus and published in 1891, that the system 31 of Ycula-pius was based upon the miracle-working of a demi-god, and not upon medical art as we now know it. The *modus operandi* was unique in some details. The patients, mostly incurables, came laden with sacrifices. After prayer, they cleansed themselves with water from the holy well, and offered up sacrifices. Certain ceremonial acts were then performed by the priests, and the patients were put to sleep on the skins of the animals offered at the altar, or at the foot of the statue of the divinity, while the priests performed further sacred rites. The son of Apollo then appeared to them in dreams, attended to the particular ailments of the sufferers, and specified further sacrifices or acts which would restore health. In many cases the sick awoke suddenly cured. Large sums of money were asked for these cures; from one inscription we learn that a sum corre-sponding to $12,000 was paid as a fee. The record of the cure was carved on the temple as at Lourdes to-day, *e.g.*:

"Some days back, a certain Caius, who was blind, learned from an oracle that he should repair to the temple, put up his fervent pray-ers, cross the sanctuary from right to left, place his five fingers on the altar, then raise his hand and cover his eyes. He obeyed, and instantly his sight was restored, amid the loud acclamations of the multitude. These signs of the omnipotence of the gods were shown in the reign of Antoninus."

32 "A blind soldier, named Valerius Apes, having consulted the oracle, was informed that he should mix the blood of a white cock with honey, to make up an ointment to be applied to his eyes for three consecutive days. He received his sight, and returned public thanks to the gods."

"Julian appeared lost beyond all hope, from a spitting of blood. The gods ordered him to take from the altar some seeds of the pine, and to mix them with honey, of which mixture he was to eat for three days. He was saved, and came to thank the gods in the presence of the people." 2

It was not until five centuries later, when credulity concerning miracles was on the wane, that the priests began to study and to apply medical means in order to sustain the reputation of the place, and to keep up its enormous revenues.

Temples similar to this one at Epidaurus existed at numerous places, among which were Rhodes, Cnidus, Cos, and one was to be found on the banks of the Tiber. The temple at Cos was rich in votive offerings, which generally represented the parts of the body healed, and an account of the method of cure adopted. From these singular clinical records, Hippocrates, a reputed descendant of Yculapius, is reported to have constructed his treatise on Dietetics.

33

For a long time after the age of Hercules and the heroic times, invalids in Greece sought relief from their sufferings from these descendants of Yculapius in the temples of that god, which an enlightened policy had raised on elevated spots, near medicinal springs, and in salubrious vicinities. Those men who pretended in right of birth to hold the gift of curing, finally learned the art of it. The preservation in the temple of the history of those diseases, the cure of which had been sought by them, aided greatly in this happy culmination.

Of Yculapius himself, it is said that he employed the trumpet to cure sciatica; he claimed that its continued sound made the fibres of the nerves to palpitate, and the pain vanished. In line with this treatment, Democritus affirmed that diseases are capable of being cured by the sound of a flute, when properly played.

Herbs were also used among the Greeks, but almost wholly in the form of charms rather than on account of what we claim now as real medicinal value. For example, great virtues were ascribed to the herb alysson which was pounded and eaten with meat to cure hydrophobia. If suspended in the house, it promoted the health of the inmates and protected both men and cattle from enchantments; when bound in a piece of scarlet flannel round the necks of the latter, it preserved them from all diseases.

34 There seems to have been no independent school of Roman medicine. From early times there was a very complicated system of superstitious medicine, as a part of the religion, which is supposed to have been borrowed from the Etruscans. This comprehended both the theory and cure of disease. The Romans got along for centuries without doctors; in fact, doctors were a Grecian importation, not made until about two centuries before Christ.

1 G. Masp麒, *Life in Ancient Egypt and Assyria*, chap. VII.

2 E. Berdoe, "A Medical View of the Miracles at Lourdes," *Nineteenth Century*, October, 1895.

35

CHAPTER III

THE INFLUENCE OF CHRISTIANITY

"The Alchemist may doubt the shining gold His crucible pours out, But faith, fanatic faith, once wedded fast To some dear falsehood, Hugs it to the last."

"Death is the cure of all diseases. There is no *catholicon* or universal remedy I know, but this, which though nauseous to queasy stomachs, yet to prepared appetites is nectar, and a pleasant potion of immortality." — Browne.

"I'll tell you what now of the Devil:
He's no such horrid creature; cloven-footed,
Black, saucer-ey'd, his nostrils breathing fire,
As these lying Christians make him." — Massinger.

"If the cure be wrought, what matters it to the happy invalid ... whether the cure is wrought by the touch of the Divine hand or the overpowering influence of a great idea upon the nervous system? If our hunger be appeased, it matters little whether it is by manna rained down from heaven, or a wheaten loaf raised from the harvest field. Miraculous water from the rock does not quench the thirst better than that which bubbles from the village spring." — Berdoe.

The advent of the Christian religion into the world, while purporting to minister especially to the spiritual life, had a wide-reaching and potent influence on the art of healing the body. We cannot sum up the effect by saying that this influence was either wholly good or bad — its relation to therapeutics was a mixed one. It can be truthfully said that nothing has retarded the science of medicine during 36 the past two thousand years so much as the iron grip of decadent orthodoxy, and, on the other hand, no power has caused men and women so to sacrifice time, money, and even life itself for the care and nurture of the sick, as the example and precepts of Jesus Christ.

For eighteen centuries this paradoxical position was held by the church, and the antithetical attitudes of hindrance and help continued to exist. As valuable as was the spirit instilled into the hearts of His followers by the tenderness of the Master, it was never sufficient to counterbalance the deterrent effects of the religion which they espoused. The retardation was caused by two related beliefs which permeated the church: The first was the doctrine of the power of demons in the lives of men, especially in the production of disease; and the second was the prevalence of the idea of the possibility and probability of the performance of miracles, particularly in the healing of diseases.

A rather complicated science of demonology had come down from primitive sources through Egyptian, Babylonian, and Greek civilization, although the demons of the Greeks were principally good spirits. At the time of Christ, however, the Jews were the most ardent advocates of demonology, and hence the chief exorcists. They expelled demons partly by adjuration and partly by means of a certain miraculous root named Baaras. They considered 37 it nothing at all out of the ordinary to meet men who were possessed by demons, and just as common an experience to see them healed by having the demon exorcised. Josephus assures us that in the reign of Vespasian he had himself seen a Jew named Eleazar perform an exorcism; by means of adjuration and the Baaras root he drew a demon through the nostrils of a possessed person, who fell to the ground on the accomplishment of the miracle, while on the command of the magician the demon, to prove that it had really left its victim, threw down a cup of water which had been placed at a distance.

Knowing as we do the close relationship between Judaism and Christianity, it does not surprise us to discover that the Christians inherited the doctrine and practice of the Jews in this matter. This is more readily understood when we remember the connection of Jesus with cases of demoniacal possession, and Paul's frequent references to the spirits of the air. Following the example of their Master, Christians everywhere became exorcists. Through the influence of Philo's writings, Jewish demonology was propagated among Christian converts, and the Gnostics quickly absorbed and spread the notion of preternatural interposition. Next to the belief in the second coming of Christ, the doctrine which most influenced the action of the early church was that of a spiritual world and its hierarchy. Terrestrial things were ruled by all sorts of spiritual beings.

38 Some philosophers, as well as the founders of different religions, expelled demons, and the Christians fully recognized the power possessed by the Jewish and gentile exorcists; the followers of Christ, however, claimed to be in many respects the superior of all others. The fathers maintained the reality of all pagan miracles as fully as their own, except that doubt was sometimes cast on some forms of healing and prophecy. Demons which had resisted all the enchantments of the pagans might be cast out, oracles could be silenced, and unclean spirits compelled to acknowledge the truth of the Christian faith by the Christians, who simply made the sign of the cross, or repeated the name of the Master.

The power of the Christian exorcists was shown by still more wonderful feats. Demons, which were sometimes supposed to enter animals, were expelled. St. Hilarion (288-371), we are told, courageously confronted and relieved a possessed camel. "The great St. Ambrose [340-397] tells us that a priest, while saying mass, was troubled by the croaking of frogs in a neighboring marsh; that he exorcised them, and so stopped their noise. St. Bernard [1091-1153], as the monkish chroniclers tell us, mounting the pulpit to preach in his abbey, was interrupted by a crowd of flies; straightway the saint uttered the sacred formula of excommunication, when the flies fell dead upon the pavement in heaps, and were cast out with shovels!

A formula of ex 39 orcism attributed to a saint of the ninth century, which remained in use down to a recent period, especially declares insects injurious to crops to be possessed of evil spirits, and names, among the animals to be excommunicated or exorcised, moles, mice, and serpents. The use of exorcism against caterpillars and grasshoppers was also common. In the thirteenth century a bishop of Lausanne, finding that the eels in Lake Leman troubled the fishermen, attempted to remove the difficulty by exorcism, and two centuries later one of his successors excommunicated all the May-bugs in the diocese. As late as 1731 there appears an entry on the municipal register of Thonon as follows: '*Resolved*, that this town join with other parishes of this province in obtaining from Rome an excommunication against the insects, and that it will contribute *pro rata* to the expense of the same.'"

Scripture was cited to prove the diabolical character of some animals during the Middle Ages. Says White: "Did anyone venture to deny that animals could be possessed by Satan, he was at once silenced by reference to the entrance of Satan into the serpent in the Garden of Eden, and to the casting of devils into swine by the Founder of Christianity himself." 3

Notwithstanding the pleasing theory adopted by 40 the earlier Christian writers that the powers of darkness were unable to harm the faithful without the permission of divinity, to whom demoniacal spirits were ultimately subjected, unlimited power was conceded to those beings who existed under divine sanction. Demoniacal 挹s or emanations were acknowledged to be the primitive source of earthly sufferings, pestilence among men, sickness and other bodily afflictions, but inflicted with the consent of God, whose messengers they were.

Early Christian writers boldly asserted that all the disorders of the world originated with the devil and his sinister companions, because they were stirred with the unholy desire to obtain associates in their miseries. It was impossible to fix a limit to the number of these malevolent spirits constantly provoking diseases and infirmities upon men. They were alleged to surround mankind so densely that each person had a thousand to his right and ten thousand to the left of him. Endowed with the subtlest activity, they were able to reach the remotest points of earth in the twinkling of an eye.

According to Salverte, Tatian, a sincere defender of Christianity, who lived in the second century, "does not deny the wonderful cures effected by the priests of the temples of the Polytheists; he only attempts to explain them by supposing that the pagan gods were actual demons, and that they introduced disease into the body of a healthy man, an 41 nouncing to him, in a dream, that he should be cured if he implored their assistance; and then, by terminating the evil which they themselves had produced, they obtained the glory of having worked the miracle." 4

So firm was the belief that Christians could exorcise these demons that from the time of Justin Martyr (100-163), for about two centuries, there is not a single Christian writer who does not solemnly and explicitly assert the reality and frequent employment of this power. In his Second Apology, Justin says: "And now you can learn this from what is under your own observation. For numberless demoniacs throughout the whole world, and in your city, many of our Christian men exorcising them in the name of Jesus Christ, who was crucified under Pontius Pilate, have healed and do heal, rendering helpless and driving the possessing demons out of the men, though they could not be cured by all the other exorcists, and those who used incantations and drugs."

Iren浩 (130-202) held that mankind, through transgressions of divine command, fell absolutely from the time of Adam into the power of Satan. On the other hand, he assures us that all Christians possessed the power of working miracles; that they prophesied, cast out devils, healed the sick, and sometimes even raised the dead; that some who had 42 been thus resuscitated lived for many years among them, and that it would be impossible to reckon the wonderful acts that were daily performed. 5

Tertullian (160-220) insisted that a malevolent angel was in constant attendance upon every person, but in writing to the pagans in a time of persecution he challenged his opponents to bring forth any person who was possessed by a demon or any of those prophets or virgins who were supposed to be inspired by a divinity. He asserted that all demons would be compelled to confess their diabolical character when questioned by any Christians, and invited the pagans, if it were otherwise, to put the Christian immediately to death, for this, he thought, was the simplest and most decisive demonstration of the faith.

Lecky tells us of the attitude of the fathers toward demonism in the following words: "Justin Martyr, Origen, Lactantius, Athanasius, and Minucius Felix, all in language equally solemn and explicit, call upon the pagans to form their own opinions from the confessions wrung from their own gods. We hear from them, that when a Christian began to pray, to make the sign of the cross, or to utter the name of his Master in the presence of a possessed or inspired person, the latter, by screams and frightful contortions, exhibited the torture that was inflicted, and by this torture the evil spirit was compelled to avow its nature. Several of the Christian writers declare that this was generally known to pagans." 6

Origen (185-254) said: "It is demons which produce famine, unfruitfulness, corruptions of the air, pestilence; they hover concealed in clouds in the lower atmosphere, and are attracted by the blood and incense which the heathen offer to them as gods." He thought, though, that Raphael had special care of the sick and the infirm. Cyprian (186-258) charged that demons caused luxations and fractures of the limbs, undermined the health, and harassed with diseases. Up to this time it was the privilege of any Christian to exorcise demons, but Pope Fabian (236-250) assigned a definite name and functions to exorcists as a separate order. To-day the priest has included in his ordination vows those of exorcist. Gregory of Nazianzus (329-390) declared that bodily pains are provoked by demons, and that medicines are useless, but that demoniacs are often cured by laying on of consecrated hands. St. Augustine (354-430) said: "All diseases of Christians are to be ascribed to these demons; chiefly do they torment fresh-baptized Christians, yea, even the guiltless newborn infants."

Baltus 7 says: "De tous les anciens auteurs eccl鳩astiques, n'y en ayant pas un qui n'ait parl頤e ce pouvoir admirable que les Chr鳺ens avoient de 44 chasser les d魯ns," and Gregory of Tours (538-594) says that exorcism was common in his time, having himself seen a monk named Julian cure by his words a possessed person. This testimony of Gregory's concerning the prevalence of exorcisms at the end of the sixth century is interesting in view of the facts that the Council of Laodicea, in the fourth century, forbade any one to exorcise, except those duly authorized by the bishop, and that in the very beginning of the fifth century a physician named Posidonius denied the existence of possession. The fathers of the church, however, ridiculed the solemn assertion of physicians that many of these alleged demoniacal infirmities were attributable to material agencies, and were fully persuaded in their own minds that demons took possession of the organism of the human body.

At about this time, such a broad-minded man as Gregory the Great (540-604) solemnly related that a nun, having eaten some lettuce without making the sign of the cross, swallowed a devil, and that, when commanded by a holy man to come forth, the devil replied: "How am I to blame? I was sitting on the lettuce, and this woman, not having made the sign of the cross, ate me along with it." This is but an example of the ideas concerning the entrance of demons into the possessed. 8 Besides the 45 possibility of being taken into the mouth with one's food, they might enter while the mouth was opened to breathe. Exorcists were therefore careful to keep their mouths closed when casting out evil spirits, lest the imps should jump into their mouths from the mouths of the patients. Another theory was that the devil entered human beings during sleep, and at a comparatively recent period a king of Spain, Charles II (1661-1700), kept off the devil while asleep by the presence of his confessor and two friars. 9

Shortly before the reign of Gregory, there came into vogue the fashion of exorcising demons by means of a written formula rather than by the earlier means of making the sign of the cross and invoking the name of Jesus. The theory of demonology was never very clear nor consistent. By some it was claimed that in the practice of the magical arts evil spirits provided cure for sickness, others maintained that they could not heal any diseases, and hence the true test of Christianity was the ability to cure bodily ills. A compromise position was that demons were only successful in eliminating diseases which they had themselves caused. There was not a little doubt in some cases about the character of the possessing spirits, and it behooved people to be careful; demons might use men as habitations, and while posing as good angels vitiate health and provoke disease.

46

At the beginning of the seventh century, we have an account of an exorcism by St. Gall (556-640), and during the Carlovingian age the healing at Monte Cassino was based on the Satanic origin of disease. When the conversion of northern races to Christianity began, demonology received a stimulus. An unlimited number of demons, similar in individuality and prowess, were substituted for the pagan demons, and the pagan gods were added as additional demons. When proselytes were taken into the church, care was taken to exorcise all evil spirits. During the baptismal service the Satanic hosts, as originators of sin, vice, and maladies, were expelled by insufflation of the officiating clergyman, the sign of the cross, and the invocation of the Triune Deity. The earliest formulas for such expulsion directed a double exhalation of the priest. 10

In all epidemics of the Middle Ages, such persons as were afflicted by pestilent diseases were declared contaminated by the devil, and carried to churches and chapels, a dozen at a time, securely bound together. They were thrown upon the floor, where they lay, according to the attestation of a pitying chronicler, until dead or restored to health.

Unsound mind was universally accepted as a 47 specific distinction of diabolical power, and caused by the corporeal presence of an impure spirit. Imbeciles and the insane were, throughout the Middle Ages, especially conceded to be the abode of avenging and frenzied demons. In aggravated cases, the actual presence of the medicinal saint was necessary; in less vexatious maladies, the bare imposition of hands, accompanied by plaintive prayer, quickly healed the diseased. 11

As early as the fifth century before Christ, Hippocrates of Cos asserted that madness was simply a disease of the brain, but notwithstanding the reiteration of this scientific truth the church repudiated it, and as late as the Reformation, Martin Luther maintained that not only was insanity caused by diabolical influences, but that "Satan produces all the maladies which afflict mankind." Even much later, however, when other diseases were assigned a physical origin, insanity was still thought to be demoniacal possession. As late as Bossuet's time, lunacy was thought to be the work of demons. The cultured and progressive Bishop of Meaux, while trying to throw off the shackles of superstition, delivered and published two great sermons in which demoniacal possession is defended. To show how the idea has clung, notwithstanding the advancement and enlightenment of 48 late years, we may notice a trial which took place at Wemding, in southern Germany, in 1892, of which White tells us.

"A boy had become hysterical, and the Capuchin Father Aurelian tried to exorcise him, and charged a peasant's wife, Frau Herz, with bewitching him, on evidence that would have cost the woman her life at any time during the seventeenth century. Thereupon the woman's husband brought suit against Father Aurelian for slander. The latter urged in his defence that the boy was possessed of an evil spirit, if anybody ever was; that what had been said and done was in accordance with the rules and regulations of the Church, as laid down in decrees, formulas, and rituals sanctioned by popes, councils, and innumerable bishops during ages. All in vain. The court condemned the good father to fine and imprisonment." 12

I cannot refrain from quoting in this connection the now famous epitaph of Lord Westbury's, suggested by the decision given by him as Lord Chancellor in the case against Mr. Wilson in which it was charged that the latter denied the doctrine of eternal punishment. The court decided that it did "not find in the formularies of the English Church any such distinct declaration upon the subject as to require it to punish the expression of a hope by a clergyman that even the ultimate pardon of the 49 wicked who are condemned in the day of judgment may be consistent with the will of Almighty God." The following is the epitaph:

"RICHARD BARON WESTBURY,

Lord High Chancellor of England.
He was an eminent Christian,
An energetic and merciful Statesman,
And a still more eminent and merciful Judge.
During his three years' tenure of office
He abolished the ancient method of conveying land,

The time-honored institution of the Insolvents' Court,
And
The Eternity of Punishment.
Toward the close of his earthly career,
In the Judicial Committee of the Privy Council,
He dismissed Hell with costs,
And took away from Orthodox members of the
Church of England
Their last hope of everlasting damnation." 13

In the Middle Ages there was a strange and incongruous mixture of medicine and exorcism. Notice the following prescriptions:

"If an elf or a goblin come, smear his forehead with this salve, put it on his eyes, cense him with incense, and sign him frequently with the sign of the cross."

"For a fiend-sick man: When a devil possesses a man, or controls him from within with disease, a spew-drink of lupin, bishopwort, henbane, garlic. Pound these together, add ale and holy water." 50
"A drink for a fiend-sick man, to be drunk out of a church bell: Githrife, cynoglossum, yarrow, lupin, flower-de-luce, fennel, lichen, lovage. Work up to a drink with clear ale, sing seven masses over it, add garlic and holy water, and let the possessed sing the *Beati Immaculati*; then let him drink the dose out of a church bell, and let the priest sing over him the *Domine Sancte Pater Omnipotens*." 14

Three methods of driving out demons from the insane were used: the main weapon against the devil and his angels has always been exorcism by means of ecclesiastical formula and signs. These formulas degenerated at one time to the vilest cursings, threatenings, and vulgarities. A second means was by an effort to disgust the demon and wound his pride. This might simply precede the exorcism proper. To accomplish this purpose of offending the demons, the most blasphemous and obscene epithets were used by the exorcist, which were allowable and perfectly proper when addressing demons. Most of these are so indecent that they cannot be printed, but the following are some examples:

"Thou lustful and stupid one,... thou lean sow, famine-stricken and most impure,... thou wrinkled beast, thou mangy beast, thou beast of all beasts the most beastly,... thou mad spirit,... thou bestial and foolish drunkard,... most greedy 51 wolf,... most abominable whisperer,... thou sooty spirit from Tartarus!... I cast thee down, O Tartarean boor,... into the infernal kitchen!... Loathsome cobbler,... dingy collier,... filthy sow (*scrofa stercorata*),... perfidious boar,... envious crocodile,... malodorous drudge,... wounded basilisk,... rust-colored asp,... swollen toad,... entangled spider,... lousy swineherd (*porcarie pedicose*),... lowest of the low,... cudgelled ass," etc. 15

The pride of the demon was also to be wounded by the use of the vilest-smelling drugs, by trampling underfoot and spitting upon the picture of the devil, or even by sprinkling upon it foul compounds. Some even tried to scare the demon by using large-sounding words and names.

The third method of exorcism was punishment. The attempt was frequently made to scourge the demon out of the body. The exorcism was more effective if the name of the demon could be ascertained. If successful in procuring the name, it was written on a piece of paper and burned in a fire previously blessed, which caused the demons to suffer all the torments in the accompanying exorcisms. All forms of torture were employed, and in the great cities of Europe, "witch towers," where witches and demoniacs were tortured, and "fool towers," where the more gentle lunatics were im 52 prisoned, may still be seen. The treatment of the insane in the Middle Ages is one of the darkest blots on the growing civilization.

The exorcism being completed, when some of the weaker demons were put to flight an after service was held in which everything belonging to the patient was exorcised, so that the demon might not hide there and return to the patient. The exorcised demons were forbidden to return, and the demons remaining in the body were commanded to leave all the remainder of the body, and to descend into the little toe of the right foot, and there to rest quietly.

After the Reformation, two contests shaped themselves in the matter of exorcisms. The Protestants and the Roman Catholics vied with each other in the power, rapidity, and duration of the exorcisms. Both put forth miraculous claims, and with as much energy denied the power of the other. They agreed in one thing, and that was the erroneous position and teaching of the physicians. This, however, was but a continuation of that rivalry between the advancement of science and the conservation of theology, which is as old as history. In our examination of the influence of Christianity upon mental healing, it may be well for us to glance at the discouraging attitude of Christianity toward medicine. 16

53

The usurpation of healing by the church, which was a most serious drawback to the therapeutic art, will be traced in the following chapters; there are, however, some other ways in which the church retarded the work of physicians. Chief among these was the theory propagated by Christians that it was unlawful to meddle with the bodies of the dead. This theory came down from ancient times, but was eagerly accepted by the church, principally on account of the doctrine of the bodily resurrection. In addition to this, surgery was forbidden because the Church of Rome adopted the maxim that "the church abhors the shedding of blood." A recent English historian has remarked that of all organizations in human history, the Church of Rome has caused the spilling of most innocent blood, but it refused to allow the surgeons to spill a drop.

Monks were prohibited the practice of surgery in 1248, and by subsequent councils, and all dissections were considered sacrilege. Surgery was considered dishonorable until the fifteenth or sixteenth centuries. The use of medicine was also discouraged. Down through the centuries a few churchmen and many others, especially Jews and Arabs, took up the study. The church authorities did everything possible to thwart it. Supernatural means were so abundant that the use of drugs was not only irreligious but superfluous. Monks who took medicine were punished, and physicians in the thirteenth century 54 could not treat patients without calling in ecclesiastical advice.

We are told that in the reign of Philip II of Spain a famous Spanish doctor was actually condemned by the Inquisition to be burnt for having performed a surgical operation, and it was only by royal favor that he was permitted instead to expiate his crime by a pilgrimage to the Holy Land, where he died in poverty and exile.

This restriction was continued for three centuries, and consequently threw medical work into the hands of charlatans among

Christians, and of Jews. The clergy of the city of Hall protested that "it were better to die with Christ than to be cured by a Jew doctor aided by the devil." The Jesuit professor, Stengal, said that God permits illness because of His wish to glorify Himself through the miracles wrought by the church, and His desire to test the faith of men by letting them choose between the holy aid of the church and the illicit resort to medicine.

There was another reason for the antagonism of the church to physicians; the physicians in this case were inside the church. The monks converted medicine to the basest uses. In connection with the authority of the church, it was employed for extorting money from the sick. They knew little or nothing about medicine, so used charms, amulets, and relics in healing. The ignorance and cupidity of the monks led the Lateran Council, un 55 der the pontificate of Calixtus II, in 1123, to forbid priests and monks to attend the sick otherwise than as ministers of religion. It had little or no effect, so that Innocent II, in a council at Rheims in 1131, enforced the decree prohibiting the monks frequenting schools of medicine, and directing them to confine their practice to their own monasteries. They still disobeyed, and a Lateran Council in 1139 threatened all who neglected its orders with the severest penalties and suspension from the exercise of all ecclesiastical functions; such practices were denounced as a neglect of the sacred objects of their profession in exchange for ungodly lucre. When the priests found that they could no longer confine the practice of medicine to themselves, it was stigmatized and denounced. At the Council of Tours in 1163, Alexander III maintained that through medicine the devil tried to seduce the priesthood, and threatened with excommunication any ecclesiastic who studied medicine. In 1215, Innocent III fulminated an anathema against surgery and any priest practising it. Even this was not effectual. 17

What we see in connection with dissection and surgery and medicine was repeated at a later date with inoculation, vaccination, and anæsthetics. There were the same objections by the church on 56 theological grounds, the same stubborn battle, and the same inevitable defeat of the theological position.

So long as disease was attributed to a demoniacal cause, so long did exorcisms and other miraculous cures continue, and so far as these cures were efficacious, they must be classed as mental healing. Probably they continued longer in insanity and mental derangement on account of the beneficent and soothing effect of religion upon a diseased mind. Priestly cures of all kinds were largely, if not wholly, suggestive, and no history of mental healing would be complete without a r鳴m額f ecclesiastical therapeutics. Many vagaries of healing which the church introduced might be mentioned to show to what extent the people may be misled in the name of religion. For example, the doctrine of signatures, to be later discussed, was disseminated by priests and monks, and if these medicines were ever effective it must have been by mental means.

The demon theory of disease, which began before the age of history, and continued down through the savage ages and religions, through the early civilizations, through the gospel history, and dominated early Christianity, was finally, in the sixteenth century, to be vigorously assailed and largely overcome. The cost of this was considerable; attached as it was to the Christian church, it seemed necessary to destroy the whole Christian fabric in order to unravel this one thread. Atheism, therefore, was rampant, 57 and science and atheism became almost synonymous, and continued so until the church freed science from its centuries of bondage and allowed it to develop so as to be again in these days a co-laborer.

In pleasing contrast to the destructive and deterrent efforts of the church against the development of medicine is the helpful care of the sick exercised by Christians. The example of Jesus as shown by his tender sympathy, his helpful acts, and his instruction to his followers, bore fruit in the relief and care of sufferers by individuals and religious asylums. About the year 1000 and later, the infirmaries which were attached to numerous monasteries, and the *hospitia* along the routes of travel which opened their doors to sick pilgrims, were but the development of a less portentous attempt on the part of individuals and societies to care for the sick. The Knights of St. John, or the Hospitalers as they were called, assumed as their special duty the nursing and doctoring of those in need of such attention, especially of sick and infirm pilgrims and crusaders.

Hospitals for the sick, orphanages for foundlings, and great institutions for the proper care of paupers developed with immense strides, and during the twelfth century expanded into gigantic proportions. In the ensuing age, the medi涡l mind was fired with a faith in the efficacy of unstinted charity; members of society, from holy pontiff to the hum 58 blest recluse by the wayside, rivalled each other in gratuities of clothing and food, founding of hospitals, and endowment of beneficent public institutions. St. Louis's highest claim to pious glory arose from his restless and unstinted charities to the indigent and sick. Even the lepers, which were shunned or segregated, were treated by Christian institutions; and saints and saintesses found pious expression for their humility in personal attendance and even loving embraces of these unsightly beings covered with repulsive sores. For the last millennium there has not been a time when Christian love and benevolence have not sought the opportunity of ministering to the sick.

One can easily recognize the effect which this fact would have on mental healing. The church fostered the ideas of exorcism and the cures by relics and shrines, and deprecated the use of medicine. If the hospitals and infirmaries were almost wholly in the hands of the monks and churchmen, there was little hope for the development of other than ecclesiastical mental healing. The untold good which Christian ministrations to the sick accomplished must be acknowledged, but it was not an unmixed benefit to the race as a whole.

We may more easily see, perhaps, the connection between the church and the development of medicine, and the despotic power of the church in this regard, when we remember that physicians were 59 formerly a part of the clergy, and it was not until 1542 that the papal legate in France gave them permission to marry. In 1552 the doctors in law obtained like permission. An early priestly physician has survived to fame by the name of Elpideus, sometimes confused with Elpidius Rusticus. He was both a deacon of the church and a skilled surgeon, and was very favorably mentioned by St. Ennodius as a person of fine culture. He was sufficiently dexterous and skilful to heal the Gothic ruler, Theodoric, of a grievous illness. 18 Salverte gives us additional examples: "Richard Fitz-Nigel, who died Bishop of London, in 1198, had been apothecary to Henry II. The celebrated Roger Bacon, who flourished in the thirteenth century, although a monk, yet practised medicine. Nicolas de Farnham, a physician to Henry III, was created Bishop of Durham; and many doctors of medicine were at various times elevated to ecclesiastical dignities." 19

The grip of the church accomplished its purpose, and science, especially the science of medicine, was strangled, almost to the death. Even the people of the time recognized the shortcomings of the physicians. Henricus Cornelius Agrippa (1486-1535), writing in 1530, said with pleasant irony that physic was "a certaine Arte of manslaughter," and that 60 "well neare alwaies there is more daunger in the Physition and the Medicine than in the sicknesse itselfe." He also gives the following picture of a fashionable doctor of his time: "Clad in brave apparaile, having ringes on his fingers glimmeringe with pretious stoanes, and which hath gotten fame and credence for having been in farre countries, or having an obstinate manner of vaunting with stiffe lies that he hath great remedies, and for having continually in his mouth many wordes halfe Greeke and barbarous.... But this will prove to be true, that Physitians moste commonlye be naught. They have one common honour with the hangman, that is to saye, to kill menne and to be recompensed therefore." 20

3 A. D. White, *History of the Warfare of Science with Theology*, II, p. 113.

4 E. Salverte, *Philosophy of Magic* (trans. Thompson), II, p. 94.

5 W. E. H. Lecky, *History of European Morals*, I, p. 378.

6 *Ibid.*, I, p. 383.

7 R*é*nse a l'histoire des oracles, p. 296.

8 A. D. White, *History of the Warfare of Science with Theology*, II, p. 101.

9 H. T. Buckle, *History of Civilization in England*, II, p. 270.

10 G. F. Fort, *History of Medical Economy During the Middle Ages*, p. 201.

11 For a full discussion of this subject, see A. D. White, *History of the Warfare of Science with Theology*, II, pp. 97-134.

12 A. D. White, *History of the Warfare of Science with Theology*, II, p. 128.

13 Nash, *Life of Lord Westbury*, II, p. 78.

14 Cockayne, *Leechdoms, Wort-cunning, and Star-craft of Early England*, II, p. 177.

15 M. H. Dziewicki, "Exorcizo Te," *Nineteenth Century*, XXIV, p. 580.

16 For a full discussion of this subject, see A. D. White, *History of the Warfare of Science with Theology*, II, pp. 1-167.

17 T. J. Pettigrew, *Superstitions Connected with the History and Practice of Surgery and Medicine*, pp. 51 f.

18 G. F. Fort, *History of Medical Economy During the Middle Ages*, pp. 142 f.

19 E. Salverte, *Philosophy of Magic* (trans. Thompson), II, p. 96.

20 E. A. King, "Medieval Medicine," *Nineteenth Century*, XXXIV, p. 151.

For further references to the effect of demonism, see J. F. Nevius, *Demon Possession and Allied Themes*; J. M. Peebles, *The Demonism of the Ages and Spirit Obsessions*; articles on "Demon," "Demonism," "Demoniacal Possession," and "Devil," in the *Catholic Encyclopedia*, the *New International Encyclopedia*, and the *Encyclopedia Britannica*.

61

CHAPTER IV

RELICS AND SHRINES

"A fouth o' auld knick-knackets, Rusty airn caps and jinglin' jackets, Wad haud the Lothians three, in tackets, A towmond guid; An' parritch pats, and auld saut backets, Afore the flood." — Burns.

"For to that holy wood is consecrate A virtuous well, about whose flowery banks The nimble-footed fairies dance their

rounds By the pale moonshine, dipping oftentimes Their sto-
len children, so to make them free From dying flesh and dull
mortality." — Fletcher.

"Ne was ther such another pardoner, For in his male he hadde a pilwebeer, Which that he saide was oure lady veyl; He
seide, he hadde a gobet of the seyl That seynt Peter hadde,
whan that he wente Uppon the see, til Jhesu Crist him pente.
He hadde a cros of latoun ful of stones, And in a glas he
hadde pigges bones. But with these reliques, whanne that he
fond A poure persoun dwelling uppon lond, Upon a day he
gat him more moneye Than that the persoun gat in monthes
tweye. And thus with feyned flaterie and japes, He made the
persoun and the people his apes." — Chaucer.

A wide-spread movement developed in the early church as a result of which innumerable miracles of healing were credited to the
power of saints, indirectly through the medium of streams and
pools of water which were reputed to have some connec 62 tion
with a particular saint, or through the efficacy still clinging to the
relics of holy persons.

On account of the growth of the belief in demonism in the Christian church, and the need of supernatural means to counteract diabolic diseases, saintly relics came into common use for this purpose,
and afterward when demonism was not so thoroughly credited as
the cause of diseases, relics were still considered to hold their power
over physical infirmities. In addition to this, the missionary efforts
and successes of the church had some influence in establishing and
continuing cures by relics and similar means. The missionaries
found that their converts had formerly employed various amulets
and charms for the healing of diseases, and that they continued to
have great faith in them for that purpose. To wean them from their
heathen customs, Christian amulets and charms had to be substituted, or, as was sometimes the case, the heathen fetich was continued,
but with a Christian significance.

The early Scandinavians carried effigies carved out of gold or silver as safeguards against disease, or applied those made out of certain other materials, as the mandragora root or linen or wood, to the diseased part as a cure of physical infirmities. Some of these images were carried over into Christianity, for in Charlemagne's time, headache was frequently cured by following the saintly recommendation to 63 shape the figure of a head and place it on a cross. Fort tells us that "The introduction of Christianity among the Teutonic races offered no hindrance to a perpetuation, under new forms, of those social observances with which Norse temple idolatry was so intimately associated. Offering to proselytes an unlimited number of demoniacal 搩s, similar in individuality and prowess to those peopling the invisible universe, Northern mythology readily united with Christian demonology." 21

The relics of the saints came to be the favorite substitute for the heathen charms. With the acceptance of the demoniacal cause of disease, exorcism by relics gradually grew in importance until it was firmly established and a preferred form in the sixth and subsequent centuries. Down to this time there still existed a feeble recognition of a possible system adapted to the cure of maladies, so far, perhaps, as the practice was restricted to municipalities. The rapid advancement of saintly remedies, consecrated oils, and other puissant articles of ecclesiastical appliance, enabled and encouraged numerous churchmen to exercise the Yculapian art; this, together with the ban put upon physicians and scientific means, soon gave the church the monopoly of healing. Perhaps the most thorough attestation of the contempt into which physicians had fallen, 64 compared with saintly medicists, is the fact that cures were invariably attempted after earthly medicine had been exhausted. 22

Islam, Buddhism, and other religions have their shrines where some pilgrims are undoubtedly cured, but Christianity seems to have had the most varied and numerous collection. As early as the latter part of the fourth century miraculous powers were ascribed to the images of Jesus and the saints which adorned the walls of most of the churches of the time, and tales of wonderful cures were related of them. The intercessions of saints were invoked, and their relics began to work miracles. 23

St. Cyril, St. Ambrose, St. Augustine, and others of the early church fathers of note maintained that the relics of the saints had great efficacy in the cure of diseases. St. Augustine tells us: "Besides many other miracles, that Gamaliel in a dream revealed to a priest named Lacianus the place where the bones of St. Stephen were buried; that those bones being thus discovered, were brought to Hippo, the diocese of which St. Augustine was bishop; that they raised five persons to life; and that, although only a portion of the miraculous cures they effected had been registered, the certificates drawn up in two years in the diocese, and by the orders of the saint, were nearly seventy. In the adjoining diocese of Calama 65 they were incomparably more numerous." 24 This great and intellectual man also mentions and evidently credits the story that some innkeeper of his time put a drug into cheese which changed travellers who partook of it into domestic animals, and he further asserts after a personal test that peacock's flesh will not decay.

St. Ambrose declared that "the precepts of medicine are contrary to celestial science, watching, and prayer." When the conflict between St. Ambrose and the Arian Empress Justina was at its height, the former declared that it had been revealed to him that relics were buried in a certain spot which he indicated. When the earth was removed, there was exposed a tomb filled with blood, and containing two gigantic skeletons with their heads severed from their bodies. These were pronounced to be the remains of St. Gervasius and St. Protasius, two martyrs of gigantic physical proportions, who were said to have been beheaded about three centuries before. To prove beyond doubt the genuineness of these relics, a blind man was restored to sight by coming in contact with them, and demoniacs were also cured thereby. Before being exorcised, however, the demons, who were supposed to have supernatural and indubitable knowledge, declared that the relics were genuine; that St. Ambrose was the deadly enemy of hell; that the doctrine of the Trinity was 66 true; and that those who rejected it would certainly be damned. To be sure that the testimony of the demons should have its proper weight in the controversy, on the following day St. Ambrose delivered an invective against all who questioned the miracle. 25

Late researches concerning the Catacombs of Rome have thrown much light upon the early use of relics. The former opinion of the

Catacombs was that they were used for secret worship by the persecuted Christians, but now we know that they were burial-places under the protection of Roman law, with entrances opening on the public roads. Their chapels and altars were for memorial and communion services. Great reverence was felt for the bodies of all Christians, so that for the first seven centuries the bodies were not disturbed, and relics, in the modern sense of the word, were unknown. People prayed at the tombs, or if they wished to take something away, they touched the tomb with a handkerchief, or else they took some oil from the lamps which marked the tombs. These mementos were regarded as true relics, so that when the Lombard Queen, Theodelinda, sent the abbot John for relics to put in her cathedral at Monza, he came back with over seventy little vials of oil, each with the name of the saint from whose tomb the oil was procured, and many of them are still preserved.

67 The oil from altar lamps was of therapeutic value, as St. Chrysostom tells us in speaking of the superiority of the church over ordinary houses. "For what is here," he asks, "that is not great and awful? Thus both this Table [the altar] is far more precious and delightful than that [any table at home], and this lamp than that; and this they know, as many as have put away diseases by anointing themselves with oil in faith and due season." If the body of a saint lay beneath the altar, the oil was then known as the "Oil of the Saints," and was even more efficacious for healing. Notice the following quotations on the subject taken from Dearmer's work.

"Far more common are stories of healing by oil from a lamp burnt in honor of Christ or the saints. The following examples are from the East. The wounded hand of a Saracen was healed by oil from a lamp before the icon of St. George."

"St. Cyrus and St. John appeared to a person suffering from gout, and bade him take a little oil in a small ampulla from the lamp that burnt before the image of the Saviour, in the great tetrapyle at Alexandria, and anoint his feet with it."

"Similar stories are found in Western writers. Thus Nicetius of Lyons, by means of the oil of the lamp which burnt daily at his sepulchre, restored sight to the blind, drove demons from bodies possessed, restored soundness to shrunken limbs," etc.

"An epileptic was cured by oil from the lamp that burnt night and day at the tomb of St. Severin."

68

"It was revealed to a blind woman, that oil from the lamp of St. Genevi趙 would restore her sight, if the warden of the church were to anoint her with it. A week after she brought a blind man, who was healed in the same manner." 26

At the time of Gregory of Tours, application was made of sainted reliquaries as a remedy against the devil and his demons. Gregory narrates the miraculous efficacy of a small pellet of wax, taken from the tomb of St. Martin, in extinguishing an incendiary fire started by his Satanic majesty, which was instigated by malicious envy, because this omnipotent talisman was in the custody of an ecclesiastic! This Turonese bishop records many instances of cures being effected at Martin's tomb. He himself was relieved of severe pains in the head by touching the disordered spot with the sombre pall of St. Martin's sepulchre. This remedy was applied on three different occasions with equal success. Once he was cured of an attack of mortal dysentery by simply dissolving into a glass of water a pinch of dust scraped from the tomb of St. Martin and drinking the strange concoction. At another time, his tongue having become swollen and tumefied, it was restored to its natural size and condition by licking the railing of the tomb of this saint. He knew of others who had been equally successful. An archdeacon, named Leonastes had sight restored to his blind eyes at the 69 tomb of St. Martin, but unfortunately the fact that he later applied to an Israelitish physician caused his infirmity to return. Even a toothache was cured by St. Martin's relics.

The following is an apostrophe to the relics of St. Martin by Bishop Gregory: "Oh ineffable theriac! ineffable pigment! admirable antidote! celestial purge! superior to all drugs of the faculty! sweeter than aromatics! stronger than unguents together; thou cleanest the stomach like scammony, the lungs like hyssop, thou purgest the head like pyre-thrig!" 27

From the end of the fifth century the exercise of the medical art was almost exclusively appropriated by cloisters and monasteries, whose occupants boldly vended the miraculous remedial properties of relics, chrism, baptismal fluids, holy oil, rosy crosses, etc., as of unquestioned virtue. In these early days living saints seem to have rivalled dead ones in their power over diseases, but of these we shall speak in a later chapter.

A renewed interest sprang up when pilgrims began to return from their journeys to Palestine, bringing with them, as was natural, some souvenirs of their sojourn. A most interesting quotation from Mackay reveals the condition of these times. "The first pilgrims to the Holy Land brought back to Europe thousands of apocryphal relics, in the purchase of which they had expended all their 70 store. The greatest favorite was the wood of the true cross, which, like the oil of the widow, never diminished. It is generally asserted, in the traditions of the Romish Church, that the Empress Helen, the mother of Constantine the Great, first discovered the veritable *true cross* in her pilgrimage to Jerusalem. The Emperor Theodosius made a present of the greater part of it to St. Ambrose, Bishop of Milan, by whom it was studded with precious stones and deposited in the principal church of that city. It was carried away by the Huns, by whom it was burnt, after they had extracted the valuable jewels it contained. Fragments, purporting to have been cut from it, were, in the eleventh and twelfth centuries, to be found in almost every church in Europe, and would, if collected together in one place, have been almost sufficient to have built a cathedral. Happy was the sinner who could get a sight of one of them; happier he who possessed one! To obtain them the greatest dangers were cheerfully braved. They were thought to preserve from all evils and to cure the most inveterate diseases. Annual pilgrimages were made to the shrines that contained them and considerable revenues collected from the devotees.

"Next in renown were those precious relics, the tears of the Saviour. By whom and in what manner they were preserved, the pilgrim did not enquire. Their genuineness was vouched by the Christians of 71 the Holy Land, and that was sufficient. Tears of the Virgin Mary, and tears of St. Peter, were also to be had, carefully enclosed in little caskets, which the pious might wear in their bosoms. After the tears, the next most precious relics were drops of the blood of Jesus and the martyrs, and the milk of the Virgin Mary. Hair and toe-nails were also in great repute, and were sold at extravagant prices. Thousands of pilgrims annually visited Palestine in the eleventh and twelfth centuries, to purchase pretended relics for the home market. The majority of them had no other means of subsistence than the profits thus obtained. Many a nail, cut from the filthy foot of some unscrupulous ecclesiastic, was sold at a diamond's price, within six months after its severance from its parent toe, upon the supposition that it had once belonged to a saint or an apostle. Peter's toes were uncommonly prolific, for there were nails enough in Europe, at the time of the Council of Clermont, to have filled a sack, all of which were devoutly believed to have grown on the sacred feet of that great apostle. Some of them are still shown in the cathedral of Aix-la-Chapelle. The pious come from a distance of a hundred German miles to feast their eyes upon them." 28

While some of these relics enumerated by Mackay seem to be such apparent frauds that none could credit them, they were surpassed in audacity by one 72 offered for sale at a monastery in Jerusalem. Here was presented to the prospective buyers one of the fingers of the Holy Ghost. 29

In addition to the popular relics already noted, an extensive and lucrative trade was carried on in iron filings from the chains with which, it was claimed, Peter and Paul were bound. These filings were deemed by Pope Gregory I as efficacious in healing as were the bones of saints or martyrs. 30

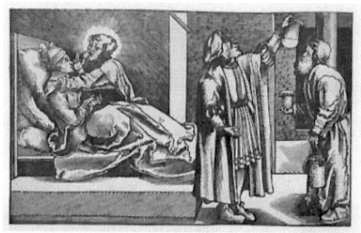

CURE THROUGH THE INTERCESSION OF A HEALING SAINT

As an example of healing at shrines in early days, I will reproduce Bede's description of a cure effected at the tomb of St. Cuthbert in 698. "There was in that same monastery a brother whose name was Bethwegan, who had for a considerable time waited upon the guests of the house, and is still living, having the testimony of all the brothers and strangers resorting thither, of being a man of much piety and religion, and serving the office put upon him only for the sake of the heavenly reward. This man, having on a certain day washed the mantels or garments which he used in the hospital, in the sea, was returning home, when on a sudden about half-way, he was seized with a sudden distemper in his body, insomuch that he fell down, and having lain some time, he could scarcely rise again. When at last he got up, he felt one-half of his body from the 73 head to the foot, struck with palsy, and with much difficulty he got home with the help of a staff. The distemper increased by degrees, and as night approached became still worse, so that when day returned, he could not rise or walk alone. In this weak condition, a good thought came into his mind, which was to go to church, the best way he could, to the tomb of the reverend Father Cuthbert, and there on his knees, to beg of the Divine Goodness either to be delivered from that disease, if it were for his good, or if the Divine Providence had ordained him longer to lie under the same for his punishment, that he might bear the pain with patience and a composed mind. He did accordingly, and supporting his weak limbs with a staff, entered the church, and prostrating himself before the body of the man of God, he with pious earnestness, prayed, that through his intercession, our Lord might be propitious to him. In the midst of his prayers he fell as it were, into a stupor, and as he was afterwards wont to relate, felt a large and broad hand touch his head where the pain lay, and by that touch all the part of his body which had been affected with the distemper, was delivered from the weakness, and restored to health down to his feet. He then awoke, and rose up in perfect health, and returning thanks to God for his recovery, told the brothers what had happened to him; and to the joy of them all, returned the more zealously, as if chastened by his 74 affliction, to the service which he was wont before so carefully to perform. The very garments which had been on Cuthbert's body, dedicated to God, either while living, or after he was dead, were not exempt from the virtue of performing cures, as may be seen in the book of his life and miracles, by such as shall read it." 31 It should be noticed that in this account God alone seemed to have been the healer.

Nearly every country had its long list of saints, each with his special power over some organ or disease. This saintly power, however, was not applied directly, but through their relics or through shrines consecrated to them. Melton, in his *Astrologaster*, says: "The saints of the Romanists have usurped the place of the zodiacal constellations in their governance of the parts of man's body, and that 'for every limbe they have a saint.' Thus St. Otilia keepes the head instead of Aries; St. Blasius is appointed to governe the necke instead of Taurus; St. Lawrence keepes the backe and shoulders instead of Gemini, Cancer, and Leo; St. Erasmus rules the belly with the entrayles, in the place of Libra and Scorpius; in the stead of Sagittarius, Capricornus, Aquarius, and Pisces, the holy church of Rome hath elected St. Burgarde, St. Rochus, St. Quirinus, St. John, and many others, which governe the thighes, feet, shinnes, and knees."

But the influence of the saints is distributed more 75 minutely, as *e.g.*, "*Right Hand*: the top joint of the thumb is dedicated to God, the second joint to the Virgin; the top joint of the fore-finger to St. Barnabas, the second joint to St. John, and the third to St. Paul; the top joint of the second finger to Simon Cleophas, the second joint to Tathideo, the third to Joseph; the top joint of the third finger to Zaccheus, the second to Stephen, the third to the evangelist Luke; the top joint of the little finger to Leatus, the second to Mark, the third to Nicodemus." Thus the body was cared for.

Pettigrew makes the following enumeration which shows the division of labor among the saints in the Middle Ages. In this, not the different portions of the body but the various diseases and infirmities are distributed.

"The following list, though doubtless very imperfect, will yet serve to show how general was the appropriation of particular diseases to the Roman Catholic saints:

St. Agatha, against sore breasts.
St. Agnan and St. Tignan, against scald head.
St. Anthony, against inflammations.
St. Apollonia, against toothache.
St. Avertin, against lunacy.
St. Benedict, against the stone, and also for poisons.
St. Blaise, against the quinsey, bones sticking in the throat, etc.
St. Christopher and St. Mark, against sudden death.
76 St. Clara, against sore eyes.
St. Erasmus, against the colic.
St. Eutrope, against dropsy.
St. Genow and St. Maur, against the gout.
St. Germanus, against diseases of children.
St. Giles and St. Hyacinth, against sterility.
St. Herbert, against hydrophobia.
St. Job and St. Fiage, against syphilis.
St. John, against epilepsy and poison.
St. Lawrence, against diseases of the back and shoulders.
St. Liberius, against the stone and fistula.
St. Maine, against the scab.
St. Margaret and St. Edine, against danger in parturition.
St. Martin, against the itch.
St. Marus, against palsy and convulsions.
St. Otilia and St. Juliana, against sore eyes and
the headache.

St. Pernel, against the ague.
St. Petronilla, St. Apollonia, and St. Lucy, against the toothache.
----, and St. Genevieve, against fevers.
St. Phaire, against hemorrhoids.
St. Quintan, against coughs.
St. Rochus, and St. Sebastian, against the plague.
St. Romanus, against demoniacal possession.
St. Ruffin, against madness.
St. Sigismund, against fevers and agues.
St. Valentine, against epilepsy.
St. Venise, against chlorosis.
St. Vitus, against madness and poisons.
St. Wallia and St. Wallery, against the stone.
St. Wolfgang, against lameness." 32

77

Wax from the tapers illuminating the altar which enclosed St. Gall's mortal remains was an instantaneous cure for toothache, diseased eyes, and total deafness; a vase used by the martyred Willabrod for bathing thrice a year, still holding its partially solidified water by divine invocation after her death, had great remedial energy in diverse ailments; the water in which the ring of St. Remigius was immersed cured certain obstinate fevers; and the wine in which the bones of the saints were washed restored imbeciles to instant health. In the thirteenth century, hairs of saints, especially of St. Boniface, were used as a purge, and a single hair from the beard of St. Vincent, placed about the neck of an idiot, restored normal mental operations. With the water in which St. Sulpicius washed her hands aggravated infirmities were instantly cured; and in the twelfth century, an invalid being advised in a dream to drink the water in which St. Bernard washed his hands, the Abbot of Clairvaux went to him, gave him the wash water, and healed an incurable disease. Flowers reposing on the tomb of a saint, when steeped in water, were supposed to be especially efficacious in various diseases, and those blooming in aromatic beauty at the tomb of St. Bernard instantly cured grievous sicknesses. 33 The belt of St. Guthlac, and the belt of St. Thomas of 78 Lancaster, were sovereign remedies for the headache, whilst the penknife and boots of Archbishop

Becket, and a piece of his shirt, were found most admirably to aid parturition. Fragments of the veil of the saintess Coleta, and the use of her well-worn cloak, immediately cured a terrible luxation, and a cataleptic patient was restored to sanity by drinking from her cup.

To show how thoroughly the idea of the efficacy of these relics must have been indued in the thought of the times, White quotes the following: "Two lazy beggars, one blind, the other lame, try to avoid the relics of St. Martin, borne about in procession, so that they may not be healed and lose their claim to alms. The blind man takes the lame man on his shoulders to guide him, but they are caught in the crowd and healed against their will." He also says: "Even as late as 1784 we find certain authorities in Bavaria ordering that anyone bitten by a mad dog shall at once put up prayers at the shrine of St. Hubert, and not waste his time in any attempts at medical or surgical cure." 34

In addition to what Dr. White says here about the treatment for threatened hydrophobia in the eighteenth century, we find a curious mixture of science and superstition in the nineteenth century in connection with the same trouble. Early in this 79 century physicians discovered that the most effectual remedy against the bite of a rabid animal was the cauterization of the wound with a red-hot iron. In Tuscany, however, the iron which they heated was one of the nails of the true cross, and in the French provinces it was the key of St. Hubert. This, though, was only to be used in the hands of those who could trace their genealogy to this noble saint. At the abbey of St. Hubert, in the diocese of Liege, the intercession of the saint still continued to be sufficient to effect a cure, provided it was seconded by some religious ceremonies, and a diet which would reassure the patient.

After the discovery of the "true cross," portions of this relic were much used for aid in any emergency. In addition to sanitary and healing powers, fragments suspended to a tree manifested the proper location of sacred edifices. St. Magnus, who seems to have carried pieces around with him, completely vanquished demons who frequented a locality selected for a chapel. Eyesight was restored to a humble merchant seeking the blood-stained marks upon the chapel of this same St. Magnus. The blind man was feeling his uncertain way to the place, where these discolorations reappeared more distinctly after each washing with heavy layers of lime.

St. Louis, almost in the agonies of earthly dissolution, with rigid body, rigorous limbs, and fluctu 80 ating spirit, was brought to full health by the application to his moribund body of a piece of the true cross, about the year 1244; and later in the century miracles took place at his tomb. M. Littré in his *Fragment de Medecine Rétrospective*, describes seven miracles which occurred at his tomb, some of which cures, however, were very gradual. We are also told that when a humble hunchback bowed the knee in adoration at the tomb of St. Andreas, his irresistible faith instantly released him from his unnatural rotundity. In 1243 a Ferrara writer was at Padua, and while attending vespers at the tomb where the sainted body of the Minorite Anthony reposed, he affirms that he saw a person who had been mute from his birth recover his voice and speak audibly.

Saintly remedies were used to cure hemorrhages, readjust luxations, unite fractures, remove calculi, moderate the agonizing pangs of parturition, restore vision to the blind, and hearing to the deaf — in fact, in an endeavor to perform cures which modern medicine and surgery are counting among their greatest and most recent triumphs. Some things even more strange were attempted: paradoxical as it may seem, they were used to cover up crime. Fort tells us that among nuns and consecrated women in convents, some erring sisters applied the preventive talismanic influence of a sacred shirt or girdle to suppress the manifestation of conventual 81 irregularities of a sexual character. Animals as well as human beings were treated for sickness, and relics were used to free captive birds and animals. At a banquet, a costly urn was shattered by ecclesiastics, and through the power of Odilo it was restored to its original integrity. At the tombs of both St. Severin and St. Gall, when the light had been quenched, miraculous fire burst forth to renew the splendor. 35

The allotment of certain diseases to certain saints did not end with the Middle Ages. I have in my hand a little manual entitled: *De l'Invocation miraculeuse des Saints dans les maladies et les besoins particuliers, par Mme. la Baronne d'Avout*, published in 1884. An invocation is given for every day in the year to some particular saint, who is thought to be especially efficacious in the cure of some specific disease. I shall quote but one for illustration.

"30 MAI
S. HUBERT DE BROIGNY
Pr賠Noyons (Oise).
Honor頧u dioc睟 de Beauvais.

"L'illustre saint Hubert, ap·· des Ardennes, fut son protecteur et lui donna son nom. Il lui obtint les plus heureuses dispositions pour la vertu. Lui aussi h鲩ta du pouvoir de gu鲩r de la rage.

"Les habitants de Noyon et des environs n'ont pas cess頤e recourir ·on intercession. Les per 82 sonnes qui touchent ses reliques ou portent sur elles son nom b鮕 esp鲩nt 饚apper pendant leur vie aux atteintes des d魯ns, de la rage et du tonnerre.

" Aire, dioc睟 de Fr骸s, on invoque aussi sainte Quit航 contre la rage.

INVOCATION

"Dieu tout-puissant, qui avez form頩e cœur de vos saints avec une admirable bont馩afin qu'ils deviennent pour nous une source de bienfaits et de consolation; assistez-nous dans le pressant besoin o nous nous trouvons et sauvez-nous de la mort, par les pri航s at les m鲩tes de saint Hubert de Br鶣gny, afin que nous puissions vous louer et vous b鮕r. Par N.-S. J.-C. Ainsi soit-il."

"*Saint Hubert, qui pr骸rvez de la morsure des b蟭s enrag餣, ou qui gu鲩ssez leur morsures mortelles, priez pour tous les afflig閣qui vous invoquent.*"

While there was probably some advance when the saints of the church took the place of the zodiacal constellations in the government of the human body, the church prevented the development along scientific lines, although there were many ramifications of saintly influence. Not the least among these was the healing efficacy of holy wells, pools, and streams, which had been empowered in some way by the saints. In some cases the bones of holy men have been buried in different parts of the continent, and after a certain lapse of time, water was said to have oozed from them, which soon formed a spring and cured all the diseases of the faithful.

83 Perhaps the cure of leprous Naaman by bathing in the Jordan, and the restoration of the sight of the blind man by washing in the Pool of Siloam may have served as examples which the credulous were only too ready to follow. We must also note, however, as a reason for their use, that in classical times the greater number of thermal waters, more frequently used then than in the present day, remained consecrated to the gods, to Apollo, to Yculapius, and, above all, to Hercules, who was named Iatricos, or the able physician. At any rate, many wells and fountains were dedicated to different saints, and various rites were performed there at Easter and other particular days, where offerings were also made to the saints.

In Ireland, many such sacred places have been visited by the sick for centuries, and England and Scotland have them also. Not only in the British Isles, but in all parts of Europe they were much frequented in the Middle Ages, and they are not without their visitors today. As late as 1805 the eminent Roman Catholic prelate, Dr. John Milner, gave a detailed account of a miraculous cure performed at a sacred well in Flintshire. Gregory of Tours was one of the first to notice the healing power of springs in connection with the saints. He asserted that the diseases of the sick and infirm were banished upon the contact of a few drops of water drawn from a spring dug by St. Martin's own hands.

84 From Fosbrooke's *British Monachism* we learn that "on a spot called Nell's Point, is a fine well, to which great numbers of women resort on Holy Thursday, and, having washed their eyes in the spring, they drop a pin into it. Once a year, at St. Mardrin's well, also, lame persons went on Corpus Christi evening, to lay some small offering on the altar, there to lie on the ground all night, drink of the water there, and on the next morning to take a good draught more of it, and carry away some of the water each in a bottle at their departure. At Muswell Hill was formerly a chapel, called our Lady of Muswell, from a well there, near which was her image; this well was continually resorted to by way of pilgrimage. At Walsingham, a fine green road was made for the pilgrims, and there was a holy well and cross adjacent, at which pilgrims used to kneel while drinking the water. It is remarkable that the Anglo-Saxon laws had proscribed this as idolatrous. Such springs were consecrated upon the discovery of cures effected by them. In fact," Fosbrooke adds,

"these consecrated wells merely imply a knowledge of the properties of mineral waters, but, through ignorance, a religious appropriation of their properties was made to supernatural causes."

"Holywell, in the county of Flint," we are informed by Salverte, "derives its name from the Holy Well of St. Winifred, over which a chapel was 85 erected by the Stanley family, in the reign of Henry VII. The well was formerly in high repute as a medicinal spring. Pennant says that, in his time, Lancashire pilgrims were to be seen in deep devotion, standing in the waters up to the chin for hours, sending up prayers, and making a prescribed number of turnings; and this excess of piety was carried so far, as in several instances to cost the devotees their lives." 36

Pennant also tells us of a small spring outside the bathing well at Whiteford, which was once famed for the cure of weak eyes. The patient made an offering of a crooked pin, and at the same time repeated some words. The well still remains, but the efficacy of its waters is lost. In recounting his tour of Wales, the same author describes the church of St. Tecla, virgin and martyr, at Llandegla. He says: "About two hundred yards from the church, in a Quillet called Gwern Degla, rises a small spring. The water is under the tutelage of the Saint, and to this day held to be extremely beneficial in the falling sickness. The patient washes his limbs in the well; makes an offering into it of four-pence; walks round it three times; and thrice repeats the Lord's Prayer. These ceremonies are never begun till after sun-set, in order to inspire the votaries with greater awe. If the afflicted be of the male sex, like 86 Socrates, he makes an offering of a cock to his Yculapius, or rather to Tecla Hygeia; if of the fair sex, a hen. The fowl is carried in a basket, first round the well; after that into the church-yard; when the same orisons and the same circumambulations are performed round the church. The votary then enters the church; gets under the communion table; lies down with the Bible under his or her head; is covered with the carpet or cloth, and rests there till break of day; departing after offering sixpence, and leaving the fowl in the church. If the bird dies, the cure is supposed to have been effected, and the disease transferred to the devoted victim." 37

"At Withersden," says Hasted, "is a well, which was once famous, being called St. Eustache's well, taking its name from Eustachius, Abbot of Flai, who is mentioned by Matt. Paris, An. 1200, to have been a man of learning and sanctity, and to have come and preached at Wye, and to have blessed a fountain there, so that afterwards its waters were endowed by such miraculous power, that by it all diseases were cured." 38 Unfortunately, wells do not always benefit the bathers. Lilly 39 relates that in 1635 Sir George Peckham died in St. Winifred's Well, "having continued so long mumbling his pater nosters and Sancta Winifreda ora pro me, that the 87 cold struck into his body, and after his coming forth of that well he never spoke more."

The people of the Highlands of Scotland regarded fountains with particular veneration. According to the Statistical Account of Scotland, the minister of Kirkmichael, Banffshire, said: "The sick who resort to them for health, address their vows to the presiding powers, and offer presents to conciliate their favor. These presents generally consist of a small piece of money, or a few fragrant flowers. The same reverence in ancient times seems to have been entertained by every people in Europe." Near Kirkmichael there was a fountain dedicated to St. Michael, and once celebrated for its cures. "Many a patient have its waters restored to health, and many more have attested the efficacy of their virtues. But, as the presiding power is sometimes capricious, and apt to desert his charge, it now lies neglected, choked with weeds, unhonored and unfrequented." 40

The most noted well in Perthshire is in Trinity Gask. Again from the Statistical Account we quote: "Superstition, aided by the interested artifices of Popish Priests, raised, in times of ignorance and bigotry, this well to no small degree of celebrity. It was affirmed that every person who was baptized with the water of this well would never be seized with the plague. The extraordinary virtue of Trin 88 ity Gask well has perished with the downfall of superstition." 41

Pinkerton, in speaking of the river Fillan in Scotland, says: "In this river is a pool consecrated by the ancient superstition of the inhabitants of this country. The pool is formed by the eddying of the stream round a rock. Its waves were many years since consecrated by Fillan, one of the saints who converted the ancient inhabitants of Caledonia from paganism to the belief of Christianity. It has ever since been distinguished by his name, and esteemed of sovereign virtue in curing madness. About two hundred persons afflicted in this way are annually brought to try the benefits of its salutary influence. These patients are conducted by their friends, who first perform the ceremony of passing with them thrice through a neighbouring cairn: on this cairn they then deposit a simple offering of clothes, or perhaps a small bunch of heath. More precious offerings used once to be brought. The patient is then thrice immerged in the sacred pool. After the immersion, he is bound hand and foot, and left for the night in a chapel which stands near. If the maniac is found loose in the morning, good hopes are conceived of his full recovery. If he is still bound, his cure remains doubtful. It sometimes happens that death relieves him, during his confinement, from the troubles of life."

89

Mrs. Macaulay, 42 speaking of a consecrated well in St. Kilda, called Tobirnimbuadh, or the spring of diverse virtues, says that "near the fountain stood an altar, on which the distressed votaries laid down their oblations. Before they could touch sacred water with any prospect of success, it was their constant practice to address the genius of the place with supplication and prayer. No one approached him with empty hands.... Shells and pebbles, rags of linen or stuffs worn out, pins, needles, or rusty nails were generally all the tribute that was paid."

Collinson 43 mentions a well in the parish Wembton, called St. John's Well, to which in 1464 "an immense concourse of people resorted: and ... many who had for years labored under various bodily diseases, and had found no benefit from physick and physicians, were, by the use of these waters (after paying their due offerings), restored to their primitive health."

Brome, in his *Travels*, 1700, observes: "In Lothien, two miles from Edinburg southward, is a spring called St. Katherine's Well, flowing continually with a kind of black fatness, or oil, above the water, proceeding (as it is thought) from the parret coal, which is frequent in these parts; 'tis of a marvellous nature, for as the coal, whereof it proceeds, 90 is very apt quickly to kindle into a flame, so is the oil of a sudden operation to heal all scabs and tumors that trouble the outward skin, and the head and hands are speedily healed by virtue of this oil, which retains a very sweet smell; and at Aberdeen is another well very efficacious to dissolve the stone, to expel sand from the reins and bladder, being good for the collick and drunk in July and August, not inferiour, they report, to the Spaw in Germany." 44

Grose tells us of a well dedicated to St. Oswald, between the towns of Alton and Newton. The neighbors have the opinion that a sick person's shirt thrown into the well will prognosticate the outcome of the disease; if it floats the sick one will recover, if it sinks he will die. To reward the saint for the information, they tear a rag off the shirt and hang it on the briers near by; "where," says the writer, "I have seen such numbers as might have made a fayre rheme in a paper-myll." Similar practices are related by other authors. Ireland formerly had a sanctified well in nearly every parish. They were marked by rude crosses and surrounded by fragments of cloth left as memorials. St. Ronague's Well, near Cork, was very popular at one time. Near Carrick-on-Suir is the holy well of Tubber Quan, the waters of which are reputed to have performed many miraculous cures. The well 91 was dedicated to two patron saints, St. Quan and St. Brogawn. These saints are supposed to exert a special influence the last three Sundays in June. "It is firmly believed," says Brand, "that at this period the two saints appear in the well in the shape of two small fishes, of the trout kind; and if they do not so appear, that no cure will take place. The penitents attending on these occasions ascend the hill barefoot, kneel by the stream and repeat a number of paters and aves, then enter it, go through the stream three times, at a slow pace, reciting their prayers. They then go on the gravel walk, and traverse it round three times on their bare knees, often till the blood starts in the operation, repeat their prayers, then traverse three times round a tree on their bare knees, but upon the grass. Having performed these exercises they cut off locks of their hair and tie them on the branches of the tree as specifics against headache."

After being three times admonished in a dream, a man washed in St. Madern's Well in Cornwall and was miraculously cured, so say Bishop Hall and Father Francis. Ranulf Higden, in his *Polychronicon*, relates the wonderful cures performed at the holy well at Basingwerk. The red streaks in the stones surrounding it were symbols of the blood of St. Wenefride, martyred by Carodoc.

The Scotch considered certain wells to have healing properties in the month of May. In the Ses 92 sions Records (June 12, 1628) it is reported that a number of persons were brought before the Kirk Sessions of Falkirk, accused of going to Christ's Well on the Sundays of May to seek their health, and the whole being found guilty were sentenced to repent "in linens" three several sabbaths. "In 1657 a number of persons were publicly rebuked for visiting the well at Airth. The custom was to leave a piece of money and a napkin at the well, from which they took a can of water, and were not to speak a word either in going or returning, nor on any account to spill a drop of the water. Notwithstanding these proceedings, many are known to have lately travelled many miles into the Highlands, there to obtain water for the cure of their sick cattle." 45

To-day, probably the most efficacious waters are to be found at the sacred fountain at La Salette and at the holy spring at Lourdes.

We have another specific form of healing which should be noticed. It was especially common in Eastern churches, and was found to some extent in the West. I refer to Incubation, or "Temple-sleep." This practice came down through early civilizations and was an adopted practice among Christians. The patient went to some church well known for its cures, which was provided with mattresses or low 93 couches, and attended by priests and assistants. Devotions being finished he lay down to sleep. Sometimes he slept immediately, at other times sleep must be wooed by fast and vigil. At any rate, during the sleep he dreamed that the saint touched him, or prescribed some remedy, and in the first case he awoke cured, and in the second the prescribed medicine brought about the relief.

Sophronius, the Patriarch of Jerusalem, wrote about 640 as follows: "Cyrus appeared to the sick man in the form of a monk, not in a dream, as he appears to many; but in a waking vision, just as he was and is represented. He told the patient to rise and to plunge into the warm water. Zosimos said it was impossible for him to move, but when the order was repeated, he slid like a snake into the bath. When he got into the water, he saw the saint at his side, but when he came out, the vision had vanished." Beside the cure of this paralytic at the church of Cyrus and John, he mentions the cure of many other diseases by this method of incubation. Among them are dumbness, blindness, barrenness, possession, scrofula, dyspepsia, a broken leg, deformities of limbs, lameness, gout, diseases of the eyes, cataract, ulcer, and dropsy.

Among the churches of Greece and southern Italy incubation is still common. The climate may have some effect in limiting the area of this practice. Miss M. Hamilton furnishes us with some modern 94 examples. In speaking of a new picture of St. George in the church at Arachova, she says: "It is a votive offering of a Russian, who came a paralytic to Arachova in July, 1905. He spent several weeks praying and sleeping in the church, and departed completely cured. The festival of St. George is held on April 23rd. They have three days of dancing and feasting, and at night all suppliants bring their rugs and sleep round the shrines in the church. Every year many of the sick are found to be cured when morning comes."

The Church of the Evangelestria, our Lady of the Annunciation, is visited by about forty-five thousand pilgrims every year. It is situated at Tenos, and Miss Hamilton tells us what she saw during her visit there in 1906:

"On the morning before Annunciation Day this year, the pilgrims could be seen making their way to the church. Among them were cripples, armless, and legless, half-rolling up the street; blind people groping their way along; men and women with deformities of every kind; one or two showing the pallor of death on their faces were being carried up on litters. These evidently were coming to Tenos as a last resource, when doctors were of no avail. Other pilgrims were ascending after their own fashion, according to vows they had made. One woman toiled laboriously along on her knees, kissing the stones of the way, and clasping a silver Madonna and Child. Last year her daughter had been seized with epilepsy, and she vowed to carry in 95 this way this offering to the Madonna of Tenos if she would cure her daughter. The girl recovered and the other now with thankful heart was fulfilling her part of the bargain.

"The eve of Annunciation Day is the time when the Panagia is believed to descend among the sick and work miraculous cures among them. Then all the patients are gathered together in the crypt or in the upper church. The Chapel of the Well is the popular place for incubation. There is more chance for miraculous cure there than in the church. The little crypt can accommodate only a comparatively small number, but they are packed together as tightly as possible. From the entrance up to the altar, they lie in two lines of three or four deep, with a passage down the middle large enough for only one person. Down the narrow way two streams of people press the whole evening. They worship at the shrines along the wall, purchase holy earth from the spot where the picture was discovered, drink at the sacred well, and are blessed by the priest at the altar. The cripples and the sick desiring healing have been engaged all day in such acts of worship; they have received bread and water from the priests in the upper church, paid homage to the all-powerful picture, offered their candles to the Madonna, and all the time sought to endue themselves with her presence. Now at night, still fixing their thoughts upon her, and permeated by this spirit of worship, they settle down to sleep in order that she may appear to them in a dream.

"Disappointment, of course, awaits the vast majority, but on the evening of the vigil all are filled with hope. They know the precedents of former years, how such things have happened to some unfortunate people among the pilgrims every year. 96 Usually eight or nine miracles take place, and lists of them are published for distribution....

"The church records contain accounts of the miracles which now amount to many hundreds. They are practically all of the type I have described—cure during a vision while incubation was being practised. For example, the case of a man from Moldavia is on record. He had become paralyzed during a night-watch, and the doctor could effect no relief. He was taken to the Chapel of the Well, and when asleep he thought he heard a voice telling him to arise. He awoke, thought it was a dream, and fell asleep again. A second time he heard a voice, and saw a white-robed woman of great beauty entering the church. In his fear he rose and walked about. His recovery was so complete that he could walk in the procession round the town the following day." 46

The medicinal power imputed to the sainted relics and shrines would naturally be considered very valuable. So it proved. Wealth flowed to a conventual treasury or a cathedral chapter where were deposited fragments of the martyred dead endowed with miraculous puissance. When the Frankish forces sacked Constantinople at the beginning of the thirteenth century, the principal object of their ferocious cruelties and vigilant searches was the acquisition of precious relics. Concerning these relics Fort gives the following account:

97 "These relics, captured in Constantinople, were divided by the troops under Marquis de Montfort, with the same justice as prevailed in the division of other booty. In this way the Venetians were enabled to enrich their metropolis with a piece of the sainted cross, an arm of St. George, part of the head of St. John the Baptist, the entire skeleton of St. Luke, that of the prophet St. Simeon, and a small bottle of Jesus Christ's blood. The Greek capital from the remotest times appears to have monopolized this traffic in sacred wares, claiming to possess a fragment of the stone on which Jacob slept, and the staff transformed into a serpent by Moses.

"Here also were guarded the Holy Virgin's vestments, her spindle, drops of her milk, the cradle in which the Saviour had lain, a tooth from his adolescent jaw, a hair of his beard, a particle of the bread used in the Last Supper, and a portion of the royal purple worn by him before Pilate. Naturally clerical adventurers among the occidental Crusaders, pending the sacking of the Byzantine city, sought out most zealously these valuable remnants of pristine glory, and in obtaining them were by no means scrupulous with menaces and violence. When scattered through Western Europe, in the monasteries and other religious places, their curative properties increased the pilgrimages thither of the sick and diseased." 47

He further gives us more in detail 48 an idea of the continual accumulation of riches which were derived from the exposure of these relics to the sick and infirm and the consequent growth in wealth of the 98 monasteries and cathedrals. The monastic system was probably most responsible for the change from the simple adoration of the early Christians to the use of relics as a miraculous means of healing. Those which were transported with elaborate ceremonies, enclosed in a magnificent stone sarcophagus, and covered by an edifice of imposing proportions were almost sure to bring to their custodians great wealth. It is said that when the body of St. Sebastian, which was legitimately obtained from Rome, together with the purloined remains of St. Gregory, reached the cloister of Soissons, so great was the crowd of invalids who were cured, and so generous were they in their donations, that the monks actually counted eighty measures of money and one hundred pounds in coin. The great value of such objects may be calculated when it is remembered that in the year 1056 securities amounting to ten thousand solidi were pledged for the production of the relics of St. Just and St. Pastor, consequent upon the legal decision of ownership between Berenger, a French ruler, and a Narbonnese archbishop. The Reichberg annals provide a further example. They state that the emperor demanded certain hostages, or the holy arm of St. George, as a suitable guarantee for the institution of a public mart in Germany.

Venetian merchants were among the first to realize the commercial value of relics, and enjoyed a lucrative traffic in this holy merchandise. It was 99 not until the eleventh century, however, that the government of Venice founded public marts or fairs for the commercial exchange of saintly relics, although Rome and Pavia had long conducted such enterprises. These fairs were placed under the tutelary protection of some patron saint, the Venetians, of course, thus honoring St. Mark. They were not always particular how these relics were procured, for it is stated that when negotiations for the exchange of a well-preserved body of St. Tairise proved unsuccessful, because the Greek monks who possessed it refused absolutely to sell or barter, these enterprising traders quietly stole the desired skeleton.

Relics provided a suitable method of acquiring ecclesiastical fortunes for denuded cloisters or impoverished nunneries; and if the old relics lost their power it was not difficult to procure episcopal assurance of the miraculous powers of new ones. For the procuring of special funds the venerated objects were taken from place to place, under priestly surveillance, presented to the sick and infirm with assurance of relief, and with the demand for large sums of money.

We can easily understand, then, why such donations were regarded as most precious presents, and chronicled in the conventual records as events of high importance. As early as the ninth century, documentary evidence of authenticity frequently 100 accompanied a gift of relics, and furnished legal proof of ownership.

The gift of St. Peter's knife to a German monastery by a benevolent abbot was deemed a most illustrious act. About the same time a noble pilgrim succeeded, after great importunity and a lavish outlay of money, in obtaining trifling particles of the relics of Abraham, Isaac, and Jacob, which he enclosed in a priceless box and donated to the monastery of St. Gall. This gift was considered the greatest event of the year, but when it is considered that this and similar presents insure in the community, where they are deposited uninterrupted peace, unstinted plenty, absence of catastrophies, and the cure of diseases, their value is explained.

The commercial aspect of ecclesiastical cures, however, was discovered by other than priestly or monkish eyes, and different forms began to be presented. Of these White says: "Very important among these was the Agnus Dei, or piece of wax from the Paschal candles, stamped with the figure of a lamb and consecrated by the Pope. In 1471 Pope Paul II expatiated to the Church on the efficacy of this fetich in preserving men from fire, shipwreck, tempest, lightning, and hail, as well as in assisting women in childbirth; and he reserved to himself and his successors the manufacture of it. Even as late as 1517 Pope Leo X issued, for a consideration, tickets bearing a cross and the following 101 inscription: 'This cross measured forty times makes the height of Christ in his humanity. He who kisses it is preserved for seven days from falling-sickness, apoplexy, and sudden death.'" 49

The enormous revenues procured through the means of relics, and the lack of certain means of identifying them, would naturally encourage the imposition of fraud. The crime would not appear so great after one experience, for the perpetrators could readily see that it really made no difference so far as efficacy in the cure of diseases was concerned, whether or not the relics were genuine. The history of some of the relics unfortunately proves them not to be relics at all, or at least not to be the relics which the faithful supposed them to be. Notice a few instances. In a magnificent shrine in the cathedral at Cologne are the skulls of the three kings, or wise men from the East, who brought gifts to the infant Lord. They have rested here since the twelfth century and have been the source of enormous wealth and power to the cathedral chapter. Not to be outdone by the cathedral, for the church of St. Gereon a cemetery has been depopulated, and the bones thus procured have been placed upon the walls and are known as the relics of St. Gereon and his Theband band of martyrs! Further competition arose in the neighboring church of St. 102 Ursula. Another cemetery was despoiled and the bones covering the interior of the walls are known as the relics of St. Ursula and her eleven thousand virgin martyrs. Anatomists now declare that many of the bones are those of men, but this made no more difference in their healing efficacy in the Middle Ages than the fact that the relics of St. Rosalia at Palermo, famed for their healing power, have lately been declared by Professor Buckland, the eminent osteologist, to be the bones of a goat.

Two different investigations have been conducted by the French courts concerning the fountain of La Salette, and in both cases the miracles which make the shrine famous were pronounced to be fraudulent. The recent restoration of the cathedral at Trondhjem has revealed a tube in the walls, not unlike the apparatus discovered in the Temple of Isis at Pompeii; the healing power of this sacred spring was augmented by angelic voices which issued from the supposedly solid walls. 50

While the golden age of the therapeutic use of relics was from the sixth to the sixteenth centuries, modern times, with its physicians, hospitals, and drugs, has not been deprived of this method of cure. Mackay, writing in the latter half of the past century, touches this subject.

At Port Royal, in Paris, is kept with great care a thorn, which the priests of that seminary assert to 103 be one of the identical thorns that bound the holy head of the Son of God. How it came there, and by whom it was preserved, has never been explained. This is the famous thorn which the long dissensions of the Jansenists and the

Molenists have made celebrated, and which worked the miraculous cure upon Mademoiselle Perier, an account of which is so interesting that I give it. The cure occurred on March 14, 1646.

"A young pensioner in the monastery, by name Margaret Perier, who for three years and a half had suffered from a lachrymal fistula, came up in her turn to kiss it; and the nun, her mistress, more horrified than ever at the swelling and deformity of her eye, had a sudden impulse to touch the sore with the relic, believing that God was sufficiently able and willing to heal her. She thought no more of the matter, but the little girl having retired to her room, perceived a quarter of an hour after that her disease was cured; and when she told her companions, it was indeed found that nothing more was to be seen of it. There was no more tumor; and her eye, which the swelling (continuous for three years) had weakened and caused to water, had become as dry, as healthy, as lively as the other. The spring of the filthy matter, which every quarter of an hour ran down from nose, eye, and mouth, and at the very moment before the miracle had fallen upon her cheek (as she declared in her deposition), was found to be quite dried up; the bone, which had been rotted and putrified, was restored to its former condition; all the stench, proceeding from it, which had been so insupportable that by order of the 104 physicians and surgeons she was separated from her companions, was changed into a breath as sweet as an infant's; and she recovered at the same moment her sense of smell....

"Mons. Felix, Chief Surgeon to the King, who had seen her during the month of April, was curious enough to return on the 8th of August, and having found the cure as thorough and marvellous as it had seemed to him at the time, declared under his hand that 'he was obliged to confess that God alone had the power to produce an effect so sudden and extraordinary.'" 51

Mackay gives the following account of the distribution of relics about the middle of the nineteenth century: "Europe still swarms with these religious relics. There is hardly a Roman Catholic Church in Spain, Portugal, France, or Belgium, without one or more of them. Even the poorly endowed churches of the villages boast the possession of miraculous thighbones of the innumerable saints of the Romish calendar. Aix-la-Chapelle is proud of the veritable *ch□e*, or thighbone of Charlemagne, which cures lameness. Halle has a thighbone of the Virgin Mary; Spain has seven or eight, all said to be undoubted relics. Brussels at one time preserved, and perhaps does now, the teeth of St. Gudule. The faithful who suffered from the toothache, had only to pray, look at them, and be cured." 52

105

The miracles performed at the tomb of the Deacon Paris in the cemetery of St. Médard are of comparatively recent occurrence, and well attested. For example, we have the case of "la demoiselle Coirin," which, to say the least, is out of the ordinary. "In 1716," says Dearmer, "this lady, then aged thirty-one, fell from her horse; paralysis and an ulcer followed; by 1719 the ulcer was in a horrible condition; in 1720 her mother refused an operation preferring to let her die in peace. In 1731 — after fifteen years of an open breast — she asked a woman to say a novena at the tomb of François de Paris, to touch the tomb with her shift, and to bring back some earth. This was done on August 10th; on the 11th she put on the shift and at once felt improved; on the 12th she touched the wound with the earth and it at once began to heal. By the end of August the skin was completely healed up, and on September 24th she went out of doors." 53

Among the most noted relics at the present time are the Holy Coat of Treves, 54 the Winding-sheet of Christ at Besançon, and the Santa Scala at Rome. The last are said to be the steps which Jesus ascended and descended when he was brought before Pontius Pilate, and are held in great veneration. It is sacrilegious to walk upon them; the knees of the faithful alone must touch them, and that only 106 after they have reverently kissed them. Cures are still performed by all these relics.

The two shrines at present best known and which have proved most efficacious are those of Lourdes in France 55 and St. Anne de Beaupré in the province of Quebec. Lourdes owes its reputed healing power to a belief in a vision of the Virgin received there during the last century. Over 300,000 persons visit there every year, and no small proportion of them return with health restored as a reward for their faith. At Lourdes and many other shrines bathing forms a part of the ceremony, and on account of the unsanitary conditions in the former place, there is some danger that the French Government will cause its abandonment. Charcot, who established the Salpêtrière hospital where hypnotism was so successfully used, sent fifty or sixty patients to Lourdes every year. He was firmly convinced of the healing power of faith. One commendable feature of the management at Lourdes is the opportunity given for investigation; in fact, this is courted. Most of the sick bring medical details of their diseases; an examining committee of medical men 107 examine them after they arrive there and after the cure. About two hundred and fifty doctors visit there every year, and the widest opportunity is given to them for examination of the cases, regardless of their nationality or religious belief or scepticism. This attitude might well be assumed by these in control of other shrines or of healing cults.

In America thousands flock to the shrine of St. Anne de Beaupré annually. Here are to be found bones, supposed to be the wrist bones of the holy mother of the Virgin, and many sufferers are able to testify to their value in the healing of various diseases.

On all parts of the Continent there are shrines of more or less renown as healing centres. In Normandy the springs of Fécamp or Grand-Andely are much frequented; in Austria, at Mariazell, Styria, the church is visited by two hundred thousand pilgrims a year, and has been a centre of healing since 1157; in Italy, the church of S. Maria dell' Arco, near Naples, has been a local Lourdes for four hundred years, and here, as at Amalfi, Palermo, and other places, the ancient practice of incubation is still prevalent. The adherents of the Eastern Church also have their shrines, and among the visitors to the shrines of Greece, many pilgrims are rewarded for their faith by being healed.

It is curious to remark the avidity manifested in all ages, and in all countries, to obtain possession of 108 some relic of any person who had been much spoken of, if for nothing more than for his crimes. 56 Snuff-boxes made from Shakespeare's mulberry-tree, twigs from Napoleon's willow, or bullets from the field of Waterloo have all been much sought after. Souvenirs of everything and anything are still much in demand. It is within the last decade that a foreign war-ship anchored in New York harbor, and after the officers courteously opened the ship for the inspection of visitors they found that even their silver toilet articles and plate had been carried away by the relic maniacs. A United States admiral, rather more facetiously than patriotically, remarked that "the American people of to-day would steal anything but a cellarful of water." I suppose the remark, so far as it applies to the relic-crazed crowd, would be as applicable to any other people of any other time.

We have a right to ask, in closing this chapter, how it was possible for men to believe in the power of relics to cure diseases. The practice seems to have developed from the reasoning that the saints who helped men while in the imperfections of the flesh, could be of even more benefit when they were with God in the perfections of the spiritual life. St. Augustine (426), for example, speaks of comparing the wonders performed by pagan "deities with our dead men," and that the miracles wrought 109 by idols "are in no way comparable to the wonders wrought by our martyrs." Some might agree with this, and yet find no warrant for using relics. There was, however, the remembrance of the dead man who was restored to life by contact with the bones of Elisha, and of the handkerchiefs and aprons which touched Paul's body and were thereby filled with healing efficacy. Even to-day we do not fail to recognize the value of the association of places and objects, and one finds it difficult to enter Westminster Abbey, for instance, without feeling a thrill on account of the sacred clay reposing there. When we remember the beginning of the use of relics in the catacombs we can better understand the development of the practice.

21 G. F. Fort, *History of Medical Economy During the Middle Ages*, p. 201.

22 *Ibid.*, pp. 142 and 156.

23 G. P. Fisher, *History of the Christian Church*, p. 117.

24 W. E. H. Lecky, *History of European Morals*, I, pp. 378 f.

25 *Ibid.*, I, p. 379.

26 P. Dearmer, *Body and Soul*, pp. 268 f.

27 J. Moses, *Pathological Aspects of Religions*, p. 133.

28 C. Mackay, *Extraordinary Popular Delusions*, II, pp. 303 f.

29 J. W. Draper, *History of the Conflict Between Religion and Science*, p. 270.

30 J. Moses, *Pathological Aspects of Religions*, pp. 132 f.

31 Bede, *Ecclesiastical History*, ed. J. A. Giles, bk. IV, chap. XXXI.

32 T. J. Pettigrew, *Superstitions Connected with the History and Practice of Medicine and Surgery*, pp. 55-57.

33 G. F. Fort, *History of Medical Economy During the Middle Ages*, pp. 224 f., 273-277, 457.

34 A. D. White, *History of the Warfare of Science with Theology*, II, pp. 40 f.

35 G. F. Fort, *History of Medical Economy During the Middle Ages*, p. 273.

36 E. Salverte, *The Philosophy of Magic* (trans. Thompson), II, p. 93.

37 *Tour of Wales*, I, p. 405.

38 Hasted, *Kent*, III, p. 176.

39 *History of His Life and Times*, p. 32.

40 *Statistical Account of Scotland*, VII, p. 213, and XII, p. 464.

41 *Ibid.*, XVIII, p. 487.

42 C. S. Macaulay, *History of St. Kilda*, p. 95.

43 *Somersetshire*, III, p. 104.

44 I am much indebted to J. Brand, *Popular Antiquities*, pp. 1-17, for some of the quotations used in the discussion of this subject.

45 *Superstitions Connected with ... Medicine and Surgery*, pp. 57-61.

46 I am indebted to P. Dearmer, *Body and Soul*, pp. 278-281, 314-318, for the material on incubation. For fuller study, see L. Deubner, *De Incubatione*, and M. Hamilton, *Incubation*.

47 G. F. Fort, *History of Medical Economy During the Middle Ages*, p. 227.

48 *Ibid.*, pp. 210-214, 226 f., 278.

49 A. D. White, *History of the Warfare of Science with Theology*, II, p. 30.

50 *Ibid.*, II, pp. 21, 29, 43.

51 P. Dearmer, *Body and Soul*, pp. 374 f.

52 C. Mackay, *Extraordinary Popular Delusions*, II, p. 304.

53 P. Dearmer, *Body and Soul*, pp. 105 f.

54 R. F. Clarke, *The Holy Coat of Treves*.

55 A. T. Myers and F. W. H. Myers, "Mind Cure, Faith Cure, and the Miracles at Lourdes," *Proceedings Society Psychical Research*, IX, pp. 160-409; E. Berdoe, "A Medical View of the Miracles at Lourdes," *Nineteenth Century*, October, 1895; J. B. Estrade, *Les apparitions de Lourdes, Souvenirs intimes d'un t🐟in*; H. Bernheim, *Suggestive Therapeutics*, pp. 200-202; A. Imbert-Gourbyzee, *La Stigmatisation, l'extase divine, et les miracles de Lourdes*, II, chaps. XXI and XXVII; E. Zola, *Lourdes*.

56 C. Mackay, *Extraordinary Popular Delusions*, II, p. 306.

110

CHAPTER V

HEALERS

"This is an art Which doth mend nature—but The art itself is nature." —*Winter's Tale.*

"Some are molested by Phantasie; so some, again, by Fancy alone and a good conceit, are as easily recovered.... All the world knows there is no virtue in charms, &c., but a strong conceit and opinion alone, as Pomponatius holds, which forceth a motion of the humours, spirits, and blood, which takes away the cause of the malady from the parts affected. The like we may say of the magical effects, superstitious cures, and such as are done by montebanks and wizards. As by wicked incredulity many are hurt (so saith Wierus), we find, in our experience, by the same means, many are relieved."

In discussing the subject of healers one must keep in mind the fact that the healers of the first millennium of our era were almost wholly exorcists, on account of the prevailing theory, and even after that time exorcism, on the one hand, and the faith in relics and shrines on the other, formed the principal means of cure. It is therefore difficult to differentiate the other healers from the exorcists, and to decide whether certain cures were performed by healers or by relics.

Another difficulty confronts us. Many authentic cures have probably been wrought by saints, but unfortunately most of those performed by them 111 have little contemporary evidence to support them, but rest on the very shaky testimony of tradition. White, 57 in a keen analysis, shows how the legends of miraculous cures have grown around great benefactors of humanity, taking Francis Xavier as a pertinent example.

We must also remember, however, that what are called miracles formed part of the evidence which led to the canonization of a saint, and a large number of healing miracles was usually included in the list. The procedure of the court connected with the canonization was conducted with the greatest rigor. Sitting as examiners were learned and upright men from all nations, and the witness must be irreproachable as far as character was concerned. The two witnesses required for each miracle must testify concerning the nature of the disease and the cure, and sign the deposition after it had been read to them. Following that, the examiners sifted the evidence in a hypercritical way and emphasized the weak places. Benedict XIV justly said: "The degree of proof required is the same as that required for a criminal case, since the cause of religion and piety is that of the commonweal." Some consideration must be thus given to this testimony, but the value of it depends on the number of years elapsing after the cures were performed and the 112 direct connection of the witnesses with the cure in question.

The craving for the miraculous in bodily cures prejudiced many historians, especially when the desire to emphasize the importance of the church was uppermost in the minds of the writers. We can consider, though, the material at hand, always recognizing that marvellous cures can be performed when the authority of the physician has all the weight of an infallible church behind it and the patient is credulous. We must notice in this connection that the healers up to the time of the magnetizers depended on religious ceremonies for their efficiency, with the exception of those who endorsed and propagated "sympathetic cures."

As we well know, the first healing among Christians was done by Jesus himself and the apostles; after this for two centuries the exorcists performed most of the cures. We have accounts of one non-Christian healer whose cures have probably been handed down to us on account of his exalted position. Tacitus and Suetonius describe how Vespasian (9-79) healed in at least two cases. The first was a blind man well known in Alexandria. In the second case the historians disagree; one says it was a leg and the other a hand which was diseased and cured. According to the story, the god Serapis revealed to the patients that they would be cured by the emperor. Tacitus says that Vespasian 113 did not believe in his own power and it was only after much persuasion that he was induced to try the experiment. 58

The Christians, however, were not to be outdone as healers. Irenæus (130-202) gives a long list of infirmities which were cured by the representatives of the church, and in writing, about the year 180, draws a comparison between them and the heretics. "For they [the heretics] can neither confer sight on the blind nor hearing on the deaf, nor chase away all sorts of demons (except those which are sent into others by themselves—if they can ever do as much as this): nor can they cure the weak, or the lame, or the paralytic; or those who are distressed in any other part of the body, as has often been done in regard to bodily infirmity. Nor can they furnish effective remedies for those external accidents which may occur. And so far are they from being able to raise the dead, as the Lord raised them (and the Apostles did by means of prayer, as has been frequently done in the brotherhood on account of some necessity—the entire church in that particular locality entreating with much fasting and prayer, the spirit of the dead man has returned, and he has been bestowed in answer to the prayers of the saints—) that they do not even believe that this could possibly be done." He further says: "Others again heal the sick by laying their hands upon them, 114 and they are made whole. Yea, moreover, as I have said, the dead even have been raised up, and remained among us for many years."

The great Origen (185-254), writing when he would be certain to have his words most severely criticised, says, after referring to the miracles of the apostles: "And there are still preserved among Christians traces of that Holy Spirit which appeared in the form of a dove. They expel evil spirits, and perform many cures, and foresee certain events, according to the will of the Logos." In another of his works we find the following: "For they [the Jews] have no longer prophets or miracles, traces of which to a considerable extent are still found among Christians, and some of them more remarkable than ever have existed among the Jews; and these we ourselves have witnessed."

As has already been seen, different methods were used by various healers, and we must not omit a brief account of healing by unction. The very definite instructions laid down in the Epistle of James were evidently strictly carried out in the early church, but the first definite mention of anointing after that made by Mark and James is found in the writings of Tertullian (160-220). He speaks of the pagan emperor Severus being graciously mindful of Christians: "For he sought out the Christian Proculus, surnamed Torpacion, the steward of Euhodias, and in gratitude for his having once cured him 115 by anointing, he kept him in his palace till the day of his death." 59

If the Christians anointed pagans it is legitimate to suppose that they also anointed fellow-Christians, and that if this was performed without special mention about the end of the second century, it must have been common from the time of James to that period. It is probable that during the first seven centuries of our era the practice of praying with the sick and anointing them with oil never ceased. There may be some objection to our considering the subject of anointing with oil as purely mental healing, but according to the instructions given for its use there was scarcely enough oil employed to be of benefit otherwise, and especially as food. Mental healing, then, is the rationale of the cures.

Puller 60 gives us three of the earliest incidents of healing by unction, the original accounts all being written by contemporaries and friends. Some time between the years 335 and 355, St. Parthenius, Bishop of Lampsacus, anointed a man who was described as "altogether withered." The account says: "Then getting up, he gently and gradually softened the man's body with the holy oil, and straightway made him to rise up healed." Refinus, a well-known writer and an eye-witness to this heal 116 ing, tells of St. Macarius of Alexandria and four monks restoring, about the year 375, "a man, withered in all his limbs and especially in his feet." He says: "But when he had been anointed all over by them with oil in the Name of the Lord, immediately the soles of his feet were strengthened. And when they said to him, 'In the name of Jesus Christ ... arise, and stand on thy feet, and return to thy house,' immediately arising and leaping, he blessed God." Some years later, Palladius, the friend of St. Chrysostom, writes of another of St. Macarius's cures which he witnessed: "But at the time that we were there, there was brought to him from Thessalonica a noble and wealthy virgin, who during many years had been suffering from paralysis. And when she had been presented to him, and had been thrown down before the cell of the blessed man, he, being moved with compassion for her, with his own hands anointed her during twenty days with holy oil, pouring out prayers for her to the Lord, and so sent her back cured to her own city."

The Sacramentary of Serapion, Bishop of Thmuis, Egypt, written about 350, provides for the consecration of bread and water, as well as oil, for healing; and in a prayer concerning oil and water there contained, the following words are used: "Grant healing power upon these creatures, that every fever and every demon and every sickness may depart through the drinking and the anointing, and that 117 the partaking of these creatures may be a healing medicine and a medicine of complete soundness in the Name of the Only begotten, Jesus Christ," etc. The Apostolic Constitutions of about 375 contain a prayer of consecration used over oil and water brought by members of the congregation, as follows: "Do thou now sanctify this water and this oil, through Christ, in the name of him that offered or of her that offered, and give to these things a power of producing health and of driving away diseases, of putting to flight demons, of dispersing every snare through Christ our Hope," etc.

About 390, St. Jerome wrote a life of St. Hilarion (291-371) in which the latter is thus set forth as a healer: "But lo! that parched and sandy district, after the rain had fallen, unexpectedly produced such vast numbers of serpents and poisonous animals that many, who were bitten, would have died at once if they had not run to Hilarion. He therefore blessed some oil, with which all the husbandmen and shepherds touched their wounds and found an infallible cure."

Oil was not always employed for anointing, but might be drunk by the sick, and this use of it was made in healing a girl, by St. Martin of Tours, about 395. St. Germain, Bishop of Auxerre (418-448), when the physicians were powerless during a plague, blessed some oil and anointed the swollen jaws of those who were sick, whereupon they recovered; 118 and St. Genevieve of Paris, who died about 502, used to heal the sick with oil.

In Bede's biography of St. Cuthbert we find an instance of this saint healing a girl about the year 687. A young woman was troubled for a whole year with an intolerable pain in her head and side which the physicians were unable to relieve. Cuthbert "in pity anointed the wretched woman with oil. From that time she began to get better, and was well in a few days."

At the beginning of the eighth century the anointing of the sick began to decline, largely on account of the changed attitude of the church. At this time this ceremony began to be used for spiritual ills rather than for bodily diseases. Before long, anointing was monopolized by the church for spiritual advantage, and is still so used by the Roman Catholic Church in the ceremony of Extreme Unction.

In returning to the more direct methods of healing, we find that St. Gregory of Nazianzus (329-390) confirmed the reports of the marvellous cures wrought by the martyrs, Cosmo and Damian, who were beheaded in 303. During the life of Gregory of Tours (538-594), the healing efficacy of the saints' relics was rivalled by the miraculous aid rendered to the sick by St. Julian. The solitude of the holy anchorite was interrupted by the persistent and despairing clamor of the sick to whom he gave 119 health. The great Turonese pontiff also tells us that one day Aredius, traversing Paris, found Chilperic prostrate with a grievous fever. The royal sufferer sought the saint's prayers as an irresistible curative.

The daughter of a Teutonic nobleman was brought to St. Gall (556-640) seriously ill with an incurable disorder, presenting the livid appearance of an animated cadaver. The saint approached the unconscious invalid as she reclined on her mother's knee, and assuming the bended attitude of invocation by her side, made a fervent prayer and evoked the demon producing the sickness to instantly depart. The effort was all that was desired. Shortly after this, about the year 648, St. Vardrille, the founder of Fontanelle, exercised his remedial potency in healing the palsied arm of a forester whose indiscreet zeal had induced him to transfix the sainted abbot with a lance.

We have rather a strange case from the beginning of the seventh century, where the moral and mental element seems to have been strong. Abbe Eustasius returning from Rome, whither a mission of Clothair II had called him, was urgently summoned by the sorrowful parent of a Burgundian maiden, in the last agonies of a frightful malady, to appear and cure the moribund daughter. On answering the call he found that the child had in her youth been consecrated by the vows of chastity, and on account 120 of this shrunk from a marriage sanctioned by her parents. Eustasius reproached the father for his efforts to violate the solemn obligations of the0 virgin, and upon obtaining a formal renunciation of further attempts to coerce her into matrimony, the saint, by personal intercession, obtained a complete cure.

It was found that certain remedies in the hands of certain saints were efficacious, but they did not have the same power if administered by others. For instance, Franciscus de Paula succored an anchylosed joint by the energetic surgery of three dried figs which he gave the suffering patient to eat. Similarly, a maiden grieving under a cancerous disease which surgical skill had frankly admitted was incurable, was restored to robust vigor by the administering of some mild herbs. This savored rather too much of medicine, and other holy healers used more orthodox means. Hugo the Holy abstracted a serpent from the infirm body of a woman by the use of holy water, and Coleta, the saintess, awakened from the dreamless slumber of death more than one hundred slain infants by the efficacy of a cross.

Even such a serious disorder as leprosy was said to have been healed by saintly care. St. Martin, who gave special attention to sufferers with this disease, cured a leper by kissing him, we are told. Toward the middle of the sixth century, St. Rade 121 gonde displayed her faith by first washing the repulsive sores and afterward applying her pure lips to them. On one occasion an insolent leper asserted that unless his putrefying limbs were kissed by this candidate for canonical honors he could not be cured. 61

Bede (673-735), the great English historian, in his careful way tells us of cures performed by St. John of Beverly during the first part of the eighth century. According to this record, St. John cured a dumb youth, who had never spoken a word, by the sign of the cross on his tongue, and he afterward had "ready utterance." He used holy water on a woman so that, like Peter's wife's mother, she arose and ministered to them, healed a friend who was injured by being thrown from a horse, cured a nun of a grievous complaint, and restored a servant, an account of which I shall give in Bede's words:

"The bishop went in and saw him in a dying condition, and the coffin by his side, whilst all present were in tears. He said a prayer, blessed him, and on going out, as is the usual expression of comforters, said, 'May you soon recover.' Afterwards when they were sitting at table, the lad sent to his lord, to desire he would let him have a cup of wine, because he was thirsty. The earl, rejoicing that he 122 could drink, sent him a cup of wine, blessed by the bishop; which, as soon as he had drunk, he immediately got up, and shaking off his late infirmity, dressed himself, and going in to the bishop, saluted him and the other guests, saying, 'He would also eat and be merry with them.' They ordered him to sit down with them at the entertainment, rejoicing at his recovery. He sat down, ate and drank merrily, and behaved himself like the rest of the company; and living many years after, continued in the same state of health." 62

Skipping a few centuries, we find that Bernard of Clairvaux (1091-1153), the most prominent figure of the twelfth century, performed an abundance of cures, as his biographers testify. "The cures were so many that the witnesses themselves were unable to detail them all. At Doningen, near Rheinfeld, where the first Sunday of Advent was spent, Bernard cured, in one day, nine blind persons, ten who were deaf or dumb, and eighteen lame or paralytic. On the following Wednesday, at Schaffhausen, the number of miracles increased." 63 Concerning these cures Morison says: "Thirty-six miraculous cures in one day would seem to have been the largest stretch of supernatural power which Bernard permitted to himself. The halt, the blind, the deaf, and the dumb were brought from all parts to be touched by Bernard. The patient was presented 123 to him, whereupon he made the sign of the cross over the part affected, and the cure was perfect." 64

The following case in which details are more fully given is of much interest: "At Toulouse, in the church of St. Saturninus, in which we were lodged, was a certain regular canon, named John. John had kept his bed for seven months, and was so reduced that his death was expected daily. His legs were so shrunken that they were scarcely larger than a child's arms. He was quite unable to rise to satisfy the wants of nature. At last his brother canons refused to tolerate his presence any longer among them, and thrust him out into the neighbouring village. When the poor creature heard of Bernard's proximity, he implored to be taken to him. Six men, therefore, carrying him as he lay in bed, brought him into a room close to that in which he was lodged. The abbot heard him confess his sins, and listened to his entreaties to be restored to health. Bernard mentally prayed to God: 'Behold, O Lord, they seek for a sign, and our words avail nothing, unless they be confirmed with signs following.' He then blessed him and left the chamber, and so did we all. In that very hour the sick man arose from his couch, and running after Bernard, kissed his feet with a devotion which cannot be imagined by any one who did not see it. One of the canons, meeting 124 him, nearly fainted with fright, thinking he saw his ghost."

St. Francis of Assisi (1182-1226), the great founder of the Franciscan Order, was not less famed for his miracles of healing than for his Christ-like life and his stigmata. Among those cured were epileptics, paralytics, and the blind. A typical case of cure by this humble saint is given to show his method and its results: "Once when Francis the Saint of God was making a long circuit through various regions to preach the gospel of God's kingdom he came to a city called Toscanella. Here ... he was entertained by a knight of that same city whose only son was a cripple and weak in all his body. Though the child was of tender years he had passed the age of weaning; but he still remained in a cradle. The boy's father, seeing the man of God to be endued with such holiness, humbly fell at his feet and besought him to heal his son. Francis, deeming himself to be unprofitable and unworthy of such power and grace, for a long time refused to do it. At last, conquered by the urgency of the knight's entreaties, after offering up prayer, he laid his hand on the boy, blessed him, and lifted him up. And in the sight of all, the boy straightway arose whole in the name of the Lord Jesus Christ, and began to walk hither and thither about the house." 65

125

St. Thomas of Hereford (1222-1282) was the last Englishman to be officially canonized. The extant documents of his canonization record no less than four hundred and twenty-nine miracles alleged to have been performed by him. The following case of resurrection from the dead occurred, however, twenty-one years after his death. I quote the account in full:

"On the 6th of September, 1303, Roger, aged two years and three months, the son of Gervase, one of the warders of Conway Castle, managed to crawl out of bed in the night and tumble off a bridge, a distance of twenty-eight feet; he was not discovered till the next morning, when his mother found him half naked and quite dead upon a hard stone at the bottom of the ditch, where there was no water or earth, but simply the rock, which had been quarried to build the castle. Simon Waterford, the vicar, who had christened the child, John de Bois, John Guffe, all sworn witnesses, took their oaths on the Gospel that they saw and handled the child dead. The King's Crowners (Stephen Ganny and William Nottingham) were presently called and went down into the moat. They found the child's body cold and stiff, and white with hoar-frost, stark dead, indeed. While the Crowners, as their office requires, began to write what they had seen, one John Syward, a near neighbour, came down and gently handled the child's body all over, and finding it as dead as ever any, made the sign of the cross upon its forehead, and earnestly prayed after this manner: 'Blessed St. Thomas Cantelope, you by whom God has wrought innumerable miracles, 126 show mercy unto this little infant, and obtain he may return to life again. If this grace be granted he shall visit your holy sepulchre and render humble thanks to God and you for the favor.' No sooner had Syward spoken these words, than the child began to move his head and right arm a little, and forthwith life and vigor came back again into every part of his body. The Crowners, and many others who were standing by, saw the miracle, and in that very place, with great admiration, returned humble thanks to God and St. Thomas for what they had seen. The mother, now overjoyed, took the child in her arms, and went that day to hear mass in a church not far off, where, upon her knees, she recognized with a grateful heart that she owed the life of her infant to God and St. Thomas. Her devotion ended, she returned home, and the child, feeling no pain at all, walked as he was wont to do up and down the house, though a little scar still continued in one cheek, which after a few days, quite vanished away." 66

St. Catharine of Siena (1347-1380) obtained considerable reputation as a healer, principally, however, in the line of exorcism; this, though, meant the cure of any disease. Like St. Paul, she was one of a large number of saints who healed others but did not cure herself; she died at the age of thirty-three. A woman was presented to the immaculate saintess for prompt remedy; by the virtue of divine magic a demon was forced from each part of her body where he had taken refuge, but resisting ab 127 solute ejectment from this carnal abode, made a desperate conflict in the throat, where by uninterrupted scratches he reproduced himself in the form of an abscess.

On another occasion the saint was more successful. Laurentia, a maiden of youthful years, placed by her father within the sheltering walls of a cloister, to assume ultimately monastic vows, was quickly captured by an errant demon. As an irrefutable demonstration of the impure origin of her infirmity, an annalist asserts, this spirit promptly answered in elegant Latinity all questions propounded; but the strongest confirmation of this belief was the miraculous ability which enabled her to disclose the most secret thoughts of others, and divulge the mysterious affairs of her associates. St. Catharine at length liberated the suffering female from her diabolical tenant. More extraordinary claims are made for her. It is said that she stayed a plague at Varazze, and healed a throng at Pisa. 67

Raimondo da Capua, her faithful friend and constant companion, wrote her biography and gives us different instances of remarkable cures performed by her. For example, he tells us that Father Matthew of Cenni, the director of the Hospital of la Misericordia, was stricken when the plague was raging in Siena in 1373, and of his marvellous cure.

128

Perhaps we had better allow him to tell of Catharine's power in his own words:

"One day on entering, I saw some of the brothers carrying Father Matthew like a corpse from the chapel to his room; his face was livid, and his strength was so far gone that he could not answer me when I spoke to him. 'Last night,' the brothers said, 'about seven o'clock, while ministering to a dying person, he perceived himself stricken, and fell at once into extreme weakness.' I helped to put him on his bed; ... he spoke afterwards, and said that he felt as if his head was separated into four parts. I sent for Dr. Senso, his physician; Dr. Senso declared to me that my friend had the plague, and that every symptom announced the approach of death. 'I fear,' he said, 'that the House of Mercy (Misericordia) is about to be deprived of its good director.' I asked if medical art could not save him. 'We shall see,' replied Senso, 'but I have only a very faint hope; his blood is too much poisoned.' I withdrew, praying God to save the life of this good man. Catharine, however, had heard of the illness of Father Matthew, whom she loved sincerely, and she lost no time in repairing to him. The moment she entered the room, she cried, with a cheerful voice, 'Get up, Father Matthew, get up! This is not a time to be lying idly in bed.' Father Matthew roused himself, sat up on his bed, and finally stood on his feet. Catharine retired; and the moment she was leaving the house, I entered it, and ignorant of what had happened, and believing my friend to be still at the point of death, my grief urged me to say, 'Will you allow a person so dear to us, and so useful to others, to die?' She appeared annoyed at my words, and replied, 'In 129 what terms do you address me? Am I like God, to deliver a man from death?' But I, beside myself with sorrow, pleaded, 'Speak in that way to others if you will, but not to me; for I know your secrets; and I know you obtain from God whatever you ask in faith.' Then Catharine bowed her head, and smiled just a little; after a few minutes she lifted up her head and looked at me full in the face, her countenance radiant with joy, and said, 'Well, let us take courage; he will not die this time,' and she passed on. At these words I banished all fear, for I understood that she had obtained some favor from heaven. I went straight to my sick friend, whom I found sitting on the side of his bed. 'Do you know,' he cried, 'what she has done for me?' He then stood up and narrated joyfully what I have here written. To make the matter more sure, the table was laid, and Father Matthew seated himself at it with us; they served him with vegetables and other light food, and he, who an hour before could not open his mouth, ate with us, chatting and laughing gaily."

None of Catharine's biographers fail to relate wonderful instances of her healing power. 68

Martin Luther (1483-1546), the great leader of the Reformation, and St. Francis Xavier (1506-1552), the leader of the Counter-Reformation, were both healers, so it is said. Luther's cure of his friend and helper, Melanchthon, by prayer for and encouragement of the patient, is well known. Xavier's miracles were legion, but have been somewhat 130 discredited by a recent author. 69 I add but one example. "A certain Tom預aninguem, a fencing-master, says, I knew Antonio de Miranda, who was a servant of the Father Francis, and assisted him when saying Mass. He told me that when going one night on business to Combature, he was bitten by a venomous serpent. He immediately fell down as though paralyzed and became speechless. He was found thus lying unconscious. Informed of the fact, Father Francis ordered Antonio to be carried to him: and when he was laid down speechless and senseless, the Father prayed with all those present. The prayer finished, he put a little saliva with his finger on the bitten place on Antonio's foot, and at the same moment, Antonio recovered his senses, his memory and his speech, and felt himself healed. I have since heard details of this occurrence from the mouths of several eye-witnesses." 70

If we accept G · ·s's account, 71 the most remarkable instance of curative power possessed by a saint is that afforded by St. Sauveur of Horta (1520-1567). Outside of this one work I have been unable to find any reference to this saint, so I will give a sketch of his apparently remarkable life. He 131 was born in Catalonia, and received the first part of his name from a presentiment of his sponsors that he was to be a savior of men, and the second part because he entered the monastery at Horta. A short time after he finished his novitiate, people in some way got the idea that he had a wonderful gift of healing, and soon patients came to him in crowds from all parts of the country. He continued healing for several years. At one time during the feast of the Annunciation he cured six thousand persons, and at another time he found ten thousand patients, from viceroy to laborer, waiting for him at Valencia before the convent of St. Marie de Jesus. Notwithstanding his apparently great success, his brother monks complained to the bishop concerning the dirt and disorder caused by the crowds, and after a reprimand he was sent at midnight to the monastery at Reus, where he was known as Alphonse and assigned to the kitchen. In spite of this, crowds continued to come and he was transferred from monastery to monastery, but always with the same result—the crowd sought him to be healed. He was known as simple, open, and obedient in his relations with men, and austere toward himself. He was patient and resigned, compassionate toward the poor and sick, and full of zeal for their conversion. The number of patients he is said to have cured is incredible, and it is even said that he resuscitated three dead persons. After his death 132 miracles were performed at his tomb. Why he was not in favor with his superiors and his brother monks is unknown; his friends say they were jealous; his enemies, that his cures were not genuine.

St. Philip Neri (1551-1595), the founder of the Oratorians, was renowned as a healer. He cured Clement VIII of gout by touching and prayer, a woman of cancer of the breast by the mere touch and assurance, a man of grievous symptoms such as loss of speech and internal pain by simply laying on of hands, and many similar and equally serious cases. The following case was counted nearly equal to a resurrection: "In 1560 Pietro Vittrici of Parma, being in the service of Cardinal Boncompagni, afterward Pope Gregory XIII, fell dangerously ill. He was given up by the physicians, and was supposed to be as good as dead. In this extremity he was visited by Philip who, as soon as he entered the sick man's room, began, as was his wont, to pray for him. He then put his hand on Pietro's forehead, and at the touch he instantly revived. In two days' time he was out of the house perfectly well and strong and went about telling people how he had been cured by Father Philip." 72

George Fox (1624-1691), the founder of the Quakers, performed some simple cures of which he himself tells us. The most famous case was that of the cure of a lame arm by command, the account 133 of which we take from his pen. He thus records it: "After some time I went to the meeting at Arnside where Richard Meyer was. Now he had been long lame of one of his arms; and I was moved by the Lord to say unto him, among all the people, 'Prophet Meyer stand up upon thy legs' (for he was sitting down) and he stood up and stretched out his arm that had been lame a long time, and said: 'Be it known unto all you people that this day I am healed.' But his parents could hardly believe it, but after the meeting was done, had him aside and took off his doublet; and then they saw it was true. He soon after came to Swarthmore meeting, and there declared how the Lord had healed him. But after this the Lord commanded him to go to York with a message from him; and he disobeyed the Lord; and the Lord struck him again, so that he died about three-quarters of a year after." 73 The cure evidently was not permanent.

Valentine Greatrakes (1628-1683) was born in Affane, Ireland. He was the son of an Irish gentleman, had a good education, and was a Protestant. In 1641, at the outbreak of the Irish rebellion, he fled to England, and from 1649-1656 he served under Cromwell. In 1661, after a period of melancholy derangement, he believed that God had given him power of curing "king's evil" by touching or stroking and prayer. After some success with this 134 disease, he added to his list ague, epilepsy, convulsions, paralysis, deafness, ulcers, aches, and lameness, and for a number of years he devoted three days in every week, from 6 A. M. to 6 P. M., to the exercise of his healing gifts. The crowds which thronged around him were so great that the neighboring towns were not able to accommodate them. He thereupon left his house in the country and went to Youghal, where sick people, not only from all parts of Ireland but from England, continued to congregate in such great numbers that the magistrates were afraid they would infect the place with their diseases.

VALENTINE GREATRAKES

In some instances he exorcised demons; in fact, he claimed that all diseases were caused by evil spirits, and every infirmity was, with him, a case of diabolic possession. The church endeavored to prohibit his operations but without avail. He was invited to London, and, notwithstanding that an exhibition before the nobility failed, thousands flocked to his house in Lincoln's Inn Fields. In the "Miscellanies" of St. Evremond a graphic sketch is given of his work. The results of his healing are there summed up as follows:

"So great was the confidence in him, that the blind fancied they saw the light which they did not see—the deaf imagined that they heard—the lame that they walked straight, and the paralytic that they had recovered the use of their limbs. An idea 135 of health made the sick forget for a while their maladies; and imagination, which was not less active in those merely drawn by curiosity than in the sick, gave a false view to the one class, from the desire of seeing, as it operated a false cure on the other from the strong desire of being healed. Such was the power of the Irishman over the mind, and such was the influence of the mind over the body. Nothing was spoken of in London but his prodigies; and these prodigies were supported by such great authorities that the bewildered multitude believed them almost without examination, while more enlightened people did not dare to reject them from their own knowledge."

That there were real cures, however, seems most probable. The Bishop of Dromore testifies thus from his own observation: "I have seen pains strangely fly before his hands till he had chased them out of the body; dimness cleared, and deafness cured by his touch. Twenty persons at several times, in fits of the falling sickness, were in two or three minutes brought to themselves.... Running sores of the 'King's evil' were dried up; grievous sores of many months' date in a few days healed, cancerous knots dissolved, etc." 74

The celebrated Flamstead, the astronomer, when a lad of nineteen, went into Ireland to be touched by Greatrakes, and he testifies that he was an eyewitness of several cures, although he himself was not benefited. In a letter to Lord Conway, Great 136 rakes says: "The King's doctors, this day (for the confirmation of their majesties' belief), sent three out of the hospital to me, who came on crutches; but, blessed be God! they all went home well, to the admiration of all people, as well as the doctors." 75

Several pamphlets were issued by medical men and others criticising his work, and in 1666 he published a vindication of himself entitled "A Brief Account." This contained numerous testimonials by Bishop Wilkins, Bishop Patrick, Dr. Cudworth, Dr. Whichcote, and others of distinction and intelligence. After the retirement of Greatrakes, John Leverett, a gardener, succeeded to the "manual exercise," and declared that after touching thirty or forty a day, he felt so much goodness go out of him that he was fatigued as if he had been digging eight roods of ground.

About the same time that Greatrakes was working among the people of London, an Italian enthusiast, named Francisco Bagnone, was operating in Italy with equal success. He had only to touch the sick with his hands, or sometimes with a relic, to accomplish cures which astonished the people.

Hardly less famous than Greatrakes was Johann Jacob Gassner (1727-1779). He was born at Bratz, near Bludenz, and became Roman Catholic priest 137 at Klⵧⵧrle. He believed that most diseases were caused by evil spirits which could be exorcised by conjuration and prayer. He began practising and soon attracted attention. In 1774 he received a call from the bishop at Ratisbon to Ellwangen, where by the mere word of command, "Cesset" (Give over), he cured the lame and blind, but especially those who were afflicted with epilepsy and convulsions, and who were thereby supposed to be obsessed. His cures were not permanent in some cases, and before he died he lost power and respect.

57 A. D. White, *History of the Warfare of Science with Theology*, II, pp. 5-22.

58 W. E. H. Lecky, *History of European Morals*, I, pp. 347 f.

59 P. Dearmer, *Body and Soul*, pp. 252 f. I am indebted to this excellent book for my material on the subject of Unction, as well as for many other quotations in this chapter.

60 F. W. Puller, *Anointing of the Sick*, pp. 155-158.

61 G. F. Fort, *History of Medical Economy During the Middle Ages*, gives this and the other incidents just quoted. See pp. 155, 160, 272, 275, 327.

62 Bede, *Ecclesiastical History*, bk. V, chap. V.

63 Quoted by P. Dearmer, *Body and Soul*, p. 359.

64 J. Cotter Morison, *Life and Times of St. Bernard*, pp. 422 and 460, for this and the following incident.

65 Thomas of Celano, *Lives of St. Francis of Assisi* (trans. A. G. F. Howell).

66 *Dublin Review*, January, 1876, pp. 8-10.

67 G. F. Fort, *History of Medical Economy During the Middle Ages*, pp. 278 f.

68 See J. Butler, *Life of St. Catharine of Siena*, for many examples.

69 See A. D. White, *History of the Warfare of Science with Theology*, already referred to.

70 Jos. Marie Cros, *St. Fran篩s de Xavier, Sa vie et ses lettres*, II, p. 392.

71 G · ·s, *La mystique divine naturelle et diabolique* (trans. Saintefoi), I, pp. 470-473.

72 P. J. Bacci, *Life of St. Philip Neri* (trans. Antrobus), II, p. 168.

73 G. Fox, *Journal*, I, p. 103.

74 J. Moses, *Pathological Aspects of Religions*, p. 188.

75 E. Salverte, *The Philosophy of Magic* (trans. Thompson), II, p. 81.

138

CHAPTER VI

TALISMANS

"He had the ring of Gyges, the talisman of invisibility." — Hamerton.

"The quack astrologer offers, for five pieces, to give you home with you a Talisman against Flies; a Sigil to make you fortunate at gaining; and a Spell that shall as certainly preserve you from being rob'd for the future; a sympathetic Powder for violent pains of the Tooth-ache." — *Character of a Quack Astrologer.*

"So far are they distant from the true knowledge of physic which are ignorant of astrology, that they ought not rightly to be called physicians, but deceivers; for it hath been many times experimented and proved that that which many physicians could not cure or remedy with their greatest and strongest medicines, the astronomer hath brought to pass with one simple herb, by observing the moving of the signs." — Fabian Withers.

In the minds of most persons the terms talisman, amulet, and charm are synonymous. This may be more or less true as far as they are used to-day, but in the days when these terms meant something in real life there was a distinction. The talisman was probably at first an astronomical figure, but later the term became more comprehensive. Pope portrays this astrological import in his couplet,

> "Of talismans and sigils knew the power, And carefully watch'd the planetary hour."

The amulet was always carried about the person, while the other two might be in the possession of 139 the person in the case of the talisman, or, in the case of the charm, if a material object it could be placed entirely outside of one's care. The talisman and amulet must be a compound of some substance, the charm might be a gesture, a look, or a spoken word. Notice the example of charms according to Tennyson's words,

> "Then, in one moment, she put forth the charm Of woven paces and of waving hands."

They were all used for defensive purposes, *i. e.*, to keep away evil, in the form of demons, disease, or misfortune, but they might, especially the talisman, also attract good. Their power was of a magical character, and was exercised in a supernatural manner.

The idea of the talisman probably originated from the belief that certain properties or virtues were impressed upon substances by planetary influences. "A talisman," says Pettigrew, "may in general terms be defined to be a substance composed of certain cabalistic characters engraved on stone, metal, or other material, or else written on slips of paper." Hyde quotes a Persian writer who defines the Telesm or Talismay as "a piece of art compounded of the celestial powers and elementary bodies, appropriated to certain figures or positions, and purposes and times, contrary to the usual manner."

140 We are told by Maimonides that images or idols were called Tzelamim on account of the power or influence which was supposed to reside in them, rather than on account of their particular

figure or form. Townley has opined that the reason for the production of astrological or talismanic images was probably the desire of early peoples to have some representation of the planets during their absence from sight, so that they might at all times be able to worship the planetary body itself or its representative. To accomplish this purpose, the astrologers chose certain colors, metals, stones, trees, etc., to represent certain planets, and constructed the talismans when the planets were in their exaltation and in a happy conjunction with other heavenly bodies. In addition to this, incantations were used in an endeavor to inspire the talisman with the power and influence of the planet for which it stood.

Pettigrew says: "The Hebrew word for talisman (magan) signifies a paper or other material, drawn or engraved with the letters composing the sacred name Jehovah, or with other characters, and improperly applied to astrological representations, because, like the letters composing 'The Incomparable Name,' they were supposed to serve as a defence against sickness, lightning, and tempest. It was a common practice with magicians, whenever a plague or other great calamity infested a country, to make a supposed image of the destroyer, either 141 in gold, silver, clay, wax, etc., under a certain configuration of the heavens, and to set it up in some particular place that the evil might be stayed." 76

The Jewish phylacteries must therefore be considered talismans and not amulets. The writings contained in them are portions of the law and are prepared in a prescribed manner. Three different kinds are used: one for the head, another for the arm, and the third is attached to the door-posts. The following is a Hebrew talisman supposed to have considerable power: "It overflowed—he did cast darts—Shadai is all sufficient—his hand is strong, and is the preserver of my life in all its variations." 77

Arnot gives an account of some Scottish talismans not unlike the phylacteries of the Jews, which were for use on the door-posts. "On the old houses still existing in Edinburgh," he says, "there are remains of talismanic or cabalistical characters, which the superstitious of earlier days had caused to be engraven on their fronts. These were generally composed of some text of Scripture, of the name of God, or, perhaps, of an emblematic representation of the resurrection." 78

The connection of astrology, or, as he calls it, "astronomy," and the talisman with medicine is 142 well portrayed by Chaucer in his picture of a good physician of his day. He says:

> "With us there was a doctor of phisike; In al the world, was thar non hym lyk To speke of physik and of surgerye, For he wos groundit in astronomie. He kept his pacient a ful gret del In hourys by his magyk naturel; Wel couth he fortunen the ascendent Of his ymagys for his pacient."

Fosbrooke has divided talismans into five classes, examples of some of which I have already given. They are: "1. The *astronomical*, with celestial signs and intelligible characters. 2. The *magical*, with extraordinary figures, superstitious words, and names of unknown angels. 3. The *mixed*, of celestial signs and barbarous words, but not superstitious, or with names of angels. 4. The *sigilla planetarum*, composed of Hebrew numeral letters, used by astrologers and fortune-tellers. 5. *Hebrew names and characters*. These were formed according to the cabalistic art."

The doctrine of signatures bears a close resemblance to talismans, and some believe that talismans have largely grown out of this doctrine. Dr. Paris 79 defines the doctrine as the belief that "every natural substance which possesses any medical virtues indicates, by an obvious and well-marked external 143 character, the disease for which it is a remedy or the object for which it should be employed." Southey says, 80 "The signatures [were] the books out of which the ancients first learned the virtues of herbs—Nature having stamped on divers of them legible characters to discover their uses." Some opined that the external marks were impressed by planetary influences, hence their connection with talismans; others simply reasoned it out that the Almighty must have placed a sign on the various means which he had provided for curing diseases.

Color and shape were the two principal factors in interpreting the signatures. White was regarded as cold and red as hot, hence cold and hot qualities were attributed to different medicines of these colors respectively. Serious errors in practice resulted from this opinion. Red flowers were given for disorders of the sanguiferous system; the petals of the red rose, especially, bear the "signature" of the blood, and blood-root, on account of its red juice, was much prescribed for the blood. Celandine, having yellow juice, the yellow drug, turmeric, the roots of rhubarb, the flowers of saffron, and other yellow substances were given in jaundice; red flannel, looking like blood, cures blood taints, and therefore rheumatism, even to this day, although many do not know why *red* flannel is so efficacious.

Lungwort, whose leaves bear a fancied resem 144 blance to the surface of the lungs, was considered good for pulmonary complaints, and liverwort, having a leaf like the liver, cured liver diseases. Eye-bright was a famous application for eye diseases, because its flowers somewhat resemble the pupil of the eye; bugloss, resembling a snake's head, was valuable for snake bite; and the peony, when in bud, being something like a man's head, was "very available against the falling sickness." Walnuts were considered to be the perfect signature of the head, the shell represented the bony skull, the irregularities of the kernel the convolutions of the two hemispheres of the brain, and the husk the scalp. The husk was therefore used for scalp wounds, the inner peel for disorders of the meninges, and the kernel was beneficial for the brain and tended to resist poisons. Lilies-of-the-valley were used for the cure of apoplexy, the signature reasoning being, as Coles says, "for as that disease is caused by the drooping of humors into the principal ventrices of the brain, so the flowers of this lily, hanging on the plants as if they were drops, are of wonderful use herein."

Capillary herbs naturally announced themselves as good for diseases of the hair, and bear's grease, being taken from an animal thickly covered with hair, was recommended for the prevention of baldness. Nettle-tea is still a country remedy for nettle rash; prickly plants like thistles and holly were pre 145 scribed for pleurisy and stitch in the side, and the scales of the pine were used in toothache, because they resemble front teeth. "Kidney-beans," says Berdoe, "ought to have been useful for kidney diseases, but seem to have been overlooked except as articles of diet." Poppy-heads were used "with success" to relieve diseases of the head, and the root of the "mandrake," from its supposed resemblance to the human form, was a very ancient remedy for barrenness and was evidently so esteemed by Rachel, in the account given in Genesis 30:14 ff.

In the treatment of small-pox red bed coverings were employed in order to bring the pustules to the surface of the body. The patient must be indued with red; the bed furniture and hangings should be red and red substances were to be looked upon by the patient; burnt purple, pomegranate seeds, mulberries or other red ingredients were dissolved in their drink. John of Gladdesden, physician to Edward II, prescribed the following treatment as soon as the eruption appeared: "Cause the whole body of your patient to be wrapped in scarlet cloth, or any other red cloth, and command everything about the bed to be made red." He further says that "when the son of the renowned King of England (Edward II) lay sick of the small-pox I took care that everything around the bed should be of a red color; which succeeded so completely that 146 the Prince was restored to perfect health, without a vestige of a pustule remaining."

The Emperor Francis I, when infected with smallpox, was rolled up in a scarlet cloth, by order of his physicians, as late as 1765; notwithstanding this treatment he died. Kampfer says that "when any of the Japanese emperor's children are attacked with the small-pox, not only the chamber and bed are covered with red hangings, but all persons who approach the sick prince must be clad in scarlet gowns." By a course of reasoning similar to that used in the treatment of small-pox, it was supposed that flannel dyed nine times in blue was efficacious in removing glandular swellings. 81

The astrological factor in talismans was most important because it was considered that certain stars and planets in certain relations produced certain diseases and contagious disorders. Astrologers, for example, attributed the plague to a conjunction of Saturn and Jupiter in Sagittarius, on the tenth of October, or to a conjunction of Saturn and Mars in the same constellation, on the twelfth of November. Burton makes the most generous melancholy, as that of Augustus, to come from the conjunction of Saturn and Jupiter in Libra; the bad, as that of 147 Catiline, from the meeting of Saturn and the moon in Scorpio. If these disorders were produced by planets it was reasonable to suppose that they could be cured by planets.

The virtue of herbs depended upon the planet under which they were sown or gathered. For example, verbena or vervain should be gathered at the rising of the dog-star, when neither the sun nor the moon shone, but an expiatory sacrifice of fruit and honey should previously have been offered to the earth. If this was carried out it had power to render the possessor invulnerable, to cure fevers, to eradicate poison, and to conciliate friendship. Notice also, that black hellebore, to be effective, was to be plucked not cut, and this with the right hand, which was then to be covered with a portion of the robe and secretly to be conveyed to the left hand. The person gathering it was to be clad in white, to be barefooted, and to offer a sacrifice of bread and wine.

Not only the planets and the stars, but the moon has had a potent influence on medicine. For instance, mistletoe was to be cut with a golden knife, and when the moon was only six days old. Brand 82 quotes from *The Husbandman's Practice, or Prognostication Forever*, published in 1664, the following curious passage, "Good to purge with electuaries, the moon in Cancer; with pills, the moon in Pisces; 148 with potions, the moon in Virgo; good to take vomits, the moon being in Taurus, Virgo, or the latter part of Sagittarius; to purge the head by sneezing, the moon being in Cancer, Leo, or Virgo; to stop fluxes and rheumes, the moon being in Taurus, Virgo, or Capricorne; to bathe when the moon is in Cancer, Libra, Aquarius, or Pisces; to cut the hair off the head or beard when the moon is in Libra, Sagittarius, Aquarius, or Pisces."

The Loseley manuscripts provide us with further examples. "Here begyneth ye waxingge of ye mone, and declareth in dyvers tymes to let blode, whiche be gode. In the furste begynynge of the mone it is profetable to yche man to be letten blode; ye ix of the mone, neyther be nyght ne by day, it is not good." They also tell of a physician named Simon Trippe, who wrote to a patient in excuse for not visiting him, as follows: "As for my comming to you upon Wensday next, verely my promise be past to and old pacient of mine, a very good gentlewoman, one Mrs. Clerk, wch now lieth in great extremity. I cannot possibly be with you till Thursday. On Fryday and Saterday the signe wilbe in the heart; on Sunday, Monday, and Tuesday, in the stomake; during wch time it wilbe no good dealing with your ordinary physicke untill Wensday come sevenight at the nearest, and from that time forwards for 15 or 16 days passing good." 83

149

Not unlike this is an incident of the year 686, given by Bede, where "a holy Bishop having been asked to bless a sick maiden, asked 'when she had been bled?' and being told that it was on the fourth day of the moon, said: 'You did very indiscreetly and unskilfully to bleed her on the fourth day of the moon; for I remember that Archbishop Theodore, of blessed memory, said that bleeding at that time was very dangerous, when the light of the moon and the tide of the ocean is increasing; and what can I do to the girl if she is like to die?'" 84

"So great, indeed," says Fort, "became the abuse of medical astrology, whether by the direct juxtaposition of stellar influence, or through apposite images, that a celebrated Church Council at Paris declared that images of metal, wax, or other materials fabricated under certain constellations or according to fixed characters — figures of peculiar form, either baptized, consecrated, or exorcised, or rather desecrated by the performance of formal rites at stated periods which it was asserted, thus composed, possessed miraculous virtues set forth in superstitious writings — were placed under the ban and interdicted as errors of faith." 85

We shall see that magnetism developed from astrology, and some other forms of mental healing 150 from magnetism. One of these, sympathetic cures, was talismanic in its character, and therefore I give a brief account of its method of working, in this place.

Sympathetic cures probably started with Paracelsus, although Von Helmont tells us that the secret was first put forth by Ericcius Wohyus, of Eburo. As a development from magnetism the former originated the "weapon salve" which excited so much attention about the middle of the seventeenth century. The following was a receipt given by him for the cure of any wound inflicted by a sharp weapon, except such as had penetrated the heart, the brain, or the arteries. "Take the moss growing on the head of a thief who has been hanged and left in the air; of real mummy; of human blood, still warm — of each, one ounce; of human suet, two ounces; of linseed oil, turpentine, and Armenian bole — of each, two drachms.

Mix all well in a mortar, and keep the salve in an oblong, narrow urn." With the salve the weapon (not the wound), after being dipped in blood from the wound, was to be carefully anointed, and then laid by in a cool place. In the meantime, the wound was washed with fair, clean water, covered with a clean soft linen rag, and opened once a day to cleanse off purulent matter. A writer in the *Foreign Quarterly Review* says there can be no doubt about the success of the treatment, "for surgeons at this moment 151 follow exactly the same method, *except* anointing the weapon!"

SIR KENELM DIGBY

The weapon-salve continued to be much spoken of on the Continent, and Dr. Fludd, or A Fluctibus, the Rosicrucian, introduced it into England. He tried it with great success in several cases, but in the midst of his success an attack was made upon him and his favorite remedy, which, however, did little or nothing to diminish the belief in its efficacy. One "Parson Foster" wrote a pamphlet entitled

"Hyplocrisma Spongus; or a Spunge to wipe away the Weapon-salve," in which he declared that it was as bad as witchcraft to use or recommend such an unguent; that it was invented by the devil, who, at the last day, would seize upon every person who had given it the least encouragement. "In fact," said Parson Foster, "the Devil himself gave it to Paracelsus; Paracelsus to the emperor; the emperor to the courtier; the courtier to Baptista Porta; and Baptista Porta to Dr. Fludd, a doctor of physic, yet living and practising in the famous city of London, who now stands tooth and nail for it." Dr. Fludd, thus assailed, took up his pen and defended the unguent in a caustic pamphlet.

The salve changed into a powder in the hands of Sir Kenelm Digby, the son of Sir Edward Digby who was executed for his participation in the Gunpowder Plot. Sir Kenelm was an accomplished scholar and an able man, but at the same time a 152 most extravagant defender of the powder of sympathy for the healing of wounds. This powder came into sudden and public notoriety through an accident to a distinguished person. Mr. James Howell, the well-known author of the Dendrologia, in endeavoring to part two friends in a duel, received a severe cut on the hand. Alarmed by the accident, one of the combatants bound up the cut with his garter and conveyed him home. The king sent his own surgeon to attend Mr. Howell, but in four or five days the wound was not recovering very rapidly and he made application to Sir Kenelm. The latter first inquired whether he possessed anything that had the blood upon it, upon which Mr. Howell produced the garter with which his hand had been bound. A basin of water in which some powder of vitriol had been dissolved was procured, and the garter immediately immersed in it, whereupon, to quote Sir Kenelm, Mr. Howell said, "I know not what ails me, but I find that I feel no more pain. Methinks that a pleasing kind of freshness, as it were a wet cold napkin, did spread over my hand, which hath taken away the inflammation that tormented me before." He was then advised to lay away all plasters and keep the wound clean and in a moderate temperature.

To prove conclusively the efficacy of the powder of sympathy, after dinner the garter was taken out of the basin and placed to dry before the fire. No 153 sooner was this done than Mr. Howell's servant came running to Sir Kenelm saying that his master's hand was again inflamed, and that it was as bad as before. The garter was again placed in the liquid and before the return of the servant all was well and easy again. In the course of five or six days the wound was cicatrized and a cure performed.

This case excited considerable attention at court, and on inquiry Sir Kenelm told the king that he learned the secret from a much-travelled Carmelite friar who became possessed of it while journeying in the East. Sir Kenelm communicated it to Dr. Mayerne, the king's physician, and from him it was known to even the country barbers. Even King James, the Prince of Wales, the Duke of Buckingham, and many other noble personages believed in its efficacy.

It would be a waste of time, had we space, to present fully Sir Kenelm's profound and lengthy explanation of the cure. He tried to make the cure more reasonable and acceptable by bringing forth certain alleged phenomena which he thought proved sympathy, and were therefore analogous in character. Surgeon-General Hammond calls attention to the fact that these inferences were invariably false. "It is a very curious circumstance," says he, "that of these, there is not one which is true. Thus he is wrong when he says that if the hand be severely burnt, the pain and inflammation are re 154 lieved by holding it near a hot fire; that a person who has a bad breath is cured by putting his head over a privy and inhaling the air which comes from it; that those who are bitten by vipers or scorpions are cured by holding the bruised head of either of those animals, as the case may be, near the bitten part; that in times of great contagion, carrying a toad, or a spider, or arsenic or some other venomous substance, about the person is a protection; that hanging a toad about the neck of a horse affected with farcy dissipates the disease; that water evaporated in a close room will not be deposited on the walls, if a vessel of water be placed in the room; that venison pies smell strongly at those periods in which the 'beasts which are of the same nature and kind are in rut'; that wine in the cellar undergoes a fermentation when the vines in the field are in flower; that a table-cloth spotted with mulberries or red wine is more easily whitened at the season in which the plants are flowering than at any other; that washing the hands in the rays of moonlight which fall into a polished silver basin (without water) is a cure for warts; that a vessel of water put on the hearth of a smoky chimney is a remedy for the evil, and so on—not a single fact in all that he adduces. Yet these circumstances were regarded as real, and were spoken of at the times as irrefragable proofs of the truth of Sir Kenelm's views." 86

155

We need have no doubt concerning the operation of sympathetic cures, for Sir Kenelm has told us of their virtue in his own words. 87 His method was what was called the cure by the wet way, but the cure could also be effected in a dry way. Straus, in a letter to Sir Kenelm, gives an account of a cure performed by Lord Gilbourne, an English nobleman, upon a carpenter who had cut himself severely with his axe. "The axe, bespattered with blood, was sent for, besmeared with an anointment, wrapped up warmly, and carefully hung up in a closet. The carpenter was immediately relieved, and all went well for some time, when, however, the wound became exceedingly painful, and, upon resorting to his lordship it was ascertained that the axe had fallen from the nail by which it was suspended, and thereby become uncovered."

Dryden in "The Tempest" (Act V, Sc. I) makes Ariel say, in reference to the wound received by Hippolito from Ferdinand:

> "He must be dress'd again, as I have done it. Anoint the sword which pierced him with this weapon-salve, and wrap it close from air, till I have time to visit him again."

And in the next scene we have the following dialogue between Hippolito and Miranda:

156

"*Hip.* O my wound pains me.

Mir. I am come to ease you.

[*She unwraps the sword.*

Hip. Alas! I feel the cold air come to me;
My wound shoots worse than ever.

[*She wipes and anoints the sword.*

Mir. Does it still grieve you?

Hip. Now methinks, there's something
Laid just upon it.

Mir. Do you find ease?

Hip. Yes, yes, upon the sudden, all the pain
Is leaving me. Sweet heaven, how I am eased!"

Werenfels says: "If the superstitious person be wounded by any chance, he applies the salve, not to the wound, but, what is more effectual, to the weapon by which he received it. By a new kind of art, he will transplant his disease, like a scion, and graft it into what tree he pleases."

The practice at the time was varied and general. All sorts of disgusting ingredients were gathered together to form the salve. Some idea of the condition of the science of medicine at that time may be gathered when we remember that a serious discussion was long maintained between two factions in the sympathetic school concerning the question "whether it was necessary that the moss should grow absolutely in the skull of a thief who had hung on the gallows, and whether the ointment, while compounding, was to be stirred with a murderer's knife."

157 There is no doubt that the sympathetic cures were really the most rapid and effective. The modern surgeon wonders how a wound ever healed prior to this treatment. There seemed to be little that could be imagined to prevent a wound from healing that the pre-sympathetic surgeon did not try. When the manipulations, doses, and treatments were transferred from the wound to the weapon, they did not injure the weapon, and did give the wound a chance to heal. In fact, leaving out the weapon part of the treatment, which could have none but a mental influence, the treatment would be recommended to-day. The wound was kept clean, the edges were

brought in apposition, temperature was modified, and rest given. Under these circumstances, wounds which the surgeon had irritated so as to take weeks to heal, united in as many days. Mark this, however: the wounds treated were simple incisions, the ones which most readily united if cleansed, brought together, and left alone. Gunshot and similar wounds were not treated by this process. 88

76 T. J. Pettigrew, *Superstitions Connected with ... Medicine and Surgery*, pp. 63 f.

77 *Gentleman's Magazine*, LVIII, pp. 586 and 695.

78 H. Arnot, *History of Edinburgh*.

79 *Pharmacologia*, p. 51.

80 *The Doctor*, p. 59.

81 For a discussion on the doctrine of signatures see T. J. Pettigrew, *Superstitions*, etc., pp. 33 f.; E. Berdoe, *Origin and Growth of the Healing Art*, pp. 327 and 416 f.; A. D. White, *History of the Warfare of Science with Theology*, II, pp. 38 f.; Eccles, *Evolution of Medical Science*, pp. 140 f.

82 J. Brand, *Popular Antiquities*, III, p. 153. In references to this work, the edition used was that edited by W. Carew Hazlitt.

83 *The Loseley Manuscripts*, pp. 263 f., quoted by Berdoe.

84 Bede, *Ecclesiastical History*, bk. V, chap. III.

85 G. F. Fort, *History of Medical Economy During the Middle Ages*, p. 299

86 W. A. Hammond, *Spiritualism and Nervous Derangement*, p. 175.

87 Sir Kenelm Digby, *A late discovery made in solemne assembly of nobles and learned men, at Montpellier, in France, touching the cure of wounds, by the Powder of Sympathy*, etc.

88 I am indebted to T. J. Pettigrew, *Superstitions Connected with the History and Practice of Surgery and Medicine*, pp. 201-213; C. Mackay, *Extraordinary Popular Delusions*, pp. 266-268; W. A. Hammond, *Spiritualism and Nervous Derangement*, pp. 170-176; for the material on the subject of sympathetic cures.

158

CHAPTER VII

AMULETS

"He loved and was beloved; what more could he desire as an amulet against fear?" — Bulwer-Lytton.

"Such medicines are to be exploded that consist of words, characters, spells, and charms, which can do no good at all, but out of a strong conceit, as Pomponatius proves; or the Devil's policy, who is the first founder and teacher of them." — Burton.

"Old wives and starres are his councellors; his nightspell is his guard, and charms his physician. He wears Paracelsian characters for the toothache; and a little hallowed wax is his antidote for all evils." — Bishop Hall.

"Neither doth Fansie only cause, but also as easily cure Diseases; as I may justly refer all magical and jugling Cures thereunto, performed, as is thought, by Saints, Images, Relicts, Holy-Waters, Shrines, Avemarys, Crucifixes, Benedictions, Charms, Characters, Sigils of the Planets and of Signs, inverted Words, &c., and therefore all such Cures are rather to be ascribed to the Force of the Imagination, than any virtue in them, or their Rings, Amulets, Lamens, &c." — Ramesey.

Attention has already been called to the fact that the characteristic of the amulet is that it must be worn about the person, while the talisman may simply be in possession of a person wherever it may be, or deposited at a certain place by or for the person. The Arabic equivalent of the word Amulet means "that which is suspended."

The derivation of the word is uncertain, but there are at least two Latin antecedents claimed for it. Some claim that it is derived from the barbarous 159 Latin word "amuletum," from amolior, to remove; others consider that it comes from "amula," the name of a small vessel with lustral water in it, which the Romans sometimes carried in their pockets for purification and expiation. Pliny says that many of these amul样ere carved out of pieces of amber and hung about children's necks. Whatever the derivation of the word, it is doubtless of Eastern origin.

There is also little doubt concerning the early belief in the efficacy of an amulet to ward off diseases, and to protect against supernatural agencies. So powerful were they supposed to be that an oath was formerly administered to persons about to fight a legal duel "that they had ne charme ne herb of virtue." St. Chrysostom and others of the church fathers condemned the practice very severely, and the Council of Laodicea (366) wisely forbade the priesthood from studying and practising enchantments, mathematics, astrology, and the binding of the soul by amulets. 89

Burton has the following passage on the subject: "Amulets, and Things to be borne about, I find prescribed, taxed by some, approved by Renodeus, Platerus, and others; looke for them in Mizaldus, Porta, Albertus, &c. ... A Ring made of the Hoofe of an Asse's right fore-foot carried about, &c.

160

I say with Renodeus they are not altogether to be rejected. Piony doth help epilepsies. Pretious Stones, most diseases. A Wolf's dung carried about helps the Cholick. A spider, an Ague, &c. ... Some Medicines are to be exploded, that consist of Words, Characters, Spells, and Charms, which can do no good at all, but out of a strong conceit, as Pomponatius proves; or the Devil's policy, who is the first founder and teacher of them." 90

"To this kind," says Bingham, "belong all Ligatures and Remedies, which the Schools of Physitians reject and condemn; whether in Inchantments or in certain marks, which they call Characters, or in some other things which are to be hanged and bound about the Body, and kept in a dancing posture. Such are Ear-rings hanged upon the tip of each ear, and Rings made of an Ostriche's bones for the Finger; or, when you are told, in a fit of Convulsions or shortness of Breath, to hold your left Thumb with your right hand." 91

Unfortunately the wearing of amulets did not stop with the early civilizations or even with the Middle Ages. People in our own supposedly enlightened age indulge in them. The negro carries the hind foot of a rabbit, and the children see great virtue in a four-leafed clover; men carry luck pennies, and certain stones are worn in rings and scarf 161 pins; camphor is worn about the person to avert febrile contagion, and anodyne necklaces of "Job's tears" and other equally harmless and inefficacious substances are placed on babies to assist them in teething. The camphor and necklaces are probably not supposed to be endowed with magical power, but a mistaken medical virtue is assigned to them.

There was neither rule nor reason for the composition of most amulets, and one would have to be well acquainted with the superstitions of the various ages to account for them. Sometimes the shape, rather than the material of which they were composed or the inscription on them, was the efficacious factor. Perhaps material, shape, and inscription would be combined in one object; or many objects, each purporting to contain magical properties, might be grouped for special efficacy, as when inscribed pieces of different stones of peculiar shape were formed into necklaces or bracelets.

Precious stones were often employed as amulets, and some even ground them up and took them internally in order to be more sure of their magical effects. "Butler quotes from Encelius, who says that the Garnet, if hung about the neck or taken in drink, much assisteth sorrow and recreates the heart; and the chrysolite is described as the friend of wisdom and the enemy of folly. Renodeus admires precious stones because they adorn king's crowns, grace the fingers, enrich our household stuff, defend 162 us from enchantments, preserve health, cure diseases, drive away grief, cares, and exhilarate the mind." 92

Some further quotations portray to us the efficacy of other stones:

"Heliotropius stauncheth blood, driveth away poisons, preserveth health; yea, and some write that it provoketh raine, and darkeneth the sunne, suffering not him that beareth it to be abused."

"A topaze healeth the lunaticke person of his passion of lunacie."

"Corneolus (cornelian) mitigateth the heate of the minde, and qualifieth malice, it stancheth bloodie fluxes."

"A sapphire preserveth the members and maketh them livelie, and helpeth agues and gowts, and suffereth not the bearer to be afraid; it hath virtue against venoms, and staieth bleeding at the nose, being often put thereto."

Aetius "attributed great obstetrical properties to the lapis aetites, and gagates stone. The sapphire when taken as a potion pulverized in milk, cured internal ulcers and checked excessive perspiration. The amargdine was highly recommended for strabismus...."

"Jasper, hematite and hieratite stones were strongly recommended for unusual sanative virtues, but the sapphire excelled as a remedy for scorpion bites."

"The Bezoar stone had a great reputation in melancholic affections. Manardus says it removes sadness and makes him merry that useth it."

163

"Noblemen wore the smargdum attached to a chain, in the belief of its potential virtues against epilepsy. The sard prevented terrible dreams, and the cornelian worn on the finger or suspended from the neck pacified anger and provoked contentment. Onyx superinduced troubled sleep, but fastened to the throat, stimulated the salivary glands. Saphirs cured internal ulcers and excessive perspiration, when taken as a potion dissolved in lacteal fluids."

"Of the stone which hight agate. It is said that it hath eight virtues. One is when there is thunder, it doth not scathe the man who hath this stone with him. Another virtue is, on whatsoever house it is, therein a fiend may not be. The third virtue is, that no venom may scathe the man who hath the stone with him. The fourth virtue is, that the man, who hath on him secretly the loathly fiend, if he taketh in liquid any portion of the shavings of the stone, then soon is exhibited manifestly in him, that which before lay secretly hid. The fifth virtue is, he who is afflicted with any disease, if he taketh the stone in liquid, it is soon well with him. The sixth virtue is, that sorcery hurteth not the man who has the stone with him. The seventh virtue is, that he who taketh the stone in drink, will have so much the smoother body. The eighth virtue of the stone is, that no bite of any kind of snake may scathe him who tasteth the stone in liquid."

Even as late as 1624, Sir John Harrington, writing in his "School of Salerne," says: "Alwaies in your hands use eyther Corall or yellow Amber, or a chalcedonium, or a sweet Pommander, or some like precious stone to be worne in a ring upon the little finger of the left hand; have in your rings eyther a 164 Smaragd, a Saphire, or a Draconites, which you shall bear for an ornament; for in stones, as also in hearbes, there is great efficacie and vertue, but they are not altogether perceived by us; hold sometime in your mouth eyther a Hyacinth, or a Crystall, or a Garnat, or pure Gold, or Silver, or else sometimes pure Sugar-candy. For Aristotle doth affirme, and so doth Albertus Magnus, that a Smaragd worne about the necke, is good against the Falling-sickness; for surely the virtue of an hearbe is great, but much more the vertue of a precious stone, which is very likely that they are endued with occult and hidden vertues."

Precious metals as well as precious stones were used in the manufacture of amulets. The Scandinavians carried metal effigies carved out of gold or silver, or incised upon tiles, perpetually as amulets. They were safeguards against diseases and physical infirmities. They were also administered internally in cases where powerful cures were needed. Chaucer says:

> "For gold in physic is a cordial, Therefore he loved gold in special."

The Basilideans, and other sects developed from the Gnostic systems, assigned great power to stone amulets, and prepared them for their initiates, who used them for identification and for curative purposes. They quickly acquired a celebrity undi 165 minished for ages, and were known under the general name of Abraxas. They were composed of various materials, glass, paste, sometimes metals, but principally of various kinds of stones. Through the irresistible might of Abrax, their supreme divinity, the Basilideans were protected and cured. Clement of Alexandria strictly interdicted the use of gems for personal ornamentation, with evident allusion to the Abraxas stones. These stones had various inscriptions carved upon them, most of which had some hidden meaning of great puissance. One of them, for example, is engraven with Armenian letters, and contains a standing invocation for fruitful delivery; in its medicinal property it was evidently a cure for sterility. 93

From the stone itself the word "Abraxas" came to be used as an amulet when written on paper. The numerical equivalent of the Greek letters when added together thus, A = 1, B = 2, P = 100, A = 1, Ξ = 60, A = 1, Σ = 200, is 365. The significance of this was that the deity was the ruler of 365 heavens, or of the angels inhabiting these heavens; he was also ruler over the 365 days of the year. Notwithstanding the fact that it was referred to by the Greek fathers, the name was evidently Egyptian in origin, some of the figures on the stones being strictly Egyptian.

166

Amulets in the form of inscriptions were called "Characts," the word Abraxas being an example. The very powerful word "Abracadabra" was derived from Abraxas, and when written in the proper way and worn about the person was supposed to have a magical efficacy as an antidote against ague, fever, flux, and toothache. Serenus Samonicus, a physician in the reign of Caracalla, recommends it very highly for ague, instructing how it should be written, and commanding it to be worn around the neck. It might be written in either of two ways: reading down the left side and up the right must spell the same word as at the top; or, having the left side always start the same, reading up the right side should be the same as the top line. Below are the two forms:

ABRACADABRA
BRACADABR
RACADAB
ACADA
CAD
A

ABRACADABRA
ABRACADABR
ABRACADAB
ABRACADA
ABRACAD
ABRACA
ABRAC
ABRA
ABR
AB
A

Julius Africanus says that pronouncing the word in the same manner is as efficacious as writing it. The 167 Jews attributed an equal virtue to the word "Aracalan" employed in the same way. 94

Bishop Pilkington, writing in 1561, protests against a then current practice in this way: "What wicket blindenes is this than, to thinke that wearing Prayers written in rolles about with theym, as S. Johns Gospell, the length of our Lord, the measure of our Lady, or other like, thei shall die no sodain death, nor be hanged, or yf he be hanged, he shall not die. There is so manye suche, though ye laugh, and beleve it not, and not hard to shewe them with a wet finger." The same author observes that our devotion ought to "stande in depe sighes and groninges, wyth a full consideration of our miserable state and Goddes majestye, in the heart, and not in ynke or paper: not in hangyng writtin Scrolles about the Necke, but lamentinge unfeignedlye our Synnes from the hart."

The following charact was found in a linen purse belonging to a murderer named Jackson, who died in Chichester jail in February, 1749. He was "struck with such horror on being measured for his chains that he soon after expired."

> "Ye three holy Kings, Gaspar, Melchior, Balthasar, Pray for
> us now, and in the hour of our death."

168

"These papers have touched the three heads of the holy Kings at Cologne. They are to preserve travellers from accidents on the road, headaches, falling sickness, fevers, witchcraft, all kinds of mischief, and sudden death."

Belgrave prescribes a cure of agues, by a certain writing which the patient wears, as follows: "When Jesus went up to the Cross to be crucified, the Jews asked him, saying Art thou afraid? or hast thou the ague? Jesus answered and said, I am not afraid, neither have I the ague. All those which bear the name of Jesus about them shall not be afraid, nor yet have the ague. Amen, sweet Jesus, Amen, sweet Jehovah, Amen." He adds: "I have known many who have been cured of the ague by this writing only worn about them; and I had the receipt from one whose daughter was cured thereby, who had the ague upon her two years." 95

Among other written amulets, the first Psalm, when written on doeskin, was supposed to be efficacious in childbirth. It was necessary, however, for the writer of such amulets to plunge into a bath as soon as he had written one line, and after every new line it was thought necessary that he should repeat the plunge.

The following process for avoiding inflamed eyes is taken from Marcellus, 380 A. D.: "Write on a 169 clean sheet of paper ουβαικ, and hang this round the patient's neck, with a thread from the loom. In a state of purity and chastity write on a clean sheet of paper φυρφαραν and hang it round the man's neck; it will stop the approach of inflammation. The following will stop inflammation coming on, written on a clean sheet of paper: ρουβος, ρυονειας ρηελιος ως' καντεφορα και παντες ηακοτει; it must be hung to the neck by a thread; and if both the patient and operator are in a state of chastity, it will stop inveterate inflammation. Again, write on a thin plate of gold with a needle of copper, ορνω ουρωδη; do this on a Monday; observe chastity; it will long and much avail." 96

In Africa, prayers taken from the Koran are written and worn as amulets at the present time.

After the death of the philosopher Pascal some manuscript was found sewed in his doublet. This was a "profession of faith" which he always wore stitched in his clothing as a sort of amulet.

In the East, generally, the amulet consists of certain names of the Deity, verses of the Koran, or particular passages compressed into a very small space, and is to be found concealed in the turban. The Christians wore amulets with verses selected from the Old and New Testaments, and particularly from the Gospel of John. The amulets or charms, called "grigris" by the African priests, are of similar 170 description. These were used for preservatives against thunderbolts and diseases, to procure many wives and to give them easy deliveries, to avert shipwreck or slavery, and to secure victory in battle. One, to be used for the last purpose, which had belonged to a king of Brak, in Senegal, was found on his body after he had the misfortune to be killed in battle with the amulet upon him. It had the following sentences from the Koran: "In the name of the merciful God! Pray to God through our Lord Mohammed. All that exists is so only by his command. He gives life, and also calls sinners to an account. He deprives us of life by the sole power of his name: these are undeniable truths. He that lives owes his life to the peculiar clemency of his Lord, who by his providence takes care of his subsistence. He is a wise prince or governor." 97

The Jews used as amulets some sacred name, such as the true pronunciation of the name of Jehovah, written down. The Mischna permitted the Jews to wear amulets provided they had been found efficacious in at least three cases by an approved person. One of the most famous amulets is that known as "Solomon's Seal."

Ligatures, similar to the earlier amulets, a heritage from the northern pagan races, were freely applied for the prevention and cure of maladies.

171

After imposing invocations and the addition of mystical characters, these medical charms were presumed to be of the greatest efficacy, and ready for suspension from the neck. Their efficacy was admitted by Christians, but they were condemned on account of their pagan and consequently satanic origin.

Alexander of Tralles recommended a number of amulets, some of which I will mention later, but admits that he had no faith in them, but merely ordered them as placebos for rich and fastidious patients who could not be persuaded to adopt a more rational treatment. Baas tells us that "A regular Pagan amulet was found in 1749 on the breast of the prince bishop Anselm Franz of Wrzburg, count of Ingolstadt, after his death."

Amulets were also worn to protect the wearer from charms exercised by others. The "Leech Book" gives us one to be worn and another to be taken internally for this purpose. To be used "against every evil rune lay, and one full of elvish tricks, writ for the bewitched man, this writing in Greek letters: Alfa, Omega, Iesvm, BERONIKH. Again, another dust and drink against a rune lay; take a bramble apple, and lupins, and pulegium, pound them, then sift them, put them in a pouch, lay them under the altar, sing nine masses over them, administer this to drink at three hours."

The powers of the mandragora, as an amulet, place it almost in a class by itself. Fort tells us that 172 in addition to its power to protect herds of cattle and horses, to prevent misfortunes of various kinds, to preserve the exhilarating wine and beer against loss of their intoxicating property, to render successful commercial negotiations, and promote infallibly, rapid and enormous influence, "other virtues of a surprising character were awarded the omnipotent mandragora. It conciliated affection and maintained friendship, preserved conjugal fealty and developed benevolence. The immensity of worth inherent in this mystical medicament, its vital essence, was by no means confined to sustaining health and providing certain remedies for infirmities; its power manipulated tribunals and secured judicial favor at court; and when this resistless amulet was held under the arm by a suitor at law, however unjust his cause, the vegetable Rune controlled the forum and obtained the verdict." 98

It may be well at this point to enumerate at least a number of the most noted amulets, according to the disease for which they were supposed to be efficacious.

Ague. — On account of the periodic character of this disease it was considered to be a supernatural complaint and hence many unnatural cures were suggested, among which were a number of amulets. The Abracadabra amulet was supposed to be es 173 pecially efficacious in ague. The chips of a gallows put into a bag and worn around the neck, or next the skin, have been said to have served as a cure, at least, so reports Brand. 99 Millefolium or yarrow, worn in a little bag on the pit of the stomach is reported to have cured this disease, and Alexander of Tralles advises, for a quartan ague, that the patient must carry about some hairs from a goat's chin. 100

Elias Ashmole, in his Diary, April 11, 1681, has entered the following: "I tooke early in the morning a good dose of Elixir, and hung three spiders about my neck, and they drove my Ague away. Deo Gratias!" 101

Wristbands, called pericarpia, were employed in the cure. Robert Boyle says he was cured of a violent quotidian ague, after having in vain resorted to medical aid, by applying to his wrists "a mixture of two handfuls of bay salt, the same quantity of fresh English hops, and a quarter of a pound of blue currants, very diligently beaten into a brittle mass, without the addition of anything moist, and so spread upon linen and applied to his wrists." 102

Burton gives us a leaf from his own experience. 103 "Being in the country in the vacation time, not many years since, at Lindly, in

Leicestershire, my 174 father's house, I first observed this amulet of a spider in a nut-shell, wrapped in silk, &c., so applyed for an ague by my mother; whom, although I knew to have excellent skill in chirurgery, sore eyes, aches, &c., and such experimental medicines, as all the country where she dwelt can witness, to have done many famous and good cures upon divers poor folks that were otherwise destitute of help, yet among all other experiments, this methought was most absurd and ridiculous. I could see no warrant for it. *Quid aranea cum Febre?* For what antipathy? till at length rambling amongst authors (as I often do), I found this very medicine in Dioscorides, approved by Matthiolus, repeated by Aldrovandus, *cap. de Aranea, lib. de Insectis,* I began to have a better opinion of it, and to give more credit to amulets, when I saw it in some parties answer to experience."

A narrative of not a little interest, concerning Sir John Holt, Lord Chief Justice of the Court of King's Bench, 1709, should be given in this connection. He was extremely wild in his youth, and being once engaged with some of his rakish friends in a trip into the country, in which they had spent all their money, it was agreed they should try their fortune separately. Holt arrived at an inn at the end of a straggling village, ordered his horse to be taken care of, bespoke a supper and a bed. He then strolled into the kitchen, where he observed a little girl of 175 thirteen shaking with ague. Upon making inquiry respecting her, the landlady told him that she was her only child, and had been ill nearly a year, notwithstanding all the assistance she could procure for her from physic. He gravely shook his head at the doctors, bade her be under no further concern, for that her daughter should never have another fit. He then wrote a few unintelligible words in a court hand on a scrap of parchment, which had been the direction fixed to a hamper, and rolling it up, directed that it should be bound upon the girl's wrist and there allowed to remain until she was well. The ague returned no more; and Holt, having remained in the house a week, called for his bill. "God bless you, sir," said the old woman, "you're nothing in my debt, I'm sure. I wish, on the contrary, that I was able to pay you for the cure which you have made of my daughter. Oh! if I had had the happiness to see you ten months ago, it would have saved me forty pounds." With pretended reluctance he accepted his accommodation as a recompense, and rode away. Many years elapsed, Holt advanced in his profession of the law, and went a circuit, as one of the judges of the Court of King's Bench, into the same county, where, among other criminals brought before him, was an old woman under a charge of witchcraft. To support this accusation, several witnesses swore that the prisoner had a spell with which she could either 176 cure such cattle as were sick or destroy those that were well, and that in the use of this spell she had been lately detected, and that it was now ready to be produced in court. Upon this statement the judge desired that it might be handed up to him. It was a dirty ball, wrapped round with several rags, and bound with packthread. These coverings he carefully removed, and beneath them found a piece of parchment which he immediately recognized as his own youthful fabrication. For a few moments he remained silent. At length, recollecting himself, he addressed the jury to the following effect: "Gentlemen, I must now relate a particular of my life, which very ill suits my present character and the station in which I sit; but to conceal it would be to aggravate the folly for which I ought to atone, to endanger innocence, and to countenance superstition. This bauble, which you suppose to have the power of life and death, is a senseless scroll which I wrote with my own hand and gave to this woman, whom for no other reason you accuse as a witch." He then related the particulars of the transaction, with such an effect upon the minds of the people that his old landlady was the last person tried for witchcraft in that county. 104

Calculus. — Boyle tells us 105 that the *Lapis Nephriticus*, a species of jasper, when bound to the left 177 wrist, was a cure for this trouble. Others have borne evidence to its efficacy.

Childbirth. — Among the ancient Britons, when a birth was difficult or dangerous, a girdle, made for this purpose, was put around the woman and afforded immediate relief. Until quite recently they were kept by many families in the Highlands of Scotland. They were marked with certain figures and were applied with certain ceremonies derived from the Druids. Women in labor were also supposed to be quickly delivered if they were girded with the skin which a snake has sloughed off. 106

Cholera. — Bontius declared the *Lapis Porcinus* to be good for cholera, but dangerous to pregnant women. If the females of Malaica held the stone in their hands an abortion was produced. When cholera was prevalent during the early part of the last century, it was common in many parts of Austria, Germany, and Italy to wear an amulet at the pit of the stomach, in contact with the skin. Pettigrew describes one of these which was sent to him from Hungary. "It consists merely of a circular piece of copper two inches and a half in diameter, and is without characters."

Colic. — Says Pliny, the extremity of the intestine of the ossifrage, if worn as an amulet, is well known to be an excellent remedy for colic. A tick from 178 a dog's left ear, worn as an amulet, was recommended to allay this and all other kinds of pain, but one must be careful to take it from a dog that is black. Alexander of Tralles recommended the heart of a lark to be fastened to the left thigh as a remedy for colic. Mr. Cockayne, the editor of *Saxon Leechdoms*, gives us further remedies for colic which Alexander prescribed. "Thus for colic, he guarantees by his own experience, and the approval of almost all the best doctors, dung of a wolf, with bits of bone in it if possible, shut up in a pipe, and worn during the paroxysm, on the right arm, or thigh, or hip, taking care it touches neither the earth or a bath." 107

Cramp. — The following amulets are mentioned as specifics against cramp:

> " — Wear bone Ring on thumb, or tye Strong Pack-thread below your thigh."

The subject of cramp rings will be considered in another connection.

Demoniacal Possession. — In the sixth century exorcists frequently wrote the formula on parchment and suspended it from the neck of the patient. This was as efficacious as the uttered words.

Epilepsy. — The elder tree has been the foundation of many superstitions, chief among which have been some connected with epilepsy. Blochwick 108 179 tells us how to prepare an amulet from an elder growing on a sallow. "In the month of October, a little before the full moon, you pluck a twig of the elder, and cut the cane that is betwixt two of its knees, or knots, in nine pieces, and these pieces being bound in a piece of linen, be in a thread, so hung about the neck, that they touch the spoon of the heart, or the sword-formed cartilage; and that they may stay more firmly in that place, they are to be bound thereon with a linen or silken roller wrapt about the body, till the thread break of itself. The thread being broken and the roller removed, the amulet is not at all to be touched with bare hands, but it ought to be taken hold on by some instrument and buried in a place that nobody may touch it." Some hung a cross, made of the elder and the sallow entwined, about the children's neck.

Rings of various kinds have always been supposed to have some superstitious power. Brand 109 tells us of some of their uses. A ring made from a piece of silver collected at the communion is a cure for convulsions and fits of every kind. If the silver is collected on Easter Sunday its efficacy is greatly increased. This was the receipt in Berkshire, but in Devonshire silver was not necessary. Here they prefer a ring made from three nails or screws dug out of a church-yard, which had been used to fasten a coffin. We are also informed that another kind 180 of ring will cure fits. It must be made from five sixpences collected from five different bachelors, conveyed by the hand of a bachelor to a silversmith who is a bachelor. None of the persons who gave the sixpences, however, are to know for what purpose, or to whom, they gave them. 110

A silver ring contributed by twelve young women, and constantly worn on one of the pattens fingers, has been successfully employed in the cure of epilepsy after various medical means failed. 111 Lupton says: "A piece of a child's navel-string borne in a ring is good against the falling-sickness, the pains of the head, and the collick." 112

Alexander of Tralles recommended for epilepsy a metal cross tied to the arm, or, in lieu of that, bits of sail-cloth from a shipwrecked vessel might be tied to the right arm and worn for seven weeks; the latter was a preventive as well as a cure. Among the ancients, Serapion prescribed crocodile's dung and turtle's blood as a cure for this disease. 113 Lemius remarks that "Coral, Piony, Misseltoe, drive away the falling Sicknesse, either hung about the neck or drunk with wine."

Erysipelas. — The elder seems to have been efficacious in erysipelas as well as in epilepsy, at least so 181 we are told in the "Anatomie of the Elder." The following is the method of preparing the amulet. It is to be made of "Elder on which the sun never shined. If the piece betwixt the two knots be hung about the patient's neck, it is much commended. Some cut it in little pieces, and sew it in a knot in a piece of a man's shirt, which seems superstitious."

Evil-eye. — Coral was supposed to avert the baneful consequences of the evil-eye, and Paracelsus recommends it to be worn about the necks of children. Douce has given engravings of several Roman amulets which were intended to be used against fascinations in general, but more particularly against that of the evil-eye. 114

Eye Diseases. — Cotta relates, so says Pettigrew, "a merrie historie of an approved famous spell for sore eyes. By many honest testimonies it was a long time worne as a Jewell about many necks, written in paper and enclosed in silke, never failing to do sovereigne good when all other helpes were helplesse. No sight might dare to reade or open. At length a curious mind, while the patient slept, by stealth ripped open the mystical cover, and found the powerful characters Latin: 'Diabolus effodiat tibi oculos impleat foramina stercoribus.'"

Vivisection was practised to procure an amulet for sore eyes, according to the following prescription: "If a man have a white spot, as cataract, in 182 his eye, catch a fox alive, cut his tongue out, let him go, dry his tongue and tie it up in a red rag and hang it round the man's neck." Pliny's way was to "take the tongue of a foxe, and hange the same about his necke, so long it hangeth there his sight shall not wax feeble."

Like was also used to cure like, at least in the following directions: "Take the right eye of a Frogg, lap it in a piece of russet cloth and hang it about the neck; it cureth the right eye if it bee enflamed or bleared. And if the left eye be greved, do the like by the left eye of the said Frogg." 115

Fevers. — Charms rather than amulets were employed in fevers, yet we find that among the ancients Chrysippus believed in amulets for quartan fevers and Pliny taught that the longest tooth of a black dog cured quartan fevers.

Gout. — Alexander of Tralles has preserved for us a remedy for gout as follows: "A remedy for the gout. Write, on a golden plate at the wane of the moon, what follows, rolling round it the sinews of a crane. Put it in a little bag, and wear it near the ankles. The words are meu, treu, mor, phor, teux, za, zor, phe, lou, chri, ge, ze, ou, as the sun is consolidated in these names, and is renewed every day; so consolidate this plaster as it was before, now, now, quick, quick, for, behold, I pronounce 183 the great name, in which are consolidated things in repose, iaz, azuf, zuon, threux, bain, choog; consolidate this plaster as it was at first, now, now, quick, quick."

Headache. — Pliny's amulet for this disease was an herb picked from the head of a statue, tied with a red thread, and worn upon the body.

Hysteria. — Monardes is quoted as saying: "When hysterical persons feel an attack coming on, they may be relieved by a stone, which will prevent, if constantly worn about the person, any subsequent attack. From my knowledge of cases of this kind, I attach credit to this amulet."

Melancholy. — Burton has treated much under the name of melancholy, and in respect of cure mentions several "amulets and things to be borne about." He recommends for head melancholy such things as hypericon, or St. John's-wort, gathered on a Friday in the hour of Jupiter, "... borne or hung about the neck, it mightily helps this affection, and drives away all fantastical spirits." 116

Plague. — During the visitations of the plague, the inhabitants of London wore, in the region of the heart, amulets composed of arsenic, probably on account of the theory that one poison would neutralize the power of the other. Concerning this, however, Herring, in writing concerning preservatives against the pestilence, says: "Perceiving many 184 in this Citie to weare about their Necks, upon the region of the Heart, certaine Placents or Amulets, (as preservatives against the pestilence,) confected of Arsenicke, my opinion is that they are so farre from effecting any good in that kinde, as a preservative, that they are very dangerous and hurtfull, if not pernitious, to those that weare them." Quills of quicksilver were commonly worn about the neck for the same purpose, and the powder of toad was employed in a similar way.

Pope Adrian is reported to have continually carried an amulet composed of dried toad, arsenic, tormental, pearl, coral, hyacinth, smarag, and tragacanth. Among the Harleian Manuscripts is a letter from Lord Chancellor Hatton to Sir Thomas Smith written at a time of an alarming epidemic. Among other things he writes: "I am likewise bold to recommend my most humble duty to our dear mistress (Queen Elizabeth) by this LETTER AND RING, which hath the virtue to expel infectious airs, and is *to be worn betwixt the sweet duggs*, the chaste nest of pure constancy. I trust, sir, when the virtue is known, it shall not be refused for the value." 117

Safety from Wounds. — Pettigrew gives us the two following examples: "De Barros, the historian, says that the Portuguese in vain attempted to destroy 185 a Malay so long as he wore a bracelet containing a bone set in gold, which rendered him proof against their swords. This amulet was afterward transmitted to the Viceroy Alfonso d'Alboquerque, as a valuable present.

"In the travels of Marco Polo, we read that in an attempt by Kublai Khan to make a conquest of the island of Zipangu, a jealousy arose between the two commanders of the expedition, which led to an order for putting the whole of the inhabitants of the garrison to the sword; and that in obedience thereto, the heads of all were cut off, excepting of eight persons, who, by the efficacy of a diabolical charm, consisting of a jewel or amulet introduced into the right arm, between the skin and the flesh, were rendered secure from the effects of iron, either to kill or wound. Upon this discovery being made, they were beaten with a heavy wooden club, and presently died." 118

Scrofula. — Lupton says: "The Root of Vervin hanged at the neck of such as have the King's Evil, it brings a marvellous and unhoped help." To this Brand adds: "Squire Morley of Essex used to say a Prayer which he hoped would do no harm when he hung a bit of vervain root from a scrophulous person's neck. My aunt Freeman had a very high opinion of a baked Toad in a silk Bag, hung round the neck." 119

186

Toothache.—People in North Hampshire, England, sometimes wore a tooth taken from a corpse, kept in a bag and hung around the neck, as a remedy for toothache.

Whooping-Cough.—About the middle of the last century there appeared the following in the *London Athen澤*: "The popular belief as to the origin of the mark across the back of the ass is mentioned by Sir Thomas Browne, in his 'Vulgar Errors,' and from whatever cause it may have arisen it is certain that the hairs taken from the part of the animal so marked are held in high estimation as a cure for the hooping-cough. In this metropolis, at least so lately as 1842, an elderly lady advised a friend who had a child dangerously ill with that complaint, to procure three such hairs, and hang them round the neck of the sufferer in a muslin bag. It was added that the animal from whom the hairs are taken for this purpose is never worth anything afterwards, and, consequently, great difficulty would be experienced in procuring them; and further, that it was essential to the success of the charm that the sex of the animal, from whom the hairs were to be procured, should be the contrary to that of the party to be cured by them."

The *Worcester Journal* (England), in one of its issues for 1845, had this astounding item: "A party from the city, being on a visit to a friend who lived at a village about four miles distant, had occasion to 187 go into the cottage of a poor woman, who had a child afflicted with the hooping-cough. In reply to some inquiries as to her treatment of the child, the mother pointed to its neck, on which was a string fastened, having nine knots tied in it. The poor woman stated that it was the stay-lace of the child's godmother which, if applied exactly in that manner about the neck, would be sure to charm away the most troublesome cough! Thus it may be seen that, with all the educational efforts of the present day, the monster Superstition still lurks here and there in his caves and secret places." 120

We find that not only human beings but animals profited by amulets. An amulet is used in the cure of a blind horse which could hardly have helped on the cure by his faith in it. "The root of cut Malowe hanged about the neck driveth away blemishes of the eyen, whether it be in a man or a horse, as I, Jerome of Brunsweig, have seene myselfe. I have myselfe done it to a blind horse that I bought for X crounes, and was sold agayn for XL crounes." 121 That was a trick worth knowing.

Brockett tells us that "Holy-stones, or *holed-stones*, are hung on the heads of horses as a charm against Diseases — such as sweat in their stalls are supposed to be cured by this application." The 188 efficacy of the elder also extended to animals, for a lame pig was formerly cured by boring a hole in his ear and putting a small peg into it. We are also told that "wood night-shade, or bitter-sweet, being hung about the neck of Cattell that have the Staggers, helpeth them."

89 T. J. Pettigrew, *Superstitions Connected with ... Medicine and Surgery*, pp. 51 and 66 f.

90 R. Burton, *Anatomy of Melancholy*, pt. II, sec. V.

91 J. Brand, *Popular Antiquities*, III, pp. 281 f.

92 T. J. Pettigrew, *Superstitions Connected with ... Medicine and Surgery*, p. 70.

93 G. F. Fort, *History of Medical Economy During the Middle Ages*, pp. 94-100.

94 T. J. Pettigrew, *Superstitions Connected with ... Medicine and Surgery*, pp. 74 f.

95 J. Brand, *Popular Antiquities*, III, pp. 278 f.

96 E. Berdoe, *Origin and Growth of the Healing Art*, pp. 262 f.

97 T. J. Pettigrew, *Superstitions Connected with ... Medicine and Surgery*, pp. 68 f.

98 G. F. Fort, *History of Medical Economy During the Middle Ages*, p. 182.

99 J. Brand, *Popular Antiquities*, III, p. 242.

100 E. Berdoe, *Origin and Growth of the Healing Art*, p. 252.

101 E. A. King, "Medieval Medicine," *Nineteenth Century*, XXXIV, p. 147.

102 R. Boyle, *Usefulness of Natural Philosophy*, II, p. 157.

103 R. Burton, *Anatomy of Melancholy*, pt. II, sec. V.

104 T. J. Pettigrew, *Superstitions Connected with ... Medicine and Surgery*, pp. 96-98.

105 R. Boyle, *Usefulness of Natural Philosophy*, Works II, p. 156.

106 E. Berdoe, *The Origin and Growth of the Healing Art*, pp. 257 and 259.

107 *Ibid.*, pp. 251 f and 254.

108 *Anatomie of the Elder*, p. 52.

109 J. Brand, *Popular Antiquities*, III, p. 231.

110 *Gentleman's Magazine*, 1794, p. 889.

111 *London Medical and Physical Journal*, 1815.

112 *Book of Notable Things*, p. 92.

113 E. Berdoe, *Origin and Growth of the Healing Art*, pp. 253 f and 256.

114 *Illustrations of Shakespeare*, I, p. 493.

115 E. A. King, "Medieval Medicine," *Nineteenth Century*, XXXIV, p. 147.

116 R. Burton, *Anatomy of Melancholy*, pt. II, sec. V.

117 T. J. Pettigrew, *Superstitions Connected with ... Surgery and Medicine*, p. 91.

118 *Ibid.*, p. 79.

119 J. Brand, *Popular Antiquities*, III, p. 256.

120 *Ibid.*, III, p. 238.

121 E. A. King, "Medieval Medicine," *Nineteenth Century*, XXXIV, p. 148.

189

CHAPTER VIII

CHARMS

"With the charmes that she saide, A fire down fro' the sky alight." —Gower.

"She drew a splinter from the wound, And with a charm she staunch'd the blood." — Scott.

"Thrice on my breast I spit to guard me safe From fascinating Charms." — Theocritus.

"Mennes fortunes she can tell; She can by sayenge her Ave Marye, And by other Charmes of Sorcerye, Ease men of the Toth ake by and bye Yea, and fatche the Devyll from Hell." — Bale.

"I clawed her by the backe in way of a charme,
To do me not the more good, but the less harme." — Heywood

Charms, as already noticed, are not unlike amulets in significance and similarity of power. The amulet must consist of some material substance so as to be suspended when employed, but the charm may be a word, gesture, look, or condition, as well as a material substance, and does not need to be attached to the body. The word "charm" is derived from the Latin word "carmen," signifying a verse in which the charms were sometimes written, examples of which will be given later. The medical term "carminative," a comforting medicine, really means a charm medicine, and has the same derivation.

190 A charm has been defined as "a form of words or letters, repeated or written, whereby strange things are pretended to be done, beyond the ordinary power of nature." It can be seen, though, that this definition is not sufficiently comprehensive.

For ages, people have had great faith in odd numbers. They have often been used as charms and for medicine. Some one says: "Some philosophers are of opinion that all things are composed of number, prefer the odd before the other, and attribute to it a great efficacy and perfection, especially in matters of physic: wherefore it is that many doctors prescribed always an odd pill, an odd draught, or drop to be taken by their patients. For the perfection thereof they allege these following numbers: as 7 Planets, 7 wonders of the World, 9 Muses, 3 Graces, God is 3 in 1, &c." Ravenscroft, in his comedy of "Mammamouchi or the Citizen Turned Gentleman," makes Trickmore as a physician say: "Let the number of his bleedings and purgations be odd, *numero Deus impare gaudet*" [God delights in an odd number].

Nine is the number consecrated by Buddhism; three is sacred among Brahminical and Christian people. Pythagoras held that the unit or monad is the principle and end of all. One is a good principle. Two, or the dyad, is the origin of contrasts and separation, and is an evil principle. Three, or the triad, is the image of the attributes of God. 191 Four, or the tetrad, is the most perfect of numbers and the root of all things. It is holy by nature. Five, or the pentad, is everything; it stops the power of poisons, and is dreaded by evil spirits. Six is a fortunate number. Seven is powerful for good or evil, and is a sacred number. Eight is the first cube, so is man four-square or perfect. Nine, as the multiple of three, is sacred. Ten, or the decade, is the measure of all it contains, all the numerical relations and harmonies. 122

Cornelius Agrippa wrote on the power of numbers, which he declares is asserted by nature herself; thus the herb called cinquefoil, or five-leafed grass, resists poison, and bans devils by virtue of the number five; one leaf of it taken in wine twice a day cures the quotidian, three the tertian, four the quartan fever. 123

The seventh son of a seventh son was supposed to be an infallible physician as the following quotations would indicate: "The seventh son of a seventh son is born a physician; having an intuitive knowledge of the art of curing all disorders, and sometimes the faculty of performing wonderful cures by touching only." "Plusieurs croyent qu'en France, les septi警s gar篮s, nez de l駈times mariages, sans que la suitte des sept ait est禩nterrompue par la naissance d'aucune fille, peuvent aussi gu鲩r des 192 fi趨es tierces, des fi趨es quartes, at mesme des 飲ouelles, apr賠avoir jen顂rois ou neuf jours avant que de toucher les malades. Mais ils font trop de fond sur le nombre septenaire, en attribuant au septi警 gar篮, pr穘rablement ·ous autres, une puissance qu'il y a autant de raison d'attribuer au sixi警 ou au huiti警, sur le nombre de trois, et sur celuy de neuf, pour ne pas s'engager dans la superstition. Joint que de trois que je connois de ces septi警 gar篮s il y en a deux qui ne gu鲩ssent de rien, et que le troisieme m'a avou鍊de bonne foy, qu'il avoit eu autrefois la reputation de gu鲩r de quantit頥s maux, quoique en effet il n'ait jamais guery d'aucun. C'est pourquoy Monsieur du Laurent a grande raison de rejetter ce pr騐ndu pouvoir, et de la mettre au rang des fables, en ce qui concerne la gu皖son des 飲ouelles." 124

Charms were used to avert evil and counteract supposed malignant influences of all kinds, but it is in their connection with diseases of the body that we are chiefly interested. There is scarcely a disease for which a charm has not been given, but it will be seen that those which are most affected by charms are principally derangements of the nervous system, or those periodical in character — diseases, in fact, which have proved to be most easily influenced by suggestion.

193

Charms might be of the most varied composition. The material was selected from the animal, vegetable, or mineral kingdom, and might consist of anything to which any magical property was considered to belong. Rags, old clothes, pins, and needles were frequently employed in this way. Sir Walter Scott had in his possession a pretended charm taken from an old woman who was said to charm and injure her neighbor's cattle. It consisted of feathers, parings of nails, hair, and similar material, wrapped in a lump of clay.

The theory of *similia similibus curantur* seems to have entered into medi涡l medicine, and especially into the manufacture of charms. The following prescriptions are examples: "The skin of a Raven's heel is good against gout, but the right heel skin must be laid upon the right foot if that be gouty, and the left upon the left.... If you would have man become bold or impudent let him carry about with him the skin or eyes of a Lion or Cock, and he will be fearless of his enemies, nay, he will be very terrible unto them. If you would have him talkative, give him tongues, and seek out those of water frogs and ducks and such creatures notorious for their continuall noise making." 125

King also tells us that "Hartes fete, Does Fete, Bulles fete, or any ruder beastes fete should ofte 194 be eaten; the same confort the sinewes. The elder these beastes be, the more they strengthen." It is noticeable that not age but youth is now honored, and to-day only calves' feet are accorded medicinal value.

Fort 126 gives the following account of the origin of cabbalism: "Towards the close of the fourth century an unknown scholiast collected the exegetical elucidations, explanations and interpretations produced by the Gemara, and united them to the Mishna, as a commentary out of which arose the Talmud. The word 'cabbala,' whose original significance was used in the sense of reception, or transmission, obtained at a later period the meaning of secret lore, because the metaphysical and theosophic idealities which had been developed in the Rabbinical schools, were communicated only to a few, and consequently remained the undisputed property of a limited and close organization." From this there developed a varied and complicated system of words and numbers which showed their power in all forms of magical marvels. Not the least common or puissant of these was the healing of the sick.

Knots were sometimes used as charms, and Cockayne gives us an example in the preface of *Saxon Leechdoms*: "As soon as a man gets pain in his eyes, tie in unwrought flax as many knots as there 195 are letters in his name, pronouncing them as you go, and tie it round his neck."

Long before and long after New Testament days when Jesus used spittle on the blind, and the time when Vespasian healed the blind by the same means, spittle was considered a most efficacious remedy for various diseases. Levinus Lemnius tells us: "Divers experiments shew what power and quality there is in Man's fasting Spittle, when he hath neither eat nor drunk before the use of it: for it cures all tetters, itch, scabs, pushes, and creeping sores: and if venomous little beasts have fastened on any part of the body, as hornets, beetles, toads, spiders, and such like, that by their venome cause tumours and great pains and inflammations, do but rub the place with fasting Spittle, and all those effects will be gone and dispersed. Since the qualities and effects of Spittle come from the humours, (for out of them is it drawn by the faculty of Nature, as Fire draws distilled Water from hearbs) the reason may be easily understood why Spittle should do such strange things, and destroy some creatures." 127

In *Saxon Leechdoms* a cure for gout runs thus: "Before getting out of bed in the morning, spit on your hand, rub all your sinuews, and say, 'Flee, gout, flee,' etc." Sir Thomas Browne, however, is not quite sure that fasting spittle really is poisonous to snakes and vipers.

196

Alexander of Tralles tells us that even Galen did homage to incantations, and quotes him as saying: "Some think that incantations are like old wives' tales; as I did for a long while. But at last I was convinced that there is virtue in them by plain proofs before my eyes. For I had trial of their beneficial operations in the case of those scorpion-stung, nor less in the case of bones stuck fast in the throat, immediately, by an incantation thrown up. And many of them are excellent, severally, and they reach their mark."

Even before our day, however, there were some sceptics. Andrews, quoting Reginald Scot, says: "The Stories which our facetious author relates of ridiculous Charms which, by the help of credulity, operated Wonders, are extremely laughable. In one of them a poor Woman is commemorated who cured all diseases by muttering a certain form of Words over the party afflicted; for which service she always received one penny and a loaf of bread. At length, terrified by menaces of flames both in this world and the next, she owned that her whole conjuration consisted in these potent lines, which she always repeated in a low voice near the head of her patient:

> 'Thy loaf in my hand, And thy penny in my purse, Thou art never the better — And I am never the worse.'"

197 Lord Northampton quite fittingly inquires: "What godly reason can any Man alyve alledge why Mother Joane of Stowe, speaking these wordes, and neyther more nor lesse,

> 'Our Lord was the fyrst Man, That ever Thorne prick'd upon: It never blysted nor it never belted, And I pray God, nor this not may,'

should cure either Beasts, or Men and Women from Diseases?" 128

Perhaps it would be well for us to treat the subject of charms as we have that of amulets, and present the different charms under the heading of the diseases which they were supposed to cure.

Ague. — Many charms were given for this disease, some of which seem to us to-day most ridiculous. Brand gives a quotation from the *Life of Nicholas Mooney* who was a notorious highwayman, executed with others at Bristol, in 1752. It is as follows: "After the cart drew away, the hangman very deservedly had his head broke for attempting to pull off Mooney's shoes; and a fellow had like to have been killed in mounting the gallows to take away the ropes that were left after the malefactors were cut down. A young woman came fifteen miles for the sake of the rope from Mooney's neck, which was given to her, it being by many apprehended 198 that the halter of an executed person will charm away the ague and perform many other cures."

Pettigrew relates that "In Skippon's account of a 'Journey through the Low Countries,' he makes mention of the lectures of Ferrarius and his narrative of the cure of the ague of a Spanish lieutenant, by writing the words FEBRA FUGE, and cutting off a letter from the paper every day, and he observed the distemper to abate accordingly; when he cut the letter F last of all the ague left him. In the same year, he says, fifty more were reported to be cured in the same manner."

Another charm for ague was only effective when said up the chimney on St. Agnes Eve, by the eldest female of the family. It was as follows:

> "Tremble and go! First day shiver and burn. Tremble and quake! Second day shiver and learn: Tremble and die! Third day never return." 129

Pliny said: "Any plant gathered from the bank of a brook or river before sunrise, provided that no one sees the person who gathers it, is considered as a remedy for tertian ague." Lodge, in glancing at the superstitious creed with respect to charms, says: 199 "Bring him but a Table of Lead, with Crosses (and 'Adonai,' or 'Elohim,' written in it), and he thinks it will heal his ague."

Mr. Marsden, while among the Sumatrans, accidentally met with the following charm for the ague: "(Sign of the cross.) When Christ saw the cross he trembled and shaked and they said unto him, hast thou ague? and he said unto them, I have neither ague nor fever; and whosoever bears these words, either in writing or in mind, shall never be troubled with ague or fever. So help thy servants, O Lord, who put their trust in thee!"

From Douce's notes, Mr. Brand informs us that it was usual with many persons about Exeter who had ague "to visit at dead of night the nearest cross road five different times, and there bury a new-laid egg. The visit is paid about an hour before the cold fit is expected; and they are persuaded that with the Egg they shall bury the Ague. If the experiment fail, (and the agitation it occasions may often render it successful) they attribute it to some unlucky accident that may have befallen them on the way. In the execution of this matter they observe the strictest silence, taking care not to speak to anyone, whom they may happen to meet. I shall here note another Remedy against the Ague mentioned as above, viz., by breaking a salted Cake of Bran and giving it to a Dog, when the fit comes on, by which means they suppose the 200 malady to be transferred from them to the Animal." 130 This and similar methods were designated transplantation.

Bites of Venomous Animals. — It is an old medical superstition that every animal whose bite is poisonous carries the cure within itself, but external charms were also used. It was thought that the poison of the Spanish fly existed in the body, while the head and wings contained the antidote. "A hair of the dog that bites you" is the cure for hydrophobia, the fat of the viper was the remedy for its bite, and "three scruples of the ashes of the witch, when she had been well and carefully burnt at a stake, is a sure catholicon against all the evil effects of witchcraft." 131

Serpents' bites, which were always considered very dangerous, were said to be healed by people called sauveurs, who had a mark of St. Catharine's wheel upon their palates. Snake stones, originally brought from Java, were supposed to absorb the poison by being simply placed over the bite. Russel mentions a charm against mosquitoes, used in Aleppo. It consisted of certain unintelligible characters inscribed on a little slip of paper, which was pasted over the windows or upon the lintel of the door. One family has obtained, through heredity, the power of making these charms, and they distrib 201 ute them on a certain day of the year without remuneration.

Navarette was told that the best remedy against scorpions was to make a commemoration of St. George when going to bed. This, he says, never failed, but he also rubbed the bed with garlic. The following is given as a cure for the sting of the scorpion: "The patient is to sit on an ass, with his face to the tail of the animal, by which the pain will be transmitted from the man to the beast." Or again, a person who was bitten by either a tarantulla or a mad dog must go nine times round the town on the Sabbath, calling upon and imploring the assistance of the saint. On the third night—the prayers being heard and granted, and the health restored—the madness was removed. The prayer was as follows:

> "Thou who presidest over the Apulian shores, Thou who curest the bites of mad dogs, Thou, O Sacred One, ward off this cruel plague, Get thee far hence, O madness, O fury." 132

Burns.—The following is "A Charme for a burning":

> "There came three angels out of the east; The one brought fire, the two brought frost— Out fire; in frost; In the name of the Father, and Son, and Holy Ghost. —Amen." 133

202 *Childbirth.*—Many superstitious practices have grown up around this condition. In 1554, Bonner, Bishop of London, forbade "a mydwife of his diocese to exercise any witchecrafte, charmes, sorcerye, invocations, or praiers, other than such as be allowable and may stand with the lawes and ordinances of the Catholike Church." In 1559, the first year of the reign of Queen Elizabeth, an inquiry was instituted "whether you knowe any that doe use charmes, sorcery, enchauntementes, invocations, circles, witchecraftes, southsayinge, or any lyke craftes or imaginacions invented by the devyl, and specially in the tyme of woman's travaylle." Two years before this, the midwives took an oath among themselves, so

Strype tells us, not to "suffer any other bodies' child to be set, brought, or laid before any woman delivered of child in the place of her natural child, so far forth as I can know and understand. Also I will not use any kind of sorcerye or incantation in the time of the travail of any woman."

The eagle stone and iris were supposed to promote an easy delivery, and the sardonyx was laid *inter mammas* to procure an easy birth; a sardonyx formerly belonged to the monastery of St. Albans to be used for this purpose. In some countries, during childbirth, the men lie in, keep their beds, and are attended as if really sick, sometimes as long as six weeks. 134

203 *Chorea.*—Of all the charms against this disease, St. Vitus' dance, none seemed so effectual as an application to the saint. In the translation of Naogeorgus, Barnabe Googe says:

> "The nexte is VITUS sodde in oyle, before whose ymage faire Both men and women bringing hennes for offring doe repaire: The cause whereof I doe not know, I think, for some disease Which he is thought to drive away from such as him doe please."

Colic.—This disorder was cured by a person drinking the water in which he had washed his feet; we might well consider the cure worse than the disease.

Consumption.—Shaw 135 speaks of a cure for consumptive diseases used in his time in Moray. "They pared the Nails of the Fingers and Toes of the Patient, put these Parings into a Rag cut from his clothes, then waved their Hand with the Rag thrice round his head crying *Deas soil,* after which they buried the Rag in some unknown place." Dr. Baas 136 declares that natural pills of rabbit's dung were in use on the Rhine as a cure for consumption.

"There is a disease," says the minister of Logierait, writing in 1795, "called Glacach by the Highlanders, which, as it affects the chest and lungs, is evidently of a consumptive nature. It is called Macdonald's disease, 'because there are particular tribes of Macdonalds, who were believed to cure it 204 with the Charms of their touch, and the use of a certain set of words. There must be no fee given of any kind. Their faith in the touch of a Macdonald is very great.'" 137

Cramp. — Among the many charms for cramp, the following is taken from *Pepys' Diary*: 138

> "Cramp be thou faintless, As our Lady was sinless When she bare Jesus."

Demoniacal Possession. — To know when a person is possessed, try the following, says King: "Take the harte and liver of a fysshe called a Pyck, and put them into a pot wyth glowynge hot coles, and hold the same to the patient so that the smoke may entre into hym. If he is possessed he cannot abyde that smoke, but rageth and is angry." "It is good also to make a fyre in hys chamber of Juniper wood, and caste into the fire Franckincense and S. John's wort, for the evill spirits cannot abyde thys sent, and Waxe angry, whereby may be perceived whether a man be possessed or not." 139 I am afraid that possession would be sadly common if either of these tests were applied.

Dislocation. — Among the oldest charms we have is one given by Cato the Censor for the reduction of a dislocated limb, and passed on to us by Pettigrew.

205

"A dislocation may be cured by this charm. Take a reed four or five feet long; cut it in the middle, and let two men hold the points towards each other for insertion. While this is doing repeat these words: *In Alio S. F. Motas vœta, Daries Dardaries Astataries Dissunapitur.* Now jerk a piece of iron upon the reeds at their juncture, and cut right and left. Bind them to the dislocation or fracture, and it will effect a cure." 140

Dropsy. — Toads were formed into a powder called Pulvis yhiopicus, the mode of preparation being given in Bates's Pharmacopœia. This powder was used externally, and also given internally in cases of dropsy and other diseases.

Epilepsy. — The liver of a dead athlete was a sovereign remedy against epilepsy in early days. In Lincolnshire a portion of a human skull taken from a grave was grated and given to epileptics as a cure for fits, and the water in which a corpse had been washed was given to a man in Glasgow for the same purpose. 141 Another remedy was also proposed: "If a man be greved wyth the fallinge sicknesse, let him take a he-Wolves harte and make it to pouder and use it: but if it be a woman, let her take a she-Wolves harte." 142

206

John of Gladdesden, who was court physician from 1305-1317, spoke thus concerning epilepsy: "Because there are many children and others afflicted with the epilepsy, who cannot take medicines, let the following experiment be tried, which I have found to be effectual, whether the patient was a demoniac, a lunatic, or an epileptic. When the patient and his parents have fasted three days, let them conduct him to church. If he be of a proper age, and of his right senses, let him confess. Then let him hear Mass on Friday, and also on Saturday. On Sunday let a good and religious priest read over the head of the patient, in the church, the gospel which is read in September, in the time of vintage, after the feast of the Holy Cross. After this, let the priest write the same gospel devoutly, and let the patient wear it about his neck, and he shall be cured. The gospel is, 'This kind goeth not out but by prayer and fasting.'" 143

Among some African tribes the foot of an elk is considered a splendid remedy against epilepsy. One foot only of each animal possesses virtue, and the way to ascertain the valuable foot is to "knock the beast down, when he will immediately lift up that leg which is most efficacious to scratch his ear. Then you must be ready with a sharp scymitar to lop off the medicinal limb, and you shall find an infallible remedy against the falling sickness treasured 207 up in his claws." The American Indians and medi涡l Norwegians also considered this a sure remedy. The person afflicted, however, must apply it to his heart, hold it in his left hand, and rub his ear with it. 144

Evil-eye. — Children were supposed to be most susceptible to the evil-eye. Charms and amulets were furnished against fascination in general. Certain figures in bronze, coral, ivory, etc., representing a closed hand with the thumb thrust out between the first and second fingers called the *fig*, were common. In Henry IV, Part II, Pistol says:

"When Pistol lies, do this; and fig me, like The bragging Spaniard."

Eye Diseases. — Among the early Germans, ambulatory female medicists were not uncommon, and they cured largely through charms. The following is a charm used for eye diseases:

"Three maidens once going On a verdant highway; One could cure blindness, Another cured cataract, Third cured inflammation; But all cured by one means." 145

208 *Fevers.* — This charm was used for fever: "Wryt thys Wordys on a lorell lef✝Ysmael✝Ysmael✝ adjuro vos per Angelum ut soporetur iste Homo N. and ley thys lef under hys head that he wete not therof, and let hym ete Letuse oft and drynk Ip'e seed smal grounden in a morter, and temper yt with Ale." 146

"The fever," says Werenfels, "he will not drive away by medicines, but, what is a more certain remedy, having pared his nails and tied them to a crayfish, he will turn his back, and as Deucalion did the stones from which a new progeny of men arose, throw them behind him into the next river." 147

The "Leech book" 148 says that for typhus fever the patient is to drink of a decoction of herbs over which many masses have been sung, then say the names of the four "gospellers" and a charm and a prayer. Again, a man is to write a charm in silence, and just as silently put the words in his left breast and take care not to go indoors with the writing upon him, the words being EMMANUEL VERONICA. The Loseley MSS. prescribe the following for all manner of fevers: "Take iii drops of a woman's mylke yt norseth a knave childe, and do it in a hennes egge that ys sedentere (or sitting), and let hym suppe it up when the evyl takes hym."

209

Goitre. — The dew collected from the grave of the last man buried in a church-yard has been used as a lotion for goitre, and a correspondent of *Notes and Queries* for May 24, 1851, furnishes two remedies then in use at Withyam, Sussex. "A common snake, held by its head and tail, is slowly drawn by someone standing by nine times across the front part of the neck of the person affected, the reptile being allowed, after every third time, to crawl about for awhile. Afterwards the snake is put alive in a bottle, which is corked tightly, and then buried in the ground. The tradition is, that as the snake decays, the swelling vanishes. The second mode of treatment is just the same as the above, with the exception of the snake's doom. In this case it is kidded, and its skin, sewn in a piece of silk, is worn round the diseased neck. By degrees the swelling in this case also disappears."

Headache. — In Brand's day, the rope which remained after a man had been hanged and cut down was an object of eager competition, being regarded as of great virtue in attacks of headache, and Gross says: "Moss growing on a human skull, if dried, powdered, and taken as snuff, will cure the Headach." Loadstone was also recommended as a sovereign remedy for this malady. Pliny said that any person might be immediately cured of the headache by the application of any plant which has grown on the head of a statue, provided it be folded in the 210 shred of a garment, and tied to the part affected with a red string.

Hemorrhage. — The following charm has been used to stop bleeding at the nose and other hemorrhages:

> "In the blood of Adam Sin was taken, In the blood of Christ it was all shaken, And by the same blood I do the charge, That the blood of (insert name) run no longer at large."

Pepys in his *Diary* gives us a Latin charm of which the following is a translation:

> "Blood remain in Thee, As Christ was in himself; Blood remain in thy veins, As Christ in his pains; Blood remain fixed, As Christ was on the crucifix."

Brand, the historian of Orkney, says: "They have a charm whereby they stop excessive bleeding in any, whatever way they come by it, whether by or without external violence. The name of the Patient being sent to the Charmer, he saith over some words, (which I heard,) upon which the blood instantly stoppeth, though the bleeding Patient were at the greatest distance from the Charmer. Yea, upon the saying of these words, the blood will stop in the bleeding throats of oxen or sheep, to the astonishment of Spectators. Which account we had from the Ministers of the Country."

211 Boyle says: "Having been one summer frequently subject to bleeding at the nose, and reduced to employ several remedies to check that distemper; that which I found the most effectual to stanch the blood was some moss of a dead man's skull, (sent for a present out of Ireland, where it is far less rare than in most other countries,) though it did but touch my skin, till the herb was a little warmed by it." 149

Brand gives "A charme to staunch blood: Jesus that was in Bethleem born, and baptyzed was in the flumen Jordane, as stente the water at hys comyng, so stente the blood of thys man N. thy servvaunt, thorw the virtu of thy holy Name ✝ Jesu ✝ & of thy Cosyn swete Sent Jon. And sey thys charme fyve tymes with fyve Pater Nosters, in the worschep of the fyve woundys." 150

"In the year 1853," says Berdoe, "I saw among the more precious drugs in the shop of a pharmaceutical chemist at Leamington a bottle labelled in the ordinary way with the words, Moss from a Dead-Man's Skull. This has long been used, superstitiously, dried, powdered, and taken as snuff, for headache and bleeding at the nose."

Herpes. — Turner 151 notices a prevalent charm among old women for the shingles, and which is not uncommonly heard of to-day. It was to smear on the affected part the blood from a black cat's tail. 212 He says that in the only case when he saw it used it caused considerable mischief.

Incubus. — Stones with holes through them were commonly called hag-stones, and were often attached to the key of the stable door to prevent witches riding the horses. One of these suspended at the head of the bed was celebrated for the prevention of nightmare. In the "Leech book" 152 we find the following: "If a mare or hag ride a man, take lupins, garlic, and betony, and frankincense, bind them on a fawn skin, let a man have the worts on him, and let him go into his house." Notice the following from Lluellin's poems:

> "Some the night-mare hath prest With that weight on their brest, No returnes of their breath can passe, But to us the tale is addle, We can take off her saddle, And turn out the night-mare to grasse."

Insomnia. — In the Loseley MSS. we find a receipt "For hym that may not slepe. Take and wryte yese wordes into leves of lether: Ismael! Ismael! adjuro te per Angelum Michaelum ut soporetur homo iste; and lay this under his bed, so yt he wot not yerof and use it allway lytell, and lytell, as he have nede yerto."

Jaundice. — This disease was sometimes cured by transplantation, and Paracelsus gives us a method 213 for carrying this out. Make seven or nine — it must be an odd number — cakes of the newly emitted and warm urine of the patient with the ashes of ash wood, and bury them for some days in a dunghill.

In the journal of Dr. Edward Browne, transmitted to his father, Sir Thomas Browne, we read of a magical cure for jaundice: "Burne wood under a leaden vessel filled with water; take the ashes of that wood, and boyle it with the patient's urine; then lay nine long heaps of the boyled ashes upon a board in a ranke, and upon every heap lay nine spears of crocus: it hath greater effects than is credible to any one that shall barely read this receipt without experiencing." 153

Madness. — The early inhabitants of Cornwall used "to place the disordered in mind on the brink of a square pool, filled with water from St. Nun's well. The patient, having no intimation of what was intended, was, by a sudden blow on the breast, tumbled into the pool, where he was tossed up and down by some persons of superior strength till, being quite debilitated, his fury forsook him; he was then carried to church, and certain masses were sung over him. A similar practice of the people of Perthshire is noticed by Sir Walter Scott in *Marmion*.

> "Thence to St. Fillan's blessed well, Whose spring can frenzied dreams dispel, And the crazed brain restore."

214 *Marasmus.* — Mr. Boyle relates the case of a physician whose wan face betokened a marasmus, and who was induced to try a method not unlike the sympathetic cures. "He took an egg and boiled it hard in his own warm urine; he then with a bodkin perforated the shell in many places, and buried it in an ant-hill, where it was kept to be devoured by the emmets; and as they wasted the egg, he found his distemper to abate and his strength to increase, insomuch that his disease left him." 154

Rickets. — The most common method of dealing with this disease was by drawing the children through a split tree. The tree was afterward bound up and, as it healed and grew together, the children acquired strength; at least, so 'twas said. Sir John Cullum saw the operation performed and says that the ash tree was selected as most preferable for the purpose. "It was split longitudinally about five feet: the fissure was kept open by the gardener, whilst the friend of the child, having first stripped him naked, passed him thrice through it, almost head foremost. This accomplished, the tree was bound up with packthread, and as the bark healed, so it was said the child would recover. One of the cases was of rickets, the other a rupture." Drawing the children through a perforated stone was also a cure for rickets, providing that two brass **215** pins were carefully laid across each other on the top edge of this stone. 155

Sciatica. — Sleeping on stones on a particular night was formerly practised in Cornwall to cure all forms of lameness. Boneshave was the term used for sciatica in Exmoor, where the following charm was used for its cure: The patient must lie on his back on the bank of a river or brook, having a straight staff lying by his side between him and the water, and must have the following words repeated over him:

> "Boneshave right, Boneshave straight. As the water runs by the stave Good for Boneshave." 156

Scrofula. — Scrofula, or "king's-evil," was best cured by the touch of the sovereign, but, if this could not be accomplished, a naked virgin could cure it, especially if she spit three times upon it. Stroking the affected parts nine times with the hand of a dead man, particularly of one who had suffered a violent death as a penalty of his crime, especially if it be murder, was long practised, and was said to be efficacious in curing scrofula.

Sweating Sickness. — Aubrey 157 gives a selection of the favorite prescriptions in use against the sweating sickness. Among them was the following: "Another very true medicine. — For to say every 216 day at seven parts of your body, seven paternosters, and seven Ave Marias, with one Credo at the last. Ye shall begyn at the ryght syde, under the right ere, saying the '*paternoster qui es in coelis, sanctificetur nomen tuum,*' with a cross made there with your thumb, and so say the paternoster full complete, and one Ave Maria, and then under the left ere, and then under the left armhole, and then under the left hole, and then the last at the heart, with one paternoster, Ave Maria with one Credo; and these thus said daily, with the grace of God is there no manner drede hym."

Thorns. — Three metrical charms have been used for troubles of this kind. *Pepys' Diary* records "A charme for a thorne":

> "Jesus, that was of a Virgin Born, Was pricked both with nail and thorn; It neither wealed, nor belled, rankled nor boned; In the name of Jesus no more shall this."

Another form of the same is this:

> "Christ was of a Virgin born, And he was pricked with a thorn; It did neither bell, nor swell; And I trust in Jesus this never will."

Brand gives another thus:

> "Unto the Virgin Mary our Saviour was born, And on his head he wore the crown of thorn; If you believe this true and mind it well, This hurt will never fester, nor yet swell." 158

217 *Toothache.* — King in his interesting article recites this cure: "Seeth as many little green frogges sitting upon trees as thou canst get, in water: take the fat flowynge from them, and when nede is,

anoynt the teth therwyth. The graye worms breathing under wood or stone, having many fete, these perced through with a bodken and then put into the toth, alayeth the payne." 159 A nail driven into an oak tree is reported to be a cure for this pain, and bones from a church-yard have from ancient times been used as charms against this disease.

An early idea was that toothache was caused by a worm and that henbane seed roasted would cure it. The following from "The School of Salerne" formulates this superstition:

> "If in your teeth you hap to be tormented, By meane some little wormes therein do breed, Which pain (if heed be tane) may be prevented, Be keeping cleane your teeth, when as you feede; Burne Francomsence (a gum not evil sented), Put Henbane unto this, and Onyon seed, And with a tunnel to the tooth that's hollow, Convey the smoke thereof, and ease shall follow."

Even to-day, I suppose, druggists sell henbane seed for this purpose. The seed is used by sprinkling it on hot cinders and holding the open mouth over the rising smoke. The heat causes the seed to 218 sprout, and thus there appears something similar to a maggot, which is ignorantly supposed by the sufferer to have dropped from the tooth. 160

Warts. — The cures for warts are many and varied. There have been many charms devised for their removal. Grose gives directions to "Steal a piece of beef from a butcher's shop, and rub your wart with it, then throw it down the necessary house, or bury it, and as the beef rots, your warts will decay." 161 Some have great faith in having a vagrant count them, mark the number on the inside of his hat, and then when he leaves the neighborhood he takes the warts with him. Coffin water was also considered good for them.

"For warts," says Sir Thomas Browne, "we rub our hands before the moon, and commit any magulated part to the touch of the dead. Old Women were always famous for curing warts; they were so in Lucian's time." 162

Sir Kenelm Digby, in a work already referred to, says: "One would think that it were folly that one should offer to wash his hands in a well-polished silver basin, wherein there is not a drop of water, yet this may be done by the reflection of the moonbeams only, which will afford it a competent humidity to do it; but they who have tried it, have found 219 their hands, after they are wiped, to be much moister than usually; but this is an infallible way to take away warts from the hands, if it be often used."

Black gives us several ways of charming away warts. He says: "Lancashire wise men tell us for warts to rub them with a cinder, and this tied up in paper, and dropped where four roads meet, will transfer the warts to whoever opens the parcel. Another mode of transferring warts is to touch each wart with a pebble, and place the pebbles in a bag, which should be lost on the way to church; whoever finds the bag gets the warts." A common Warwickshire custom was to rub the warts with a black snail, stick the snail on a thorn bush, and then, say the folks, as the snail dies so will the wart disappear. 163

Warts, on the other hand, seem in certain cases to be considered lucky. In "Syr Gyles Goosecappe, Knight," a play of 1606, Lord Momford is made to say: "The Creses here are excellent good: the proportion of the chin good; the little aptnes of it to sticke out; good. And the wart aboue it most exceeding good."

Wen. — A newspaper of 1777 reports: "After he (Doctor Dodd) had hung about ten minutes, a very decently dressed young woman went up to the gallows in order to have a wen in her face stroked by the Doctor's hand; it being a received opinion 220 among the vulgar that it is a certain cure for such a disorder. The executioner, having untied the Doctor's hand, stroked the part affected several times therewith."

At the execution of Crowley, a murderer of Warwick, in 1845, a similar scene is described in the newspapers: "At least five thousand persons of the lowest of the low were mustered on this occasion to witness the dying moments of the unhappy culprit.... As is usual in such cases (to their shame be it spoken) a number of females were present, and scarcely had the soul of the deceased taken its farewell flight from its earthly tabernacle, than the scaffold was crowded with members of the 'gentler sex' afflicted with wens in the neck, with white swellings in the knees, &c., upon whose afflictions the cold clammy hand of the sufferer was passed to and fro for the benefit of his executioner." 164

Whooping-Cough. — It was a common belief in Devonshire, Cornwall, and some other parts of England, that if one inquired of any one riding on a piebald horse of a remedy for this complaint, whatever he named was regarded as an infallible cure. In Suffolk and Norfolk, a favorite remedy was to put the head of a suffering child for a few minutes into a hole made in a meadow. It must be done in the evening with only the father and mother to witness it.

221 A child in Cornwall received the following treatment: "If afflicted with the hooping cough, it is fed with the bread and butter of a family, the heads of which bear respectively the names of John and Joan. In the time of an epidemic, so numerous are the applications, that the poor couple have little reason to be grateful to their godfathers and godmothers for their gift of these particular names. Or, if a piebald horse is to be found in the neighbourhood, the child is taken to it, and passed thrice under the belly of the animal; the mere possession of such a beast confers the power of curing the disease."

We have an account of a cure for whooping-cough in a Monmouthshire paper about the middle of the nineteenth century. "A few days since an unusual circumstance was observed at Pillgwenlly, which caused no small degree of astonishment to one or two enlightened beholders. A patient ass stood near a house, and a family of not much more rational animals was grouped around it. A father was passing his little son under the donkey, and lifting him over its back a certain number of times, with as much solemnity and precision as if engaged in the performance of a sacred duty. This done, the father took a piece of bread, cut from an untasted loaf, which he offered the animal to bite at. Nothing loath, the Jerusalem poney laid hold of the piece of bread with his teeth, and instantly the 222 father severed the outer portion of the slice from that in the donkey's mouth. He next clipped off some hairs from the neck of the animal, which he cut up into minute particles, and then mixed them with the bread which he had crumbled. This very tasty food was then offered to the boy who had been passed round the donkey so mysteriously, and the little fellow having eaten thereof, the donkey was removed by his owners. The father, his son, and other members of his family were moving off, when a bystander inquired what all these 'goings on' had been adopted for? The father stared at the ignorance of the inquirer, and then in a half contemptuous, half condescending tone, informed him that 'it was to cure his poor son's whooping-cough, to be sure!' Extraordinary as this may appear, in days when the schoolmaster is so much in request, it is nevertheless true."

There is a belief in Cheshire that, if a toad is held for a moment within the mouth of the patient, it is apt to catch the disease, and so cure the person suffering from it. A correspondent of *Notes and Queries* speaks of a case in which such a phenomenon actually occurred; but the experiment is one which would not be very willingly tried. Brand informs us that "Roasted mice were formerly held in Norfolk a sure remedy for this complaint; nor is it certain that the belief is extinct even now. A poor woman's son once found 223 himself greatly relieved after eating three roast mice!" 165

Worms. — A Scotch writer in the last half of the seventeenth century observed: "In the Miscellaneous MSS. ... written by Baillie Dundee, among several medicinal receipts I find an exorcism against all kinds of worms in the body, in the name of the Father, Son, and Holy Ghost, to be repeated three mornings, as a certain remedy." 166

122 S. B. Gould, *Curious Myths of the Middle Ages*, p. 273.

123 H. Morley, *Life of Cornelius Agrippa*, I, p. 165.

124 M. Thiers, *Traité es Superstitions*, p. 436.

125 E. A. King, "Medieval Medicine," *Nineteenth Century*, XXXIV, p. 147.

126 G. F. Fort, *History of Medical Economy During the Middle Ages*, p. 72.

127 J. Brand, *Popular Antiquities*, III, pp. 229 f.

128 *Ibid.*, III, pp. 228 and 237.

129 T. J. Pettigrew, *Superstitions Connected with ... Medicine and Surgery*, pp. 94 f.

130 J. Brand, *Popular Antiquities*, III, pp. 252 f.

131 E. Berdoe, *Origin and Growth of the Healing Art*, p. 416.

132 T. J. Pettigrew, *Superstitions Connected with ... Surgery and Medicine*, pp. 104-106.

133 *Pepys' Diary*, I, p. 323.

134 T. J. Pettigrew, *Superstitions Connected with ... Medicine and Surgery*, pp. 113-115.

135 *History of Moray*, p. 248.

136 *History of Medicine*, p. 159.

137 J. Brand, *Popular Antiquities*, III, pp. 240 and 248.

138 I, p. 324.

139 E. A. King, "Medieval Medicine," *Nineteenth Century*, XXXIV, p. 149.

140 T. J. Pettigrew, *Superstitions Connected with ... Medicine and Surgery*, p. 77.

141 E. Berdoe, *Origin and Growth of the Medical Art*, pp. 397 and 414.

142 E. A. King, "Medieval Medicine," *Nineteenth Century*, XXXIV, p. 147.

143 E. Berdoe, *Origin and Growth of the Healing Art*, p. 327.

144 T. J. Pettigrew, *Superstitions Connected with ... Medicine and Surgery*, pp. 84 f

145 G. F. Fort, *History of Medical Economy During the Middle Ages*, p. 196.

146 J. Brand, *Popular Antiquities*, III, p. 237.

147 T. J. Pettigrew, *Superstitions Connected with ... Medicine and Surgery*, p. 92.

148 II, p. 139.

149 *Ibid.*, pp. 112 f.

150 J. Brand, *Popular Antiquities*, III, pp. 237, 241, and 268.

151 *Diseases of the Skin*, p. 82.

152 II, p. 139.

153 T. J. Pettigrew, *Superstitions Connected with ... Medicine and Surgery*, p. 103.

154 *Ibid.*, p. 102.

155 J. Brand, *Popular Antiquities*, III, pp. 249 f.

156 *Ibid.*, p. 245.

157 *History of England*, II, p. 296.

158 J. Brand, *Popular Antiquities*, III, p. 264.

159 E. A. King, "Medieval Medicine," *Nineteenth Century*, XXXIV, p. 148.

160 E. Berdoe, *Origin and Growth of the Healing Art*, pp. 414 f.

161 T. J. Pettigrew, *Superstitions Connected with ... Medicine and Surgery*, p. 108.

162 J. Brand, *Popular Antiquities*, III, p. 241.

163 Berdoe, *Origin and Growth of the Healing Art*, pp. 415 f.

164 J. Brand, *Popular Antiquities*, III, p. 241.

165 *Ibid.*, p. 239.

166 *Ibid.*, p. 240.

224

CHAPTER IX

ROYAL TOUCH

"Men may die of imagination, So depe may impression be take." — Chaucer.

"When time shall once have laid his lenient hand on the passions and pursuits of the present moment, they too shall lose that imaginary value which heated fancy now bestows upon them." — Blair.

"The king is but a man, as I am; the violet smells to him as it does to me; the element shows to him as it doth to me; all his senses have but human conditions; his ceremonies laid by, in his nakedness he appears but a man; and though his affections are higher mounted than ours, yet, when they stoop, they stoop with the like wing." — Shakespeare.

*Malcolm.*Comes the king forth, I pray you?

Doctor. Ay, sir: there are a crew of wretched souls,
That stay his cure: their malady convinces
The great assay of art; but at his touch,
Such sanctity hath heaven given his hand,
They presently amend.

*Malcolm.*I thank you, doctor. [Exit *Doctor.*

Macduff. What's the disease he means?

Malcolm.'Tis call'd the evil:
A most miraculous work in this good king,
Which often, since my here remain in England,
I have seen him do. How he solicits heaven,
Himself best knows; but strangely-visited people,
All swoln and ulcerous, pitiful to the eye,
The mere despair of surgery, he cures;
Hanging a golden stamp about their necks,
Put on with holy prayers: and 'tis spoken,
To the succeeding royalty he leaves
The healing benediction. — *Macbeth*, Act iv, Sc. 3.

Perhaps we have no better example of the effect of the belief in healers than that presented by what was known as "king's touch." It is typical of the 225 cures performed by healers, and on that account I shall give a rather full account of the phenomenon.

Touching by the sovereign for the amelioration of sundry diseases was a currently accepted therapeutic measure. The royal touch was especially efficacious in epilepsy and scrofula, the latter being consequently known as "king's-evil." So far as we are able to trace this practice in history, it began with Edward the Confessor in England and St. Louis in France. There has been not a little dispute concerning its real origin. "Laurentius, first physician to Henry IV, of France, who is indignant at the attempt made to derive its origin from Edward the Confessor, asserts the power to have commenced with Clovis I, A. D. 481, and says that Louis I, A. D. 814, added to the ceremonial of touching, the sign of the cross. Mezeray also says, that St. Louis, through humility, first added the sign of the cross in touching for the king's evil." 167

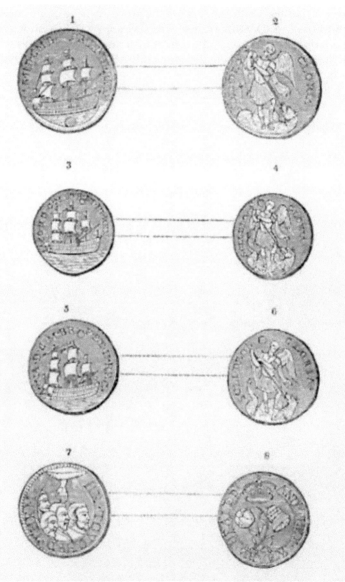

KING'S TOUCH-PIECES

William of Malmesbury gives the origin of the royal touch in his account of the miracles of Edward the Confessor. "A young woman had married a husband of her own age, but having no issue by the union, the humours collecting abundantly about her neck, she had contracted a sore disorder, the glands swelling in a dreadful manner. Admonished in a dream to have the part affected washed by the 226 king, she entered the palace, and the king himself fulfilled this labour of love, by rubbing the woman's neck with his fingers dipped in water. Joyous health followed his healing hand; the lurid skin opened, so that worms flowed out with the purulent matter, and the tumour subsided. But as the orifice of the ulcers was large and unsightly, he commanded her to be supported at the royal expense until she should be perfectly cured. However, before a week had expired, a fair new skin returned, and hid the scars so completely, that nothing of the original wound could be discovered; and within a year becoming the mother of twins, she increased the admiration of Edward's holiness. Those who knew him more intimately, affirm that he often cured this complaint in Normandy; whence appears how false is the notion, who in our times assert, that the cure of this disease does not proceed from personal sanctity, but from hereditary virtue in the royal line." 168 The fact that Edward was a saint as well as a king throws some light on the subject, for many miracles were attributed to him. Jeremy Collier maintained that the scrofula miracle is hereditary upon all his successors, but we find that not blood but royal prestige was the secret. He said "that this prince cured the king's evil is beyond dispute: and since the credit of this miracle is unquestionable, I see no reason why we should 227 scruple believing the rest.... King Edward the Confessor was the first that cured this distemper, and from him it has descended as an hereditary miracle upon all his successors. To dispute the matter of fact, is to go to the excesses of skepticism, to deny our senses, and be incredulous even to ridiculousness." 169

The quotation given above from William of Malmesbury is the earliest mention of the gift of healing by the royal touch. No historian at or near the time of Edward has alluded to the supposed power vested in him. Not even the bull of Pope Alexander III, by which Edward was canonized about two centuries after his decease, makes any allusion whatever to the cures effected by him through the imposition of hands.

English and French writers have disagreed not only regarding the origin, but also regarding the real possession of the power, the English denying it to the French kings and the French with equal vigor restricting it to their own sovereigns. There seems to be little doubt that the sovereigns of both nations made cures, but the healing was confined to these two royal families; the intermarriages in the two families probably account for the belief in the transmission of the gift, regardless of the origin.

The ability to heal certain diseases passed down 228 from reign to reign notwithstanding the religious belief, the character, or the legitimate succession of the sovereign, to the time of Queen Anne. It must not be supposed that the practice was continuous for the seven centuries from Edward the Confessor to Anne: we have no record whatever of the first four Norman kings attempting to cure any one by the imposition of hands, and we know that William III refused to attempt healing. Andrew Boorde defines king's-evil as an "euyl sickenes or impediment," and advises as follows: "For this matter let euery man make frendes to the Kynges maiestie, for it doth pertayne to a Kynge to helpe this infirmitie by the grace the whiche is geuen to a Kynge anoynted." In his *Introduction to Knowledge* (1547-1548) he continues: "The Kynges of England by the power that God hath gyuen to them, dothe make sicke men whole of a sickeness called the kynges euyll." 170

There is a curious passage in Aubrey in which he says: "The curing of the King's Evil by the touch of the king, does much puzzle our philosophers, for whether our kings were of the house of York or Lancaster, it did the cure for the most part." Sir John Fortescue, in defending the House of Lancaster against the House of York, claimed that the crown could not descend to a female because the Queen was not qualified by the form of anointing 229 her to cure the disease called the king's-evil. It must have been very comforting to all concerned to find that the power to cure disease by the royal touch had not been affected by the change of sex of the reigning sovereign.

The gift was not impaired by the Reformation, and an obdurate Roman Catholic was converted on finding that Elizabeth, after the Pope's excommunication, could cure his scrofula. Elizabeth, however, could not bring herself fully to accept the reality of these cures. She continued the practice on account of the pressure of public opinion, but upon one occasion she told a multitude of afflicted ones who had applied to her for relief, "God alone can cure your diseases." Dr. Tooker, the Queen's chaplain, though, certified freely to his own knowledge of the cures wrought by her, as did also William Cowles, the Queen's surgeon. Robert Laneham's letter, concerning the Queen's visit to Kenilworth Castle, relates how, on July 18, 1575, her Majesty touched for the evil, and that it was a "day of grace." "By her highnes accustumed mercy and charitee, nyne cured of the peynfull and daungerous diseaz, called the king's euill; for that Kings and Queenz of this Realm withoout oother medsin (saue only by handling and prayerz) only doo cure it."

James I wished to drop it as a worn-out superstition, but was warned by his advisers that to do 230 so would be to abate a prerogative of the crown; the practice therefore continued, and good testimony exists as to the cures wrought by him. The following is an extract from a letter from John Chamberlain to Sir Dudley Carleton, ambassador at The Hague, dated London, 14th November, 1618: "The Turkish Chiaus is shortly coming for the Hagh. On Tuesday last he took leave of the king, and thanked his majesty for healing his sonne of the kinges evill; which his majesty performed with all solemnity at Whitehall on Thursday was seve-night." Charles I also enjoyed the same power, notwithstanding the public declaration by Parliament "to inform the people of the superstition of being touched by the king for the evil." When a prisoner he cured a man by simply saying, "God bless thee and grant thee thy desire," the Puritans not permitting him to touch the patient. Whereupon it is asserted by Dr. John Nicholas on his own knowledge, the blotches and humors disappeared from the patient's body and appeared in the bottle of medicine which he held in his hand. Charles's blood had the same efficacy. This sovereign substituted in some cases the giving of a piece of silver instead of the gold, which was usually presented to the patient. Badger says that this king "excelled all his predecessors in the divine gift; for it is manifest beyond all contradiction, that he not only cured by his sacred touch, both with and without gold, 231 but likewise perfectly effected the same cure by his prayer and benediction only." In his reign the gift was exercised at certain seasons of the year, Easter and Michaelmas being at first set apart for this purpose. A further regulation, which is quite suggestive, was that the patient must present a certificate to the effect that he had never before been touched for the disease.

The following incident is related concerning Charles I: "A young gentlewoman of about sixteen years of age, Elizabeth Stevens, of Winchester, came (7 October, 1648) into the presence-chamber to be touched for the evill, which she was supposed to have; and therewith one of her eyes (that namely on the left side) was so much indisposed, that by her owne and her mother's testimony (who was then also present), she had not seene with that eye of above a month before. After prayers, read by Dr. Sanderson, the maide kneeled downe among others, likewise to be touched. And his majestie touched her, and put a ribbon, with a piece of money at it, in usuall manner, about her neck. Which done, his majesty turned to the lords (viz., the duke of Richmond, the earl of Southampton, and the earl of Lindsey) to discourse with them. And the said young gentlewoman of her own accord said openly: 'Now, God be praised! I can see of this fore eye.' And afterwards declared she did see more and more by it, & could, by degrees, endure the light of the 232 candle. All which his majestie, in the presence of the said lords & many others, examined himself, & found to be true. And it hath since been discovered that, some months agone, the said young gentlewoman professed that, as soon as she was come of age sufficient, she would convey over to the king's use all her land; which to the valew of about 130 *per annum*, her father deceased had left her sole heyre unto." 171

Charles II, perhaps the most unworthy of English monarchs, was by far the busiest healer, and even while in exile in the Netherlands he retained the power to cure. In one month he touched two hundred and sixty at Breda, and Lower said: "It was not without success, since it was the experience that drew thither every day a great number of those diseased even from the most remote provinces of Germany." An official register of the persons touched was kept for every month in his reign, but about two and a half years appear to be wanting. The smallest number he touched in one year was 2,983; that was in 1669. In 1682 he touched 8,500 persons. In 1684 the throng was such that six or seven of the sick were trampled to death. The total number touched in his reign was 92,107. 172 It is instructive to note, however, that while in no other reign were so many people touched for scrofula 233 and so many cures vouched for, in no other reign did so many people die of that disease. 173

John Browne, surgeon in ordinary to his majesty and to St. Thomas's Hospital, and author of many learned works on surgery and anatomy, published accounts of sixty cures due to this monarch. He says a surgeon attested the reality of the disease before the miracle was performed, to exclude impostors who were seeking the gold, for, in addition to the regular formula, the king hung about the neck of the person touched a ribbon to which was attached a gold coin. Notwithstanding these stringent measures, some were able to impose on the king, for the coins were often found in the shops, having been sold by the recipients. Says Brand: "Barrington tells us of an old man who was a witness in a cause, and averred that when Queen Anne was at Oxford, she touched him whilst a child for the evil. Barrington, when he had finished his evidence, 'asked him whether he was really cured? upon which he answered with a significant smile, that he believed himself never to have had a complaint that deserved to be considered as the Evil, but that his parents were poor, and had no objection to the bit of gold.'" 174

While it was not unknown before, the presentation of a piece of gold was first generally introduced 234 in the reign of Henry VII. It probably descended from a practice common in the time of Edward III, whose coin, the rose-noble, is said to have been worn as an amulet to preserve from danger in battle. The angel-noble of Henry VII, valued at ten shillings, appears to have been the coin given; it was in common use and not made especially for this purpose. It had the figure of the Archangel Michael on one side and a ship in full sail on the other. Before hanging it on the patient's neck the monarch always crossed the sore with it. The outlay for gold coins presented to the afflicted on these occasions rose in some years as high as 10,000. So great was the expense that after the reign of Elizabeth the size of the coin was reduced. Touching pieces of the time of Charles II are not rare even now.

In 1684 Surgeon John Browne published a curious work entitled *Adenochoiradelogia: or an Anatomick-Chirurgical Treatise on Glandules and Strum沪 or King's Evil Swellings*. In this the author traces the gift of healing from our Saviour to the apostles, and thence by a continuous line of Christian kings and governors, and holy men, commencing with Edward the Confessor, whom he regards as the first curer of scrofula by contact or imposition of hands. After referring to his majesty in most flattering terms, he continues concerning "the admirable effects and wonderful events of his royal cure throughout all nations, where not only English, 235 Dutch, Scotch, and Irish have reaped ease and cure, but French, Germans, and all countreyes whatsoever, far and near, have abundantly seen and received the same: and none ever, hitherto, I am certain, mist thereof, unless their little faith and incredulity starved their merits, or they received his gracious hand for curing another disease, which was not really evermore allowed to be cured by him; and as bright evidences hereof, I have presumed to offer that some have immediately upon the very touch been cured; others not so easily quitted from their swellings till the favor of a second repetition thereof. Some also, losing their gold, their diseases have seized them afresh, and no sooner have these obtained a second touch, and new gold, but their diseases have been seen to vanish, as being afraid of his majesties presence; wherein also have been cured many without gold; and this may contradict such who must needs have the king give them gold as well as his touch, supposing one invalid without the gift of both. Others seem also as ready for a second change of gold as a second touch, whereas their first being newly strung upon white riband, may work as well (by their favour). The tying the Almighty to set times and particular days is also another great fault of those who can by no means be brought to believe but at Good Friday and the like seasons this healing faculty is of more vigour and efficacy than at any other time, 236 although performed by the same hand. As to the giving of gold, this only shows his majesties royal well-wishes towards the recovery of those who come thus to be healed." 175 He refers to some "Atheists, Sadducees, and ill-conditioned Pharisees" who disbelieved, and he gives the letter of one who went, a complete sceptic, to satisfy his friends, and came away cured and converted.

Browne includes the following case which seems to him conclusive: "A Nonconformist child, in Norfolk, being troubled with scrofulous swellings, the late deceased Sir Thomas Browne, of Norwich, being consulted about the same, his majesty being then at Breda or Bruges, he advised the parents of the child to have it carried over to the king (his own method being used ineffectively); the father seemed very strange at this advice, and utterly denied it, saying the touch of the king was of no greater efficacy than any other man's. The mother of the child, adhering to the doctor's advice, studied all imaginable means to have it over, and at last prevailed with her husband to let it change the air for three weeks or a month; this being granted, the friends of the child that went with it, unknown to the father, carried it to Breda, where the king touched it, and she returned home perfectly healed. The child being come to its father's house, and he 237 finding so great an alteration, inquires how his daughter arrived at this health. The friends thereof assured him, that if he would not be angry with them, they would relate the whole truth; they, having his promise for the same, assured him they had the child to be touched at Breda, whereby they apparently let him see the great benefit his child received thereby. Hereupon the father became so amazed that he threw off his Nonconformity, and expressed his thanks in this manner: 'Farewell to all dissenters, and to all nonconformists; if God can put so much virtue into the king's hand as to heal my child, I'll serve that God and that king so long as I live, with all thankfulness.'" 176 It is unfortunate that we have a change of air and food to consider in this case, else we might have a good example of a real miracle.

Friday was usually set apart in this reign as the regular day for healing, but, in addition to this, special portions of the church year were reserved for the exercise of this gift. Very careful examinations were made by the surgeons, and those who were found to be suffering from the evil were presented with a ticket by the surgeon which entitled them to receive the healing touch of the king. If the king's touch were really efficacious, one might think that the disease should have been wholly exterminated during this reign, so great were the 238 number touched. On the contrary, the deaths were more numerous, and on account of the neglect of medical and surgical means it spread very widely.

James II, it is said by Dr. Heylin, also wrought cures upon babes in their mothers' arms, and the fame of these cures was so great that the year before James was dethroned, a pauper of Portsmouth, New Hampshire, petitioned the general assembly to enable him to make the voyage to England to be healed by the royal touch. In one of his progresses James touched eight hundred persons in Chester Cathedral.

William III evidently thought of the matter as a superstition, and on one occasion he touched a patient, saying to him, "God give you better health and more sense"; notwithstanding the incredulity of the sovereign, Whiston assures us that the person was healed. With honest good sense, however, William refused to exercise the power which most of his subjects undoubtedly thought he possessed, and many protests were made, and much proof was adduced concerning "the balsamic virtues of the royal hand." This refusal to continue the practice of touching brought upon him the charge of cruelty from the parents of scrofulous children, while bigots lifted up their hands and eyes in holy horror at his impiety.

Dr. Samuel Johnson was one of the last persons to receive the imposition of royal hands; when a 239 boy of four and a half years, he was touched by Queen Anne, together with about two hundred others, on March 30, 1712. In his case at least the touch was inefficacious, for he was subject to scrofula all his life. Boswell says: 177 "His mother, yielding to the superstitious notion, which, it is wonderful to think, prevailed so long in this country, as to the virtue of the royal touch; a notion which our kings encouraged, and to which a man of such inquiry and such judgment as Carte could give credit, carried him to London, where he was actually touched by Queen Anne. Mrs. Johnson, indeed, as Mr. Hector informed me, acted by the advice of the celebrated Sir John Floyer, then a physician in Litchfield." At this time few persons but Jacobites believed in king's touch as a miracle. Dr. Daniel Turner, though, relates that several cases of scrofula which had been unsuccessfully treated by himself and Dr. Charles Bernard, sergeant-surgeon to her majesty, yielded afterwards to the efficacy of the queen's touch.

During the reign of Anne the sceptics outnumbered the believers and at her death the practice was discontinued. Among the unbelievers was the above-mentioned Dr. Charles Bernard, an account of whose conversion is given by Oldmixon as follows: "Yesterday the queen was graciously pleased to touch for the King's evil some particular persons 240 in private; and three weeks after, December 19, yesterday, about twelve at noon her majesty was pleased to touch, at St. James', about twenty persons afflicted with the King's evil. The more ludicrous sort of skeptics, in this case, asked why it was not called the queen's evil, as the chief court of justice was called the Queen's Bench. But Charles Bernard, the surgeon who had made this touching the subject of his raillery all his lifetime till he became body surgeon at court, and found it a good perquisite, solved all difficulties by telling his companions with a fleer *'Really one could not have thought it, if one had not seen it.'* A friend of mine heard him say it, and knew well his opinion of it." 178

In 1745 there was an attempted revival of the practice when Prince Charles Edward exercised this prerogative of royalty.

Henry VII was the first monarch to establish a particular ceremony to be observed at the healings. He probably derived this from an old form of exorcism used for the dispossessing of evil spirits. This was altered at various times but may still be found in the prayerbook of the reign of Queen Anne. Indeed, it was not until some time after the accession of George I that the University of Oxford ceased to reprint the office of healing, together with the Liturgy.

The routes to be travelled by royal personages 241 and the days on which the miracle was to be wrought were fixed at sittings of the Privy Council, and the clergy of all the parish churches of the realm were solemnly notified. They, in turn, informed the people, and the sufferers along the way had many days in which to cherish the expectation of healing, in itself so beneficial. The ceremony was conducted with great solemnity and pomp. It has been vividly described by Macaulay as follows: "When the appointed time came, several divines in full canonicals stood round the canopy of state. The surgeon of the royal household introduced the sick. A passage of Mark 16. was read. When the words 'They shall lay their hands on the sick and they shall recover,' had been pronounced, there was a pause and one of the sick was brought to the king. His Majesty stroked the ulcers and swellings, and hung round the patient's neck a white ribbon to which was fastened a gold coin. The other sufferers were led up in succession; and as each was touched the chaplain repeated the incantation, 'They shall lay their hands on the sick and they shall recover.' Then came the epistle, prayers, antiphonies, and a benediction."

Evelyn, in his *Diary*, gives us the form employed by Charles II in July, 1660, as follows: "His Majestie first began to touch for evil according to costume, thus — His majestie sitting under his state in the Banquetting House, the Chirurgeons cause 242 the sick to be brought or led up to the throne, where they kneeling, the King strokes their faces or cheekes with both his hands at once, at which instant a Chaplaine in his formalities says: 'He put his hands on them and he healed them.' This is sayed to every one in particular. When they have all been touched they come up againe in the same order; and the other Chaplaine kneeling, and having angel-gold strung on white ribbon on his arme, delivers them one by one to his Majestie, who puts them about the necks of the touched as they passe, whilst the first Chaplaine repeats: 'That is the true light who came into the world.' Then follows an Epistle (as at first, a Gospel) with the Liturgy, prayers for the sick with some alteration, lastly the blessing: and the Lo. Chamberlaine and Comptroller of the Household, bring a basin, ewer, and towel for his Majestie to wash." 179

The belief in the efficacy of the king's touch was general, and Lecky tells us its genuineness "was asserted by the privy council, by the bishops of two religions, by the general voice of the clergy in the palmiest days of the English Church, by the University of Oxford, and by the enthusiastic assent of the people. It survived the ages of the Reformation, of Bacon, of Milton, and of Hobbes. It was by no means extinct at the age of Locke, and would probably have lasted still longer, had 243 not the change of dynasty at the Revolution assisted the tardy scepticism." 180

In France there was the same belief in the efficacy of the royal touch. Philip I exercised the gift, but the French historians say that he was deprived of the power on account of the irregularity of his life. Laurentius reports that Francis I, when a prisoner in Spain, cured a great number of people of struma (scrofula). A paraphrase of the Latin verse which Lascaris wrote concerning this event is as follows:

> "The king applies his hand, diseases fly, And though a captive, still the powers on high Regard his touch. This striking proof is giv'n, That they who bound him are the foes of Heav'n."

Concerning the touching by the kings of France, Pettigrew says: "In the church of St. Maclou, in St. Denys, Heylin (*Cosmograph.*, p. 184) says the kings of France, with a fast of nine days and other penances, used to receive the gift of healing the king's evil with nothing but a touch." Philip de Comines states, that the king always confessed before the cure of the king's evil. Butler (*Lives of the Saints*, vol. VIII, p. 394) says, 'The French kings usually only perform this ceremony on the day they have received the holy communion.' The historians who write under the first two families of the French kings are altogether silent as to the kings' curing the evil by the touching. (*Veyrard Trav.*, 244 p. 109.) Philip of Valois is reported to have cured 1400 people afflicted with the king's evil. Of Louis XIII, it was said that he had assigned all his power to Cardinal Richelieu, except that of curing the king's evil. Carte says, some of the French writers ascribe the gift of healing to their king's devotion toward the relics of St. Marculf, in the church of Corbigny, in Champagne: to which the kings of France, immediately after their coronation at Rheims, used to go in solemn procession. A veneration was also paid to this saint in England, and a room in memory of him, in the palace of Westminster, has frequently been mentioned in the Rolls of Parliament, and which was called the Chamber of St. Marculf, being, as Carte conjectures, probably the place where the kings used to touch for the evil. This room was afterward called the Painted Chamber. The French kings practised the touch extensively. Gemelli, the traveller, states, that Louis XIV touched 1600 persons on Easter Sunday, 1686. [181] The words he used were, 'Le Roy te touche, Dieu te gu鱿sse.' Every Frenchman received fifteen sous, and every foreigner thirty. The French kings kept up the practice to 1776." [182]

"Servetus," says Hammond, "who was not of a credulous mind, says in the first edition of his *Ptolemy*, published in 1535, that he had seen the king 245 touch many persons for the disease, but he had never seen any that were cured thereby. But the last clause of this sentence excited the ire of the censor, and in the next edition, published in 1541, the words '*an sanati fuerint non vidi*' were changed to '*pluresque sanatos passim audivi*': 'I have heard of many that were cured.' Testimony in support of miracles has often been manufactured, but the natural obstinacy and truthfulness of Servetus would not admit of his giving his personal endorsement at the expense of his convictions." 183

Within the last half-century we have had an example of the value of the royal touch. When cholera was raging in Naples in 1865, and the people were rushing from the city by thousands, King Victor Emmanuel went the rounds of the hospitals in an endeavor to stimulate courage in the hearts of his people. He lingered at the bedside of the patients and spoke encouraging words to them. On a cot lay one man already marked for death. The king stepped to his side, and pressing his damp, icy hand, said, "Take courage, poor man, and try to recover soon." That evening the physicians reported a diminution of the disease in the course of the day, and the man marked for death out of danger. The king had unconsciously worked a marvellous cure. 184

246 It seems certain that there was not the efficacy in king's touch which was claimed for it, or it would not have been discontinued after having held sway for over seven hundred years. No doubt the quasi-religious character of the office of the sovereign helped much in the belief, and when such men as Charles II were able to heal, little connection between religion and healing could longer be thought possible, as far as the healing by king's touch was concerned.

The Hallowing of Cramp Rings was not unlike the king's touch. It is described by Bishop Percy in his *Northumberland Household Book*, where we have the following account: "And then the Usher to lay a Carpett for the Kinge to Creepe to the Crosse upon. An that done, there shal be a Forme sett upon the Carpett, before the Crucifix, and a Cushion laid upon it for the King to kneale upon. And the Master of the Jewell Howse ther to be ready with the Booke concerning the Hallowing of the Crampe Rings, and Amner (Almoner) muste kneele on the right hand of the King, holdinge the sayde booke. When that is done the King shall rise and goe to the Alter, wheare a Gent. Usher shall be redie with a Cushion for the Kinge to kneele upon; and then the greatest Lords that shall be ther to take the Bason with the Rings and beare them after the Kinge to offer."

In the Harleian Manuscripts there is a letter from 247 Lord Chancellor Hatton to Sir Thomas Smith, dated September 11, 158-, about a prevailing epidemic, and enclosing a ring for Queen Elizabeth to wear between her breasts, the said ring having "the virtue to expell infectious airs."

Andrew Boorde, already quoted, says: "The Kynges of England doth halowe euery yere crampe rynges, the whyche rynges, worne on ones fynger, dothe helpe them the whyche hath the crampe." 185 Also, "The kynges majesty hath a great help in this matter, in hallowynge crampe rynges, and so given without money or petition."

In the account of the ceremony given by Hospinian, he states that "it was performed upon Good Friday, and that it originated from a ring which had been brought to King Edward by some persons from Jerusalem, and one which he himself hath long before given privately to a poor petitioner who asked alms of him for the love he bore to St. John the Evangelist. This ring was preserved with great veneration in Westminster Abbey, and whoever was touched by this relic was said to be cured of the cramp or of the falling sickness." Burnet informs us that Bishop Gardiner was at Rome in 1529, and that he wrote a letter to Ann Boleyn, by which it appears that Henry VIII blessed the cramp rings before as well as after the separation from Rome, and that she sent them as great presents thither. 248 "Mr. Stephens, I send you here cramp rings for you and Mr. Gregory and Mr. Peter, praying you to distribute them as you think best. — Ann Boleyn." 186

This ceremonial was practised by previous sovereigns and discontinued by Edward VI. Queen Mary intended to revive it, and, indeed, the office for it was written out, but she does not appear to have carried her intentions into effect.

167 T. J. Pettigrew, *Superstitions Connected with the History and Practice of Medicine and Surgery*, pp. 154 f.

168 E. Berdoe, *The Origin and Growth of the Healing Art*, p. 372.

169 *Ecclesiastical History of Great Britain*, I, p. 225.

170 Quoted by Berdoe, *ibid.*, p. 371.

171 J. Brand, *Popular Antiquities*, pp. 257 f.

172 T. B. Macaulay, *History of England*, III, pp. 378 f.

173 A. D. White, *History of the Warfare of Science with Theology*, II, p. 47.

174 J. Brand, *Popular Antiquities*, III, p. 256.

175 T. J. Pettigrew, *Superstitions Connected with the History and Practice of Medicine and Surgery*, pp. 182-184.

176 Quoted by H. Tuke, *Influence of the Mind upon the Body*, pp. 359 f.

177 *Life of Johnson*, I, p. 42.

178 *History of England*, II, p. 302.

179 Vol. I, p. 323.

180 W. E. H. Lecky, *History of European Morals*, I, p. 364.

181 This was at Versailles.

182 T. J. Pettigrew, *Superstitions Connected with the History and Practice of Medicine and Surgery*, pp. 156 f.

183 W. A. Hammond, *Spiritism and Nervous Derangement*, p. 150.

184 C. L. Tuckey, *Treatment by Hypnotism and Suggestion*, p. 30.

185 E. Berdoe, *The Origin and Growth of the Healing Art*, p. 371.

186 T. J. Pettigrew, *Superstitions Connected with ... Medicine and Surgery*, p. 117.

249

CHAPTER X

MESMER AND AFTER

"Some deemed them wondrous wise, And some believed them mad." — Beattie.

"A perfect medicine for bodies that be sick Of all infirmities to be relieved; This heleth nature and prolongeth lyfe eke."

Probably no one would claim that the phenomena now grouped under the head of hypnotism were unknown before the end of the sixteenth century. They are as old as man, yes, probably older, since we know that some of the same phenomena apply to animals. But the claim might well be made that while isolated facts of this kind were well known, especially in the East, no scientific collaboration and explanation were attempted until this time.

As with all other departments of science, we may trace a gradual development. Astrology of old taught the influence of the stars upon men, which doctrine was accepted by the great physician Theophrastus Paracelsus (1490-1541). This, however, was only part of his belief: the human body was endowed with a double magnetism; one portion attracted to itself the planets and was nourished by them, the result of which was the mental powers; 250 the other portion attracted and disintegrated the elements, from which process resulted the body. He also claimed that the magnetic virtue of healthy persons attracted the enfeebled magnetism of the sick. With this theory of animal magnetism, it was only natural that he should value the use of the magnet very highly in the cure of diseases. This dual theory of magnetic cures, that of the magnetic influence of men on men and of the magnet on man, was prevalent for over a century, and found its latest exponent in Mesmer.

Following Paracelsus, Glocenius, Burgrave, Helinotius, Robert Fludd, and Kircher believed that the magnet represented the universal principle by which all natural phenomena might be explained. This principle, existing as it did in the human body, was an important factor in health and disease. The great chemist Von Helmont (1577-1644) taught more precisely that a power resided in man by which he could magnetically affect others, and thereby cure the sick who were most influenced by it. He published a work on the effects of magnetism on the human frame.

About the same time Balthazar Gracian, a Spaniard, boldly proclaimed his views. "The magnet," he said, "attracts iron; iron is found everywhere; everything, therefore, is under the influence of magnetism.... It is the same agent which gives rise to sympathy, antipathy, and the passions." Baptista 251 Porta (1543-1615), one of the originators of the weapon-salve, had also great faith in the magnet. So effective was his work on the imaginations of his patients that he was considered a magician and prohibited from practising by the court of Rome. Sebastian Wirdig, professor of medicine at the University of Rostock, in Mecklenburg, wrote a treatise on "The New Medicine of the Spirits" which he presented to the Royal Society of London in 1673. He maintained that a magnetic influence took place, not only between the celestial and terrestrial bodies, but between all living things. The whole world was under the influence of magnetism: life was preserved by magnetism, death was the consequence of magnetism.

Maxwell (1581-1640) propagated somewhat the same doctrine. He was a firm believer in sympathetic cures, and assumed a vital spirit of the universe which related all bodies. It was probably from this that Mesmer got his idea of what he called the universal fluid. It would seem, however, that Maxwell was aware of the great influence of imagination and suggestion. He said: "If you wish to work prodigies, abstract from the materiality of beings—increase the sum of spirituality in bodies—rouse the spirit from its slumbers. Unless you do one or other of these things—unless you can bind the idea, you can never perform anything good or great." About the same time, in Italy, Santanelli 252 propagated the theory of a universal fluid. Everything material possessed a radiating atmosphere which operated magnetically. He also recognized, however, the great influence of the imagination.

F. A. MESMER

About the year 1771, Father Hell, a Jesuit, and professor of astronomy at the University of Vienna, became famous through his magnetic cures, and invented steel plates of a peculiar form which he applied to the naked body as a cure for several diseases. In 1774 he communicated his system to Mesmer, the man who, more than any one else, drew the world's attention to the investigation of mental healing. Various estimates have been made of Mesmer's character and he frequently has been condemned. He was fond of display, but it is doubtful if he was more avaricious than most persons who lived before and have lived since. He was evidently honest in his scientific investigations and opinions, and this is our main concern.

Friederich Antony Mesmer (1733-1815) was born at Mersbury, in Swabia, and studied medicine at the University of Vienna. He read freely the books written by the authors already mentioned, and accepted much of their teaching. His originality consisted principally in applying to the sick this universal principle, by means of contact and passes, while his predecessors infused the vital spirit through the use of talismans and of magic boxes. He took his medical degree in 1766 and chose as the subject 253 of his inaugural dissertation "The Influence of the Planets in the Cure of Diseases." In this dissertation he maintained "that the sun, moon, and fixed stars mutually affect each other in their orbits; that they cause and direct in our earth a flux and reflux not only in the sea, but in the atmosphere, and affect in a similar manner all organized bodies through the medium of a subtle and mobile fluid, which pervades the universe, and associates all things together in mutual intercourse and harmony." This influence, he said, was particularly exercised on the nervous system, and produced two states, which he called *intension* and *remission*, which seemed to him to account for the different periodical revolutions observable in several maladies.

Eight years later he met Father Hell, and after trying some experiments with his metallic plates was astonished at his success. He continued working with Hell for some time, but they finally quarrelled, and shortly afterward he stumbled upon his theory of animal magnetism. After this he no longer used the magnet in healing. The Academy of Science at Berlin examined his claims, but their report was far from favorable or flattering. Nevertheless, writing to a friend from Vienna, he said: "I have observed that the magnetic is almost the same as the electric fluid, and that it may be propagated in the same manner, by means of intermediate 254 bodies. Steel is not the only substance adapted to this purpose. I have rendered paper, bread, wool, silk, stones, leather, glass, wood, men, and dogs—in short, every thing I touched—magnetic to such a degree, that these substances produced the same effects as the loadstone on diseased persons. I have charged jars with magnetic matter in the same way as is done with electricity." About this time he was nominated a member of the Academy of Bavaria.

Leaving Vienna and travelling through Swabia and Switzerland, he met Gassner and witnessed some of his cures. Mesmer claimed that they were performed by his newly discovered magnetism. He arrived in Paris in 1778 and found this city more receptive to his arts. He at first established himself in an humble quarter of the city and began to expound his theory. The following year he published a paper in which he summed up his claims in twenty-seven assertions to which he rigidly held through his life. His doctrines were well received, and acquired an impetus at the beginning by the conversion of one of the leading physicians of the faculty of medicine, Deslon, the Comte d'Artois' first physician.

Pupils and patients now flocked to him. The crowd was so great that Mesmer employed a *valet toucheur* to magnetize in his place. This was not sufficient; he then invented the famous *baquet*, or 255 trough, around which thirty persons might simultaneously be magnetized. This *baquet* is described as follows: "A circular, oaken case, about a foot high, was placed in the middle of a large hall, hung with thick curtains, through which only a soft and subdued light was allowed to penetrate; this was the *baquet*. At the bottom of the case, on a layer of powdered glass and iron filings, there lay full bottles, symmetrically arranged, so that the necks of all converged toward the centre; other bottles were arranged in the opposite direction, with their necks toward the circumference. All these objects were immersed in water, but this condition was not absolutely necessary, and the *baquet* might be dry. The lid was pierced with a certain number of holes, whence there issued jointed and moving iron branches, which were to be held by the patients. Absolute silence was maintained. The patients were ranged in several rows round the *baquet*, connected with each other by cords passed round their bodies, and by a second chain, formed by joining hands." 187

Additional features were provided to heighten the effect of the magnetic charm. "Richly stained glass shed a dim religious light on his spacious saloons, which were almost covered with mirrors. Orange blossoms scented all the air of his corridors; incense of the most expensive kinds burned in an 256 tique vases on his chimney-pieces; Æolian harps sighed melodious music from distant chambers; while sometimes a sweet female voice, from above or below, stole softly upon the mysterious silence that was kept in the house and insisted upon from all visitors." 188

Bailly, the historian and celebrated astronomer, an eye-witness, describes the results. "Some patients remain calm and experience nothing; others cough, spit, feel slight pain, a local or general heat, and fall into sweats; others are agitated and tormented by convulsions. These convulsions are remarkable for their number, duration, and force, and have been known to persist for more than three hours. They are characterized by involuntary, jerking movements in all the limbs, and in the whole body, by contraction of the throat, by twitchings in the hypochondriac and epigastric regions, by dimness and rolling of the eyes, by piercing cries, tears, hiccough, and immoderate laughter. They are preceded or followed by a state of languor or dreaminess, by a species of depression, and even by stupor.

"The slightest sudden noise causes the patient to start, and it has been observed that he is affected by a change of time or tune in the airs performed on the pianoforte; that his agitation is increased by a more lively movement, and that his convulsions 257 then become more violent. Patients are seen to be absorbed in the search for one another, rushing together, smiling, talking affectionately, and endeavoring to modify their crises. They are all so submissive to the magnetizer that even when they appear to be in a stupor, his voice, a glance, or a sign will rouse them from it. It is impossible not to admit, from all these results, that some great force acts upon and masters the patients, and that this force appears to reside in the magnetizer. This convulsive state is termed the *crisis*. It has been observed that many women and few men are subject to such crises; that they are only established after the lapse of two or three hours, and that when one is established, others soon and successively begin.

"When the agitation exceeds certain limits, the patients are transported into a padded room; the women's corsets are unlaced, and they may then strike their heads against the padded walls without doing themselves any injury." Notwithstanding these means, thousands were healed of their diseases.

"It is impossible," says Baron Dupotet, "to conceive the sensation which Mesmer's experiments created in Paris. No theological controversy, in the earlier ages of the Catholic Church, was ever conducted with greater bitterness." He was called a quack, a fool, and a demon, while his friends were as extravagant in his praise as his foes in their 258 censure. After this great excitement, his life may largely be summed up in his challenges to different societies, the appointment of commissions, their examinations, and their reports.

On the advice of Deslon he challenged the Faculty of Medicine, proposing to select twenty-four patients, of whom twelve should be treated according to the old and approved methods and twelve magnetically, the cures to prove the efficacy of the treatment. The faculty declined to accept the conditions. Deslon asked his colleagues on the faculty to summon a general meeting to examine the matter. Through the influence of M. de Vauzesmes, the meeting was very hostile to him, and he was condemned and threatened with having his name removed from the list of licensed physicians if he did not reform.

Mesmer now wrote to Marie Antoinette suggesting that the government furnish him with houses, land, and a princely fortune to enable him to carry on his experiments untroubled. The government finally offered him a pension of 20,000 francs, and the cross of the order of St. Michael, if he had made any discovery in medicine, and would communicate it to the physicians whom the king should name. Mesmer refused the conditions and left Paris.

Deslon was then called upon to renounce animal magnetism, but instead, invited investigation. In 1784 the government appointed a commission to 259 inquire into magnetism, consisting of members from the Faculty of Medicine and the Academy of Sciences. Franklin, Lavoisier, and Bailly were members, the last named being chosen reporter. Another commission, composed of members of the Royal Society of Medicine, was charged to make a distinct report on the same subject. After experimenting for five months the first commission presented two reports, one public and the other secret, neither of which was favorable. The Royal Society of Medicine presented its report a few days later, and agreed with the first commission with the exception of one member, Laurent de Jussieu, who dissented and published a separate report of a more favorable nature. The gist of the commissions' reports was that imagination, not magnetism, accounted for the results.

Soon after the commissions started their investigations, Mesmer returned to Paris at the invitation of his friends, who proposed to open a subscription for him for 10,000 louis. Immediately it was over-subscribed by over 140,000 francs. He came with the understanding that he was to give lectures and to reveal the secret of animal magnetism. The lectures and secrets were not satisfactory. After the commission reported he left Paris and returned to his own country where he was little heard of during the remainder of his life which ended in 1815.

Whatever may be said of Mesmer, there seems to 260 be no doubt about the honesty of his most famous pupil, the Marquis de Puys騚r, and to him we are indebted for a forward step. When Mesmer left Paris, the marquis retired to his estate near Soissons, and employed his leisure in magnetizing peasants. He magnetized his gardener, a young man named Victor, and after experimenting upon him claimed that during the state Victor exhibited marvellous telepathic and clairvoyant phenomena. Unable to attend all the patients who applied to him, he followed Mesmer's plan of magnetizing a tree. An elm on the village green was chosen, and round this patients gathered on stone benches as around Mesmer's *baquet*.

Following Mesmer's theories very closely, the contribution he made was in the recognition of the likeness between the magnetized state and that of somnambulism, so that he designated this state "artificial somnambulism." He also modified the conditions of inducing this state, and simple contact or spoken orders were substituted for the use of the *baquet*. The effect was therefore milder, and instead of hysteria and violent crises accompanied by sobs, cries, and contractions, there was peaceful slumber. He recognized the rapport between operator and subject, and amnesia on awaking, and other phenomena now well known, but he still held to the Mesmeric theory of the existence of a universal fluid which saturated all bodies, especially the human 261 body. It was electric in nature, and man could display and diffuse this electric fluid at will.

While the Marquis de Puys驃r was using the elm tree near Soissons, the Chevalier de Barbarin was successfully magnetizing people without paraphernalia. He sat by the bedside of the sick and prayed that they might be magnetized; his efforts were successful. He maintained that the effect of animal magnetism was produced by the mere effort of one human soul acting upon another; and when the connection had once been established the magnetizer could communicate his influence to the subject regardless of the distance which separated them. Numerous persons adopted this view, calling themselves Barbarinists after their leader. In Sweden and Germany they were called *spiritualists*, to distinguish them from the followers of de Puys驃r, who were called *experimentalists*.

About the same time a doctor of Lyons, P鴉tin, experimented with magnetism. After his death a paper written by him was published describing catalepsy and sense transference. Numerous magnetic societies were founded in the principal cities of France. In Strasburg, the Society of Harmony, consisting of more than one hundred and fifty members, published for years the result of their work. The disturbance incident to the Revolution and the wars of the Empire which followed repressed the investigations of magnetism in France for several years.

262 In England the advent of magnetism seems to have taken place about 1788. In that year one Dr. Mainandus, who had been a pupil first of Mesmer and later of Deslon, arrived in Bristol and gave public lectures on the subject. People of rank and fortune soon came from different cities to be magnetized or to place themselves under his tuition. He afterward established himself in London where he was equally successful in attracting and curing people. So much curiosity was excited by the subject that, about the same time, a man named Holloway gave a course of lectures on animal magnetism in London. Large crowds gathered to hear him at the rate of five guineas for each pupil.

Loutherbourg, the painter, and his wife entered upon a similar work. "Such was the infatuation of the people to be witnesses of their strange manipulations," says Mackay, "that at times upwards of three thousand persons crowded round their house at Hammersmith, unable to gain admission. The tickets sold at prices ranging from one to three guineas." Loutherbourg later became a divine healer. From 1789 to 1798 magnetism attracted little or no attention in England. At the latter date a Connecticut Yankee, Benjamin Douglas Perkins, invented "metallic tractors." The Society of Friends built a hospital called the "Perkinean Institute" where all comers might be magnetized free of cost.

263 About 1786 animal magnetism appeared in two different places in Germany — on the upper Rhine and in Bremen. At this time Lavater paid a visit to Bremen and exhibited the magnetizing process to several doctors. Bremen was for a long time a focus of the new doctrine, and thereby was brought into bad repute. About the same time the doctrine spread from Strasburg over the Rhine provinces. Among those active in experiments were B□□ann of Carlsruhe, Gmelin of Heilbronn, and Pezold of Dresden. Soon it spread all over Germany. In 1789 Selle of Berlin brought forward a series of experiments made at the Charit頼Hospital), in which he confirmed some of the alleged phenomena but excluded the supernormal.

Notwithstanding the early dislike, animal magnetism flourished in Germany during the first twenty years of the nineteenth century. In 1812 the Prussian government sent Wolfart to Mesmer at Frauenfeld, to acquaint himself with the subject. He returned to Berlin an ardent adherent of Mesmer and introduced magnetism into the hospital treatment. From this magnetism flourished so much in Berlin that, as Wurm relates, the Berlin physicians placed a monument on the grave of Mesmer at M · ·urg, and theological candidates received instruction in physiology, pathology, and the treatment of sickness by vital magnetism. The well-known physician Koreff was interested in magnetism and often 264 made use of it for healing purposes. Magnetism was introduced everywhere, especially in Russia and Denmark. In Switzerland and Italy it was at first received with less sympathy, and in 1815 the exercise of magnetism was forbidden in the whole of Austria.

In 1813 the naturalist Deleuze published a book entitled *Histoire critique du magn鳩sme animal*. Like his predecessors, he was chiefly interested in the therapeutic value of magnetism, and insisted that faith was necessary for effective treatment. On account of this condition any demonstration was impossible. He still held to the idea of a pervading fluid and maintained that the depth of the magnetic sleep depended upon the amount of the magnetic charge. Shortly after the appearance of Deleuze's book, interest in animal magnetism increased, and several journals dealing exclusively with the subject were started.

With the death of Mesmer in 1815 ended the first period in the history of the phenomena known as animal magnetism. Up to this time the generally accepted theory was that of a vital fluid which permeated every thing and person and through which one person influenced another. The second period extended from 1815-1841 when Braid discovered and formulated the method of operation. The third period reached from 1841-1887 during which there was careful and scientific study of the whole 265 subject, and hypnotism came into repute as a healing measure. I am inclined to posit a fourth period, 1887 to the present time, for Myers' hypothesis of a subliminal self, or the theory of the subconsciousness, has made a great difference in the theory of hypnotism.

The second period began when Abbe Faria in 1814-15 came from India to Paris and gave public exhibitions, publishing the results of some of his experiments. He seated his subjects in an arm-chair, with eyes closed, and then cried out in a loud commanding voice, "Sleep." He used no manipulations and had no *baquet*, but he boasted of having produced five thousand somnambulists by this method. He opined that the state was caused by no unknown force, but rested in the subject himself. He agreed with the present generally accepted theory that all is subjective.

Following Faria, Bertrand and Noizet paved the way for the doctrine of suggestion notwithstanding their inclination toward animal magnetism. Experiments were performed at the H□□-Dieu in 1820 but later were prohibited. Through the influence of Foissac in 1826 the Academy of Medicine appointed a committee to examine the subject, and in 1831 a report acknowledging the genuineness of the phenomena was made, and therapeutic effects were frankly admitted. In 1837 the Academy appointed another commission to exam-

181

ine still 266 further, for the members as a whole were not convinced. The report of this commission was largely negative.

After this the younger Burdin, a member of the Academy, proposed to award from his own purse a prize of 3,000 francs to any person who could read a given writing without the aid of his eyes, and in the dark. The existence of animal magnetism must stand or fall on this test. That was the difficulty during this period: the whole dispute was waged about, and experiments consisted in tests of, clairvoyance, transposition of the sense of sight, and other mystical phenomena, instead of dealing with the state as such. This, of course, made the struggle much easier for the opponents of mesmerism, but was largely the fault of the magnetizers. The Burdin prize was not awarded, and in 1840 Double proposed that the Academy should henceforth pay no further attention to animal magnetism, but treat the subject as definitely closed. This was certainly unfair and unscientific, but was the attitude assumed.

At the beginning of this period another series of tests was being performed in Germany, but after 1820 the belief in magnetism declined more and more. It flourished longest in Bremen and in Hamburg where Siemers was its advocate. From 1830-1840 Hensler and Ennemoser were the chief exponents in Bavaria. As the scientific investiga 267 tors withdrew from the study, the charlatans and frauds entered the field, and the marvellous and occult were emphasized, so that in 1840 little general attention was paid to the subject.

Notwithstanding the efforts of the London physicians Elliotson and Ashburner, magnetism could obtain little footing in England during this period. Numerous investigations were made, however, and several publications were sent forth. Townshend, Scoresby, and Lee are names prominent in the study of the subject in England at this time. In the next period, though, an Englishman gives the impetus necessary for the successful pursuit of the study.

In 1841 the French magnetizer, La Fontaine, gave some public exhibitions in Manchester which attracted the attention of a physician by the name of James Braid. Through the aid rendered by Braid, animal magnetism blossomed into a science. He directed the subject into its proper field: he eschewed the occult and mysterious, and emphasized observation and experiment. It was Braid who gave us the word "hypnotism." At first a sceptic, he began experimenting and proved that fixity of gaze had in some way such an influence on the nervous system of the subject that he went off into a sleep. He therefore opined that the transmission of a fluid by the operator had no part in the matter.

He further showed that an assumed attitude 268 changed the subject's sentiments in harmony with the attitude, and that the degree of sleep varied with different persons, and with the same person at different times. He also noted the acuteness of the senses during hypnosis, and that verbal suggestion would produce hallucinations, emotions, paralysis, etc. Therapeutics was a subject in which he was naturally interested, and his experiments on different diseases were frequent and valuable. Braid made some mistakes, as was natural, but his discoveries covered the field so well and his ideas were so sound that too much credit cannot be ascribed to him. At first he thought hypnotism (Braidism) was identical with animal magnetism, but later made the mistake of considering it analogous, and the two flourished side by side and independently.

Animal magnetism was first introduced into America in 1836 by Mr. Charles Poyan, a French gentleman. A few years later a certain Dr. Collyer lectured upon it in New England. New Orleans was, however, for a long time its chief centre. In 1848 Grimes, working independently, appears to have arrived at about the same conclusions as Braid. He showed that most of the hypnotic phenomena could be produced in the waking state in some subjects, by means of verbal suggestion. The phenomena were known under the name of electro-biology. In 1850 Darling went to England and introduced electro-biology, but it was soon identified 269 with Braidism, and in 1853 Durand de Gros, who wrote under the pseudonym of Philips, exhibited the phenomena of electro-biology in several countries, but aroused little attention.

Azam of Bordeaux and Broca of Paris made some experiments following Braid's method, and several times performed some painless operations by this means. They were followed by numerous others in all European countries and in America. In fact, the interest in the subject became general, and as more was known about it, fewer objections were heard. Societies were formed for the study of hypnotism, publications were started devoting all their space to the exposition and discussion of it, and as this third period advanced, its scientific value was more and more recognized from the standpoints of psychology, pathology, and therapeutics.

In a brief r鳾m頬ike this it would be impossible to name even the chief experimenters in the different countries who contributed to this period, but some names stand out so prominently that they should be emphasized, for they must be reckoned in importance with Braid's. Liebeault, whose book, *Du Sommeil, etc.*, was published in 1866, has been called the founder of the therapeutics of suggestion. While suggestion in both waking and hypnotic states had been applied long before Liebeault's day, it was he who first fully and methodically recognized its value. We are also indebted to him for stimulating 270 in the study of hypnosis Bernheim and other prominent investigators. Liebeault at the head of the School of Nancy was not less known than Charcot at the Salp瑩谤.

Charcot was indefatigable in his researches, but was led away in his conclusions by artifacts. For example: three states were produced in the hypnotic subject which Charcot considered to be symptomatic and characteristic. They were catalepsy, lethargy, and somnambulism. Certain physical excitations, such as rubbing the scalp or exposing the eyes to a bright light, were thought to be all that was necessary to change the subject from one stage to another. It has since been shown that not only were the states of catalepsy, lethargy, and somnambulism produced by suggestion, but the physical stimuli were simply suggestions and signs by which the subject knew that a particular change was expected, and, in harmony with hypnotic action, the expected change came about. Not only did Charcot make this mistake, but some of his followers of the Salp瑩谤 School continued to be deceived for years afterward.

Hardly a conclusion of Charcot's remains to-day, and yet so earnest was he in his investigations and so untiring in his experiments, that many of his facts contributed much to our knowledge of the subject even if his theories have been rejected. Binet, F鯨, and other followers of his have contrib 271 uted much to the science and literature of the subject. The latter half of this period is not unknown to us to-day, and as the names connected with it are familiar, it remains for me to mention but one more name, that of the one who ushered in the fourth period, F. W. H. Myers.

From its beginning Myers was prominently connected with the Society for Psychical Research and occupied the offices of president and secretary. He held the latter position at the time of his death in 1901. In 1887 he formulated his theory of the subliminal self or subliminal consciousness, a theory which has come to be more and more accepted, and the value of which has received increasing appreciation. It has been known as the "subconscious self" or the "subconsciousness" probably more than by Myers's original title; and his theory has been modified by some subtractions and additions, but it is generally accepted to-day and its exposition has helped solve many problems in abnormal psychology. In no department has it contributed more than in that of hypnotism, for by it this state has been partially explained.

For a number of years Charcot and his followers put forward a physiological theory of hypnotism which waged war with that of the Nancy School, under Liebeault, but even before Charcot's death he recognized the validity of the Nancy claims while still clinging to his own. Few if any espouse Charcot's 272 claims to-day. The general psychological theory of Nancy, which bases the results on suggestion, is that currently accepted, while a theory not very different from that of animal magnetism has been held by some of those who accepted the spiritualistic hypothesis, notably among whom was Myers.

Hypnotism to-day is recognized as the product of a long line of erroneous theory and zigzag development, but the wheat has largely been sifted and the chaff thrown to the winds of antiquity. Its therapeutic and psychological value is duly recognized by science to-day. 189

187 Binet and F皖, *Animal Magnetism*, p. 8.

188 C. Mackay, *Extraordinary Popular Delusions*, I, p. 278.

189 Many works and encyclopedic articles on hypnotism have been consulted in the preparation of this chapter, all of which were valuable, and few of which stand out prominently.

CHAPTER XI

THE HEALERS OF THE NINETEENTH CENTURY

"Medical cannot be separated from moral science, without reciprocal and essential mutilation." — Reid.

"Man is a dupeable animal. Quacks in medicine, quacks in religion, and quacks in politics know this, and act upon that
knowledge. There is scarcely anyone who may not, like a trout, be
taken by tickling." — Southey.

"Canst thou minister to a mind diseas'd, Pluck from the memory a
rooted sorrow, Raze out the written troubles of the brain, And with
some sweet oblivious antidote Cleanse the stuff'd bosom of that
perilous stuff Which weighs upon the heart?" — Shakespeare.
"Joy, temperance, and repose, Slam the door on the doctor's nose." —
Longfellow.

There seems to have been a great development of mental healing
during the nineteenth century. The healing by shrines, relics, and
charms diminished in the latter part of the century on account of the
lessening of superstition and the better understanding of mental
laws, but additional work has thereby been laid upon the healers.
The development of hypnotism and the exposition of the laws underlying it, the collection and publication of cases of cures by mental means, the lessening of faith in noxious doses of drugs, the increase of nervous diseases which are most easily helped by suggestive 274 therapeutics, the attempted duplication of apostolic gifts on
the part of some sects and the general reaction against the material-
ism of the early part of the century as shown in the great revival of
psychical study and research have all been factors in the demand
for mental medicine.

The healers have been of various kinds. Having already dealt
with the mesmerizers and hypnotizers, we shall now look only at
the classes of independent and generally less scientific investigators
and experimenters. Some have not been regular healers but healed
only incidentally, as, *e. g.*, the revivalists; some have followed James

5:14 f. in anointing with oil and praying — of these and others, some have had institutions for housing the patients; some have been peripatetic healers; some have simply used prayer; some have established their systems on metaphysical bases and been the founders of sects; some have combined the results of scientific investigations in an endeavor to help mankind. Many of these have simply followed the ways of their predecessors of former centuries, but a few started on new lines of procedure. Whatever the method, they have all, consciously or unconsciously, depended upon the influence of the patient's mind over his own body, and the now better understood laws of suggestion.

The revivals were eighteenth and nineteenth century phenomena, and in discussing the part which 275 their leaders have taken in healing we may well include the experience of Wesley. As a mere incident in his revival work, John Wesley (1703-1791), the great founder of Methodism, appeared in the rather unenviable role of exorcist. It is to his credit that he was not led away from his primary purpose by this experience, but returned to his preaching without any effort to add healing to his gifts. The account of his encounter with the demons can best be given by quoting his own words, as found in his Journal.

"October 25 [1739]. I was sent for to one in Bristol who was taken ill the evening before. She lay on the ground furiously gnashing her teeth and after a while roared aloud. It was not easy for three or four persons to hold her, especially when the name of Jesus was named. We prayed. The violence of her symptoms ceased, though without a complete deliverance." Wesley was sent for later in the day. "She began screaming before I came into the room, then broke out into a horrid laughter, mixed with blasphemy, grievous to hear. One who from many circumstances apprehended a preternatural agent to be concerned in this, asking, 'How didst thou dare to enter into a Christian?' was answered, 'She is not a Christian, she is mine.' Then another question, 'Dost thou not tremble at the name of Jesus?' No words followed, but she shrunk back and trembled exceedingly. 'Art thou 276 not increasing thy own damnation?' It was faintly answered, 'Ay! Ay!' which was followed by fresh cursing and blasphemy ... with spitting, and all the expressions of strong aversion." Two days later Wesley called and prayed with her again, when "All

187

her pangs ceased in a moment, she was filled with peace, and knew that the son of wickedness was departed from her." On October 28 he exorcised two more demons whom he had evidently (unconsciously) been the means of producing in two neurotic girls. He had a few other experiences in healing, but always in an incidental way.

JOHN ALEXANDER DOWIE

Charles G. Finney (1792-1875) had at least one experience as a healer. During revival services at Antwerp, N. Y., in 1824, two insane women were cured, but Finney was directly concerned in the restoration of only one of them. Of this he gives an account in his memoirs. "There were two very striking cases of instantaneous recovery from insanity during this revival. As I went into meeting in the afternoon of one Sabbath, I saw several ladies sitting in a pew, with a woman dressed in black who seemed to be in great distress of mind; and they were partly holding her, and preventing her from going out. As I came in, one of the ladies came to me and told me she was an insane woman.... I said a few words to her; but she replied that she must go; that she could not hear any praying, or preaching, or singing; that hell was her portion, 277 and she could not endure anything that made her think of heaven. I cautioned the ladies, privately, to keep her in her seat, if they could, without her disturbing the meeting. I then went into the pulpit and read a hymn. As soon as the singing began, she struggled hard to get out. But the ladies obstructed her passage; and kindly but persistently prevented her escape.... As I proceeded ... all at once she startled the congregation by uttering a loud shriek. She then cast herself almost from her seat, held her head very low, and I could see that she 'trembled very exceedingly.'... As I proceeded she began to look up again, and soon sat upright, with face wonderfully changed, indicating triumphant joy and peace.... She glorified God and rejoiced with amazing triumph. About two years after, I met with her, and found her still full of joy and peace." 190

The so-called "Mountain Evangelist," George O. Barnes, who was born in 1827, added healing to his other revival efforts. After leaving the Presbyterian Church he did his work mostly in Kentucky as an independent minister, and there anointed with oil according to James 5:14 f. In his records little is said about the cures, but the daily number of anointings is given, amounting to at least five thousand in all. He believed that the devil, not God, sends sickness: God is the great healer. The 278 anointing was simply a matter of faith. His formula varied and was very simple, as *e. g.*, "Dear daughter, in Jesus's precious name I anoint thee with this oil of healing for thy maladies. Oh, go on thy way rejoicing. Be of good cheer. He is the great healer. He will make thee whole. He hath commanded it. Lean thy whole weight on Him." 191 His views may be judged by the following extract from a sermon of his on "Our Healer": "Oh, the hospitals and drug-stores, the bitter doses, the pains and racks, the tortures — great God, may this people believe to-day that thou hast nothing to do with this, that all came in with sin, and the devil manages it all; and wherever we are afflicted God stands by wringing His hands, and saying, '...Return to me, O backsliding children. Come back to me, and I will keep the devil off of you.'" 192 I take also some extracts from his daily record.

"July 19 [1881]. John and I took a long walk.... I shall not repeat the experiment, for I got many chiggers on me, which are tormenting me from head to foot while I write, I think because I trusted the pennyroyal to keep them off me instead of the Lord. It was not wilful, but a slip of forgetfulness, yet a door wide enough for Satan to enter a little bit. Now, instead of trying pennyroyal to get me rid of them, I will trust the Lord only.

279

"July 20. The chiggers gave exquisite torment. I shall never trust in pennyroyal again.

"July 21. Satan tried to get me wavering on the eye question, but the dear Lord set me up more firmly than ever.

"July 24. We have gotten into a little trouble by carelessly trying to help the dear Lord take care of his little organ. A key was silent, and yesterday Marie tried to remedy it. There was a good deal of taking out of keys, and dusting — result, two keys silent now, and one that won't be silent, but goes on in a bass wail through every song. So much for meddling with the dear Lord's work. We trust Him, when the lesson is learned, to set the little machine all right again.... The dear Lord cured the little organ this afternoon while we were at dinner; at least it was all right, as Marie with a happy smile informed me before she began to sing the first song. I gave thanks for it in the opening prayer, and then told the people all about it.

"July 27. Satan is not a little busy with me, injecting doubts as to the right to trust for eyes. Faith still quenches all his fiery darts, although it sorely tries me to be thus inactive in these long summer days, without reading my beautiful edition of Young's Concordance, useless at the bottom of my trunk. My Revised New Testament I can only get at through others." 193

Leaving now the revivalists, let us take up the cases of others not revivalists who used anointing for healing. In her native hamlet of Maennedorf, Switzerland, Dorothea Trudel (1813-1862), the de 280 scendant of some generations of faith healers, cured many. Soon people began to come to her from near and far and, finally, at the solicitation of a "patient" of rank, she purchased a home where the afflicted could be near her. In 1856 the health authorities interfered. She was fined; an appeal was taken and, finally, she was permitted to carry on her work in connection with the home under some formal restrictions. During the course of the trial some authenticated cases of cure were produced: "one stiff knee, pronounced incurable by the best surgeons of France, Germany, and Switzerland; a leading physician testified to the recovery of a hopeless patient of his own; a burned foot, which was about to be amputated to prevent impending death, was healed without means. The evidence was incontrovertible, and the cases numerous. The cure was often contemporaneous with the confession of Christ by the unbelieving patient; but duration of the sickness varied with each case. Lunatics were commonly sent forth cured in a brief while." Nothing miraculous was claimed and no war was waged against physicians. It was not asserted that a cure was infallibly made, but it was pointed out as a simpler and more direct method. The means employed were gentleness, discipline, Bible reading, prayer, and anointing. After the death of Dorothea the home continued under the supervision of Mr. Samuel Zeller.

281 Charles Cullis (1833-1892), a young physician of Boston, suffered a crushing bereavement in the death of his wife shortly after their marriage, and then vowed to devote his life to charity. Inspired by Mller's *Life of Trust* he established a number of charitable institutions, relying on prayer and faith for their support. Some of these institutions were for the cure of the sick, and in connection with these, and otherwise, Dr. Cullis anointed and prayed with all who came to him. Every summer a camp-meeting was held at Old Orchard Beach, Maine, where the large collections gathered were the subject of annual comment. He was followed in his work by Rev. A. B. Simpson, of New York, who now conducts it. The latter was formerly a Presbyterian minister but is now an independent. He still heals and takes up collections. From the efforts of Cullis and

Simpson have come the Christian and Missionary Alliance and other similar organizations with Pentecost as the text and apostolic gifts as the much-sought-after prize. The proof of success is found in healing, speaking with tongues, trances, visions, and other abnormal phenomena.

The "Holy Ghost and Us" movement, with headquarters at Shiloh, Maine, was an outgrowth of the Christian and Missionary Alliance propaganda. Rev. F. W. Sanford (1863-) was born on Bowdoinham Ridge, Maine. He graduated at Bates Col 282 lege in 1886 and attended Cobb Divinity School for a short time. His ordination took place in 1887, after which he held two pastorates of three years each, presumedly in Free Baptist churches. In 1891, while attending meetings at Old Orchard, he was inspired to start "a movement on strictly apostolic lines, which was to sweep the entire globe." He started on this new work early in 1893 with Shiloh, Maine, as the centre. Relying on faith alone, several buildings were erected and paid for, among which is Bethesda—a Home of Healing: "For those who believe God told the truth when He said, 'The prayer of Faith shall save the sick.'" In an account of the healing we read: "We have seen ... in at least one case, the restoration of the dead to life." Quite a following embraced the doctrine at one time, but lately there has been a considerable decline.

An institution for faith healing was established in the north of London by Rev. W. E. Boardman (1810-1886). He called it "Bethshan" or the "Nursery of Faith" and refused to permit it to be called a hospital. The usual method of treatment was by anointing with oil and prayer, but it was claimed that many also were healed by correspondence. The results professed were very extravagant, among the cases being cancer, paralysis, advanced consumption, chronic rheumatism, and lameness of different kinds. As a proof of the cure of the last 283 named affliction, numerous canes and crutches left behind by the healed were on exhibition. 194

It is said that Lord Radstock practised healing through anointing in Australia about the same time.

There have been a number of prominent healers who have used prayer, and perhaps the laying on of hands, as the means for healing, and have usually eschewed anointing. Among these was Prince

Hohenlohe (1794-1849). His was probably the greatest name in mental healing in the nineteenth century. He was born in Waldenburg and educated at several institutions. He was ordained priest in 1815 and officiated at Olmtz, Munich, and other places. In 1820 he met a peasant, Martin Michel, who had performed some wonderful cures, and in connection with him effected a so-called miraculous cure on a princess of Schwarzenberg who had been for some years a paralytic. 195 From this experience he became enthusiastic in healing, and he acquired such a fame as a performer of miraculous cures that multitudes flocked from different countries to receive the benefit of his supposed supernatural gifts. In one year (1848-49) there were eighteen thousand people who obtained access to him. His name and his titles probably had not a little to do with his wide influence. They were 284 Alexander Leopold Franz Emmerich, Prince of Hohenlohe-Waldenburg-Schillingsfrst, Archbishop and Grand Provost of Grosswardein, Hungary, and Abbot of St. Michael's at Gaborjan.

The testimony concerning his cures is from reliable witnesses. Notice the letter written by the ex-King of Bavaria to Count von Sinsheim, describing his own case:

My dear Count:

There are still miracles. The ten last days of the last month, the people of Wrzburg might believe themselves in the times of the Apostles. The deaf heard, the blind saw, the lame freely walked, not by the aid of art, but by a few short prayers, and by the invocation of the name of Jesus.... On the evening of the 28th, the number of persons cured, of both sexes, and of every age, amounted to more than twenty. These were of all classes of the people, from the humblest to a prince of the blood, who, without any exterior means, recovered, on the 27th at noon, the hearing which he had lost from his infancy. This cure was effected by a prayer made for him during some minutes, by a priest who is scarcely more than twenty-seven years of age — the Prince Hohenlohe. Although I do not hear so well as the majority of the persons who are about me, there is no comparison between my actual state and that which it was before. Besides, I perceive daily that I hear more clearly.... My hearing, at present, is very sensitive. Last Friday, the music of the troop which defiled in the square in front of the palace, struck my tympanum so strongly, that for the first time, I was obliged to close the window of my cabinet.

285 The inhabitants of Wrzburg have testified, by the most lively and sincere acclamations, the pleasure which my cure has given them. You are at liberty to communicate my letter, and to allow any one who wishes, to take a copy of it.

Bruckenau, *July 3d, 1822*. Louis, *Prince Royal.*

Professor Onymus, of the University of Wrzburg, reported a number of cases cured by Prince Hohenlohe, which he himself witnessed. He gives the following:

"Captain Ruthlein, an old gentleman of Thundorf, 70 years of age, who had long been pronounced incurable of paralysis, which kept his hand clenched, and who had not left his room for many years, has been perfectly cured. Eight days after his cure he paid me a visit, rejoicing in the happiness of being able to walk freely.

"A man, of about 50, named Bramdel, caused himself to be carried by six men from Carlstadt to the Court at Stauffenburg. His arms and legs were utterly paralyzed, hanging like those of a dead man, and his face was of a corpse-like pallor. On the prayer of the Prince he was instantly cured, rose to his feet, and walked perfectly, to the profound astonishment of all present.

"A student of Burglauer, near Murmerstadt, had lost for two years the use of his legs; he was brought in a carriage, and though he was only partially relieved by the first and second prayer of the Prince, at the third he found himself perfectly well.

"These cures are real and they are permanent. If any one would excite doubts of the genuineness of the cases operated by Prince Hohenlohe, it is 286 only necessary to come hither and consult a thousand other eye and ear witnesses like myself. Every one is ready to give all possible information about them." 196

The Mormons, under the leadership of Joseph Smith, Jr. (1805-1844), were healing the sick about the time that Prince Hohenlohe was performing his miracles on the other side of the water. Smith was born in Sharon, Vermont. The Mormon Church (The Church of

Jesus Christ of Latter Day Saints) was founded in 1830 in Palmyra, New York, and moved from there to Kirkland, Ohio; Independence, Missouri; Nauvoo, Illinois; and thence to Utah. Smith was successively first elder, prophet, seer, and revelator. The year the church was founded Smith began his healing career as an exorcist, casting the devil out of Newel Knight in Colesville, New York. Following this, there was a firm belief in demoniacal possession, and exorcism was practised by both Smith and his followers, principally by means of command. This exorcism led up to faith healing.

Smith's maternal uncle, Jason Mack, was a firm believer in healing by prayer and practised it; later, the Oneida Community of Perfectionists in western New York cured by faith; both of these facts would be known to the founder of Mormonism. After adopting faith healing he soon became proficient in 287 the art. Numerous well-attested cures were performed by Smith and his followers in other places. Elder Richards advertised in England "Bones set through Faith in Christ," and Elder Phillips made the additional statement that "while commanding the bones, they came together, making a noise like the crushing of an old basket." All forms of disease were treated, but not always successfully, as may be inferred from Smith's own words: "The cholera burst forth among us, even those on guard fell to the earth with their guns in their hands.... At the commencement I attempted to lay on hands for their recovery, but I quickly learned by painful experience, that when the great Jehovah decrees destruction upon any people, makes known His determination, man must not attempt to stay his hand." The means employed varied, but included at different times prayer, command, laying on of hands, consecrated handkerchiefs and other cloths, baptism, and infrequently anointing. 197

Crossing the ocean again, we find Johann Christolph Blumhardt (1805-1880) performing wonderful acts of healing. He assumed his first independent charge in 1838 when he became pastor of the village church at Moettlinger, Wurtemberg. He was known afterward as Pastor Blumhardt. Among his parishioners was Gottliebin Ditters, generally thought to be possessed by an evil spirit. After two years 288 prayer and care for this woman, he saw her restored to peace of mind. This was the beginning of a life of faith in the efficacy of prayer for healing. After the restoration of Gottliebin a spontaneous and entirely unexpected revival took place in Moettlinger. Multitudes came from afar to hear this sincere man preach his simple sermons, and in many cases bodily disease left those who confessed and upon whom Blumhardt laid his hands. It became noised about that those who repented, with whom the pastor prayed and upon whom he laid his hands, would be healed. "One morning a mother rushed to his house, saying that she had by an accident scalded her child with boiling soup. The infant was found screaming with agony. He took the child in his arms, prayed over it, and it grew quiet. It had no further pain, and the effects of the scalding were quickly gone. Another child was nearly blind with disease. A neighboring pastor, when consulted, said to the parents: 'If you believe Jesus can and will heal your child, by all means go to Blumhardt, but if you have not got the faith, don't do it on any account; let an operation be performed.' 'Well, we have faith,' they said, and went to Blumhardt. Three days after it was perfectly well." These events could not fail to attract attention, and miracles or healings from his prayers were of constant occurrence. In 1852 Blumhardt moved to Boll, Wurtemberg, and until his death he continued his healing. He did not despise human means of healing, but he stoutly held that Jesus would answer the prayer of faith uttered for and by the sick.

About the middle of the century Father Mathew (1790-1856) attracted a large number of persons who were in need of healing. He was best known as the famous apostle of temperance, and was to Ireland in the nineteenth century what Wesley was to England in the eighteenth. He also travelled over England and Scotland and spent two years in America. In one period of nine months he induced two hundred thousand persons to take the temperance pledge. Among other things he cured blindness, lameness, paralysis, hysteria, headache, and lunacy. After his death the same diseases which he had cured during his lifetime were just as effectively relieved by visiting the good father's tomb, in the firm belief that a miracle would be performed. From the following cure, his first one, it will be seen that the discovery of his healing power was rather accidental.

"A young lady, of position and intelligence, was for years the victim of the most violent headaches, which assumed a chronic character. Eminent advice was had but in vain; the malady became more intense, the agony more excruciating. Starting up one day from the sofa on which she lay in a delirium of pain, she exclaimed—'I cannot endure this torture any longer; I will go and see what Father Mathew 290 can do for me.' She immediately proceeded to Lehanagh, where Father Mathew was then sick and feeble. Flinging herself on her knees before him she besought his prayers and blessing. In fact, stung by intolerable suffering she asked him to cure her. 'My dear child, you ask me what no mortal has power to do. The power to cure rests alone with God. I have no such power.' 'Then bless me, and pray for me—place your hand on my head,' implored the afflicted lady. 'I cannot refuse to pray for you, or to bless you,' said Father Mathew, who did pray for and bless her, and place his hand upon her poor throbbing brow. Was it faith?—was it magnetism?—was it the force of imagination exerted wonderfully? I shall not venture to pronounce what it was; but that lady returned to her home perfectly cured of her distressing malady. More than that—cured completely, from that moment, forward." 198

About the same time, Mrs. Elizabeth Mix, a negro woman living in Connecticut, achieved great fame through her healing by prayer. Many testified to the efficacy of her prayers and bewailed her death.

GEORGE O. BARNES

Francis Schlatter (1856-1909) was a native of Alsace, France. He was born a Roman Catholic and, so far as he was affiliated with any denomination, always remained one. When a year old, he was blind and deaf and was cured by his mother's prayers. He came to America in 1891, and first settled at Jamestown, Long Island. Early in 1893 he moved to 291 Denver, Colorado, and in the following July he felt impelled by inner promptings to start out, he knew not whither. Probably mentally unbalanced, he wandered through the wilderness of the great Southwest without shoes or hat. Fasts, temptations, visions, arrests and imprisonments, and healings combined to furnish his experience during these wanderings, always, as he said, being led by the Father. In July, 1895, he arrived at Las Lunas, New Mexico, where he first attracted public attention as a healer. From here he went to Albuquerque, where he treated as many as six hundred persons in a day, many very effectively. After forty days' fast, which was broken by a hearty meal of solid food, he went to Denver and here reached the pinnacle of his fame and success. At the home of a sympathizer, daily from 9 A. M. to 4 P. M., he treated those who came to him, always without any remuneration. From two thousand to five thousand people would congregate in line, reaching nearly around a city block, five or six abreast, but he was never able to treat more than two thousand in a day. Crowds came from other cities, and some few from great distances, even the New England States. He stood inside a fence, and as each one came along he held the patient's hand for a short time; lifting up his eyes, he prayed and then assured the sufferer of relief within a certain time. Through the mail and in other ways he received 292 handkerchiefs which he blessed and returned with assurance of relief through them. Not all cases handled were restored to health or even noticeably eased, but large numbers testified to cures, some of which came immediately and others by degrees. He did not preach. Although he never claimed it, when asked, "Are you the Christ?" he always replied, "I am." He wore a beard and long hair, and dressed in the plainest clothes. In appearance he looked not unlike the pictures of the traditional Christ. Afterward he appeared in different parts of the United States, but never with the same success in healing as in Denver. 199

The once famous Dr. Newton arrived in Boston in 1859 on one of his visits, and caused an extraordinary sensation. Astonishing results were reported in the way of cures. The lame, having no further need of crutches, left them behind; the blind were cured, and several chronic cases were relieved. He had many followers and disciples among whom was "Dr." Bryant, who settled in Detroit and healed there. Rev. J. M. Buckley, D.D., met Dr. Newton on a Mississippi steam-boat, when the latter was returning from Havana with his daughter who was very low with consumption, and the father doubted if she would reach home alive. When asked "Doctor, why could you not heal her?" he replied "It seems as if we cannot always affect our own 293 kindred." At this time he denounced his pupil, Dr. Bryant, as an "unmitigated fraud who had no genuine healing power."

"If Bryant be an unmitigated fraud, how do you account for the cures which he makes?" asked Dr. Buckley.

"Oh!" said the doctor, "they are caused by the faith of the people and the concentration of their minds upon his operations with the expectation of being cured. Now," said he, "nobody would go to see Bryant unless they had some faith that he might cure them, and when he begins his operations with great positiveness of manner, and when they see the crutches he has there, and hear the people testify that they have been cured, it produces a tremendous influence on them; and then he gets them started in the way of exercising, and they do a good many things that they thought they could not do; their appetites and spirits revive, and if toning them up can possibly reduce the diseased tendency, many of them will get well."

Said Dr. Buckley: "Doctor, pardon me, is not that a correct account of the manner in which you perform your wonderful works?"

"Oh, no," said he; "the difference between a genuine healer and a quack like Bryant is as wide as the poles." 200

294 Father John of Cronstadt (1829-1908) was a saintly man, and furnishes us with an example of the healers among the Orthodox Church of the East. He was famed in all Russia for his sanctity, and was so thronged by crowds for his healing power that he often had to escape by side doors after celebrating the communion. His cures were many, but I choose his own account of one as an example.

"A certain person who was sick unto death from inflammation of the bowels for nine days, without having obtained the slightest relief from medical aid, as soon as he had communicated of the Holy Sacrament, upon the morning of the ninth day, regained his health and rose from his bed of sickness in the evening of the same day. He received the Holy Communion with firm faith. I prayed to the Lord to cure him. 'Lord,' said I, 'heal thy servant of his sickness.

He is worthy, therefore grant him this. He loves thy priests and sends them his gifts.' I also prayed for him in church before the altar of the Lord, at the Liturgy, during the prayer: 'Thou who hast given us grace at this time, with one accord to make our common supplication unto thee,' and before the Holy Mysteries themselves. I prayed in the following words: 'Lord, our life! It is as easy for thee to cure every malady as it is for me to think of healing. It is as easy for thee to raise every man from the dead as it is for me to think of the possibility of the resurrection of the dead. Cure, then, thy servant Basil of his cruel malady, and do not let him die; do not let his wife and children be given up to weeping.' And the Lord graciously heard, and had mercy upon him, 295 although he was within a hair's breadth of death. Glory to thine omnipotence and mercy, that thou, Lord, hast vouchsafed to hear me!" 201

For the past century and a half healing has been carried on among the Pennsylvania Germans by means of a superstitious practice known as "Pow-wow." A book called *The Sixth Book of Moses, or Black Art* is said to be the basis of the practice. The practitioners are usually women of the most ignorant, degraded, and, not infrequently, immoral class, and in harmony with this, a firm belief in witchcraft is entertained by them. Notwithstanding this, they are employed at times by intelligent and respectable people, even by those whose standing in the community might well guarantee a disbelief in such incantations. The healers treat for burns, erysipelas and all skin diseases, goitre, tumors, rheumatism, and some other similar troubles. They have different formulas for the various diseases, and the belief is current that if a healer should reveal the formula to her own sex, she would lose her power, and if she told more than one of the opposite sex, the power would be taken from her. The following is the method of operating for burns:

"Take a piece of red woolen yarn and wrap it into the shape of a ball. Pass it slowly around the burn and while doing so, repeat three times, 'The fire burneth, water quencheth, the pain ceaseth.' After 296 which reverse the movement and repeat the words again three times. Then take the yarn upstairs, pull out the chimney-stop, put the yarn in the chimney, and as soon as it disappears the burn is healed."

There have been a number of cases of local healers and I give two examples: "At the time of the prevalence of cholera in Canada, a man named Ayers, who came out of the States, and was said to be a graduate of the University of New Jersey, was given out to be St. Roche, the principal patron saint of the Canadians, and renowned for his power in averting pestilential diseases. He was reported to have descended from heaven to cure his suffering people of the cholera, and many were the cases in which he appeared to afford relief. Many were thus dispossessed of their fright in anticipation of the disease, who might, probably, but for his inspiriting influence, have fallen victims to their apprehensions. The remedy he employed was an admixture of maple sugar, charcoal, and lard." 202

"The *Month* for June, 1892, published an account, by the late Earl of Denbigh, of a cure worked by a member of a family named Cancelli of Lady Denbigh in 1850. She was suffering severely from rheumatism, and the Pope (Pius IX) mentioned to the Earl that near Foligno there was a family of

297

peasants who were credited with a miraculous power of curing rheumatic disorders. Lord Denbigh succeeded in getting one of the family, an old man, to come, and learned from him the legend of the cure. The belief was that in the reign of Nero, the Apostles Peter and Paul took refuge in the hut of an old couple named Cancelli, near Foligno, and, as a proof of gratitude, gave to the male descendants of the family living near the spot the power of curing rheumatic disorders to the end of time. Lord Denbigh described how the old man made a solemn invocation, using the sign of the cross, and, in fact, Lady Denbigh did recover at once. In a few days the pains returned, but she made an act of resignation, and they then left her, and never returned with any acuteness." 203

What we may designate "Metaphysical Healing" originated with Phineas Parkhurst Quimby (1802-1866). The movement was important, not so much on account of what Quimby himself was able to accomplish by it, as because of the work that has been carried on since by at least three of his pupils. He was born in Lebanon, New Hampshire, and in early life was a watch and clock maker. In 1840 he began experimenting with mesmerism, and accounts of these experiments were published in the Maine papers of that time. After this he developed a system of mental healing of his own, practising it 298 in different towns in Maine for some years. About 1858 he settled as a practitioner in Portland and remained there until his death. I shall quote brief extracts in his own words, which portray his system.

"My practice is unlike all medical practice. I give no medicine, and make no outward applications. I tell the patient his troubles, and what he thinks is his disease; and my explanation is the cure. If I succeed in correcting his errors, I change the fluids of the system and establish the truth, or health. The truth is the cure. This mode of practice applies to all cases."

"The greatest evil that follows taking an opinion for a truth is disease."

"Man is made up of truth and belief; and, if he is deceived into a belief that he has, or is liable to have, a disease, the belief is catching, and the effect follows it."

"Disease being made by our belief, or by our parents' belief, or by public opinion, there is no formula to be adopted, but every one must be reached in his particular case. Therefore it requires great shrewdness or wisdom to get the better of the error. Disease is our error and the work of the devil." 204

Quimby made many wonderful and mostly speedy cures, and although he wrote out his system, it has never been published. Among his patients was Mrs. Patterson from Hill, New Hampshire, who went to 299 Portland in 1862. She had been a confirmed invalid for six years. To quote her own words, published in the *Portland Evening Courier* in 1862, she made a rapid recovery. "Three weeks since I quitted my nurse and sick room en route for Portland. The belief of my recovery had died out of the hearts of those who were most anxious for it. With this mental and physical depression I first visited P. P. Quimby, and in less than one week from that time I ascended by a stairway of one hundred and eighty-two steps to the dome of the City Hall, and am improving *ad infinitum*. To the most subtle reasoning, such a proof, coupled, too, as it is with numberless similar ones, demonstrates his power to heal." Mrs. Patterson, afterward Mrs. Eddy, proclaimed after his death a doctrine very similar to Quimby's. She called it "Christian Science," a name Quimby applied to his teaching, although usually he called it "Science of Health."

Another patient of Quimby's was Julius A. Dresser, who visited him first in 1860. Of him Mr. Dresser says: "The first person in this age who penetrated the depths of truth so far as to discover and bring forth a true science of life, and publicly apply it to the healing of the sick, was Phineas Parkhurst Quimby of Belfast, Me."

Rev. W. F. Evans was still another patient and disciple of Quimby's. His testimony is as follows: "Disease being in its root a wrong belief, change that 300 belief and we cure the disease.... The late Dr. Quimby, of Portland, one of the most successful healers of this or any age, embraced this view of the nature of disease, and by a long succession of most remarkable cures ... proved the truth of the theory.... Had he lived in a remote age or country, the wonderful facts which occurred in his practice would have now been deemed either mythical or miraculous."

These three, Messrs. Evans and Dresser and Mrs. Eddy, proved to be Quimby's most famous patients and disciples. Evans became a noted and voluminous writer on mental healing, Mr. Dresser has been identified with the New Thought movement of which his son H. W. Dresser is probably the best exponent, and Mrs. Eddy ruled the Christian Scientists with a rod of iron.

Warren F. Evans visited Quimby twice in the year 1863, and at these times obtained his knowledge of Quimby's methods. Up to this time he had been a Swedenborgian clergyman, and his beliefs enabled him the better to grasp the new doctrines. On the occasion of the second visit he told his healer that he thought he could cure the sick in this way, and Quimby agreed with him. On returning home he tried it, and his first attempts were so successful that he became a practitioner, using only mental means, and continued in this work. He wrote several books on the subject of mental healing, the first one, 301 *The Mental Cure*, appearing in 1869, six years before Mrs. Eddy's *Science and Health*.

Perhaps, strictly speaking, the New Thought movement does not come within the scope of our subject, except as we see in it an outgrowth and application of the Quimby doctrine, for two reasons. In the first place, its purpose is mental hygiene rather than cure, and it is all the more valuable for that. Of course, in establishing hygienic practices many disorders are cured, but prevention is the main feature. The second reason why we might perhaps not include it in a r鴨m頹f the healers is that it is intended to be for the use of the individual to prevent his employing a healer of any kind. The same objection, however, would do away to some extent with a discussion of Christian Science. The principles of New Thought are that the mind has an influence on the body, and that good, sweet, pure thoughts have a salutary effect, but the opposite ones injure the body. Don't worry, don't think of disease, don't look for trouble, but fill the mind with the opposite positive thoughts and life will be happy and the body will be well. The doctrines are expounded differently by the various leaders, and emphasis is laid on different points, some emphasizing more fully the religious aspects of the movement, for example. The principal writers on the subject are H. W. Dresser, R. W. Trine, H. Wood, and H. Fletcher.

302 Mrs. Mary A. Morse Baker Glover Patterson Eddy (1821-1910) was born at Bow, New Hampshire. After a precocious and neurotic childhood, she united with the Congregational Church when seventeen years of age. At the age of twenty-two she married George Washington Glover, probably the best of her husbands. His death, six months later, was followed by the birth of her only child and a ten years' widowhood. During this time she stayed with her relatives and had long periods of illness, principally of an hysterical character. She then experimented to some extent with mesmerism and clairvoyance. In 1853 she married Dr. Daniel Patterson, an itinerant dentist, from whom she got a divorce, and as Mrs. Patterson she went first to "Dr." Quimby in 1862. She visited Quimby again in 1864, at which time, with some others, she studied with him. After Quimby's death she began teaching what she then called his science. For the next few years she wandered from town to town about Boston in straitened circumstances, healing, teaching, and endeavoring to found an organized society. It was not, however, until 1875 that the organization was formed in Lynn, and later in the same year appeared her *Science and Health*. The years since then have been filled with controversies in the law courts and newspapers, caresses and blows from the ruling hand of Mother Eddy, and numerous

developments from small beginnings, until now 303 over one hundred thousand are identified with the organization. These are almost without exception proselytes from other churches.

MARY BAKER EDDY

Mrs. Eddy's doctrines are founded on a metaphysical theory known as subjective idealism, and advanced centuries before her birth. It posits the all-comprehensiveness of mind and the non-existence of matter. If bodies do not exist, diseases cannot exist, and must be only mental delusions. If the mind is freed of these delusions the disease is gone. This was Quimby's method of procedure already quoted. In *Science and Health* she says that the object of treatment is "to destroy the patient's belief in his physical condition." She also advises: "Mentally contradict every complaint of the body." She continues: "All disease is the result of education, and can carry its ill effects no further than mortal mind maps out the way. Destroy fear," she says, "and you end the fever." However, as with other healers, practice and theory are two different things. Listen further: "It would be foolish to venture beyond our present understanding, foolish to stop eating, until we gain more goodness and a clearer comprehension of the living God." Again: "Until the advancing age admits the efficacy and the supremacy of Mind, it is better to leave the adjustment of broken bones and dislocations to the fingers of the surgeon, while you confine yourself chiefly to mental reconstruction, and the pre 304 vention of inflammation and protracted confinement." 205

With the exception of Christian Science, no modern religious movement has come so prominently before the public and gained so many adherents in a short time as the Christian Catholic Apostle Church of Zion, and both movements owe their popularity solely to their healing. John Alexander Dowie (1847-1907), the founder of this sect, was born in Edinburgh, Scotland, but in 1860, with his parents, he went to Australia, returning for two years to his native city for college study. In 1870 he was ordained to the Congregational ministry. He served three churches, and after some political activity was offered a portfolio in the Australian cabinet of Sir Henry Parks. In 1882 he went to Melbourne and established a large independent church, building a tabernacle for worship. About this time he became a firm believer in Divine Healing in direct answer to prayer. He arrived in San Francisco in 1888 and spent two years in organizing branches of the Divine Healing Association of which he was president. He went to Chicago in 1890 and continued there holding meetings for some years. In 1895 he broke away from the International Divine Healing Association, which he had been chiefly instrumental in organizing, and insisted that his followers should not remain in the churches. The following year 305 the Christian Catholic Church was organized. Of this organization Mr. Dowie was known as General Overseer, then as Prophet, and in 1904 as First Apostle. He also proclaimed himself in general as the messenger of the Covenant and Elijah the Restorer. In 1900 Mr. Dowie said: "About twenty-two thousand have been baptized by triune immersion up to the present, and this includes practically all the members." This, however, was a great exaggeration. In 1901 the headquarters of the church was moved to Zion City, forty-two miles north of Chicago. He preached the threefold gospel of Salvation, Healing, and Holy Living. Dowie differed from Christian Science in proclaiming the reality of disease, the distinctive feature of his doctrine being that all bodily ailment is the work of the Devil, and that Christ came to destroy the works of the Devil. His contempt for external means may be judged from the title of a pamphlet, *Doctors, Drugs, and Devils*; nevertheless, he used physicians at least to diagnose cases at different times, a licensed medical doctor, Speicher, being associated with him from the beginning of his work in Chicago. Dentists are a factor of Zion City, and it is said he also used an oculist. According to his doctrine there are four methods of cure: "The first is the direct prayer of faith; the second, intercessory prayer of two or more; the third, the anointing of the elders, with the prayer of faith; 306 and the fourth, the laying on of hands of those who believe, and whom God has prepared and called to that ministry." In addition to this, teaching is the basis of all other methods. The first ten years of his healing he is said to have laid hands on eighteen thousand sick, and he declared that the greater part of them were fully healed. In some of his later years he said in an issue of his paper: "I pray and lay hands on seventy thousand people in a year." That would make one hundred and seventy-five thousand in two and a half years; but in the time preceding the statement he reported only seven hundred cures. Evidently very few were helped. However, in Shiloh Tabernacle at Zion City are exhibited on the walls crutches, canes, surgical instruments, trusses, and almost every form of apparatus used by the medical profession, presented by people who have now no further use for them on account of their being healed. 206

Our study began with the mental therapeutics of over a millennium before the birth of Christ; let us now close with that of the twentieth century after, in giving some account of the so-called Emmanuel Movement. In 1905 there was formed in connection with Emmanuel Church, Boston, a tuberculosis class for the alleviation of unfortunates of this kind. In this experience it was found that certain psychic and social factors greatly aided in a 307 cure, and in the following year, 1906, the work expanded into what has been called the "Emmanuel Movement." It is an attempt to combine the wisdom and efforts of the physician, the clergyman, the psychologist, and the sociologist, to combat conditions most frequently met in a large city. In the medical phase of the work mental healing has had a large place, and has been emphasized most in the popular presentation of the movement, and so far as the idea has spread, it has been almost wholly in connection with this aspect. What the future of this will be is uncertain, but it seems probable that its most valuable service will be in stimulating the physicians to take up the work which properly belongs to them — the work of therapeutics in all its branches, mental and physical.

190 C. G. Finney, *Memoirs*, pp. 108 f.

191 W.T. Price, *Without Scrip or Purse, or the "Mountain Evangelist," George O. Barnes*, p. 451.

192 *Ibid.*, p. 610.

193 *Ibid.*, pp. 301 ff.

194 J. M. Buckley, "Faith Healing and Kindred Phenomena," *Century*, XXXII, pp. 221 f.

195 *Encyclopedia Britannica*, article "Hohenlohe."

196 D. H. Tuke, *Influence of the Mind upon the Body*, pp. 355 ff.

197 I. W. Riley, *The Founder of Mormonism*, chaps. VIII and IX.

198 J. F. Maguire, *Father Mathew*, pp. 529 f.

199 *Biography of Francis Schlatter, The Healer*.

200 J. M. Buckley, "Faith Healing and Kindred Phenomena," *Century*, XXXII, pp. 221 f.

201 Father John, *My Life in Christ* (trans. Goulaeff), p. 201.

202 T. J. Pettigrew, *Superstitions Connected with ... Medicine and Surgery*, p. 53.

203 E. Berdoe, *Origin and Growth of the Healing Art*, p. 482.

204 J. A. Dresser, *The True History of Mental Science*; A. G. Dresser, *The Philosophy of P. P. Quimby*.

205 G. Milmine, *Mary Baker G. Eddy*.

206 R. Harlan, *John Alexander Dowie*.

308-309